Scars of Truth

A Novel of Pontius Pilate
and the Death of Jesus of Nazareth

Chris Jesse

AmErica House
Baltimore

First printing

All Scripture references contained in the endnotes (e.g. Luke 12:14, Leviticus 2:10) are from the Holy Bible.

ISBN: 1-59129-047-3
PUBLISHED BY AMERICA HOUSE BOOK PUBLISHERS
www.publishamerica.com
Baltimore

Printed in the United States of America

Dedication

This book is dedicated to our fathers, Col. William C. Jesse and Loyd C. McGee. They were not the bumbling, simpleton fathers that we find portrayed on television, but men with a moral compass inexorably fixed on true north.

Acknowledgments

It is unfortunate that readers generally skip the acknowledgments, because so much of what is in a book comes from those who feed, nurture, and critique the author. Below are the names of some who were my sustenance. Clearly, I have not mentioned all who were critical to this effort. And to those not listed because of space constraints, I assure you that your contribution and faith are no less appreciated.

The first fruits of gratitude rightfully belong to God. I am a blessed man. I have America as a home, a wonderful family, and professional blessings beyond my abilities. Yet all of this is nothing compared to the salvation granted me from the cross. Thank you, Lord.

A special thanks to my bride, Judi. It is your faith that is the measure of difference. Thank you Amanda, Mary, and Rachel. You, my daughters, have been my greatest teachers. Thanks to my mother, Kay Jesse, and my sister, Kathy Robertson. Your contribution is the fiber of my being.

I also wish to acknowledge my indebtedness to those who cleared the way so this book might be written: Chuck Root, Mike Forster, Carl Wilson, Jim Ounsworth, Jean Temple, and Bill Patterson. Your courage and integrity are not forgotten.

The depth of support and encouragement I have received from friends is represented by the few I have chosen to list here. Thank you Nancy Dunn, Steve Kuekes, John Nelli, Teresa Poppen, Jim Taggart, Andrea Taggart, Susan Barbee, Stan Ragsdale, and Ralph Cyr. A special nod goes to those who threw themselves into the fire that I might survive. Thank you Von Painter, Tracey Minnich, Jeanann Agiovlassitis, Jae Cody, and Dawn Gerstner.

A grudging but sincere thanks to my editors, Bonnie Tilson and Allison Legge, and my agent, K. Mary Hood. You drove me crazy, but you have my unqualified love and respect. Thanks to Amanda Thompson of Porcupine Studios for the cover layout and Ashley Bromirski for the cover art.

None of this would have been possible without Rev. Paul Kibler and Rev. Elliott Robertson. These two brought me a love and knowledge of the Bible that I consider my greatest joy. I am certain that both would want me to mention that all Biblical errors contained in this text are the fault of the bonehead author and are no way a reflection of their credentials as teachers. Yeah, sure.

Oh yes, lest any of us become too focused on our contribution, I would like to offer my greatest earthly thanks to Laverne and Sophie (my dogs). You were always there with a cold nose and encouraging whimper. Thanks girls. Yes, you can have another cookie.

There you have it, a representative list of those who made this book possible. As for its failings, they are mine alone.

63 B.C. Pompey drives the Roman army south and takes control of Jerusalem. The Jews initially welcome the Romans as a means of protection from Nabateans. This welcome sours when Rome refuses to withdraw her troops. This Roman domination would spawn repeated revolts over the next hundred years.

9 B.C. Pilate's date of birth? (manuscript/historical assumption). For Pilate to rise to the station of governor (in A.D. 26), it is logical to assume that he received a substantial education. This would possibly delay his entry into the military until his twentieth year.

A.D. 11-21 Pilate's period of military service (historical assumption). To enter Roman public service, a man had to first serve at least ten years in the legions. Under the above assumptions, Pilate would have been thirty years of age before entering public service.

A.D. 21-26 Pilate leaves military service and enters public service (historical assumption). Even with a patron as powerful as Sejanus (chief administrator under the Emperor Tiberius) it is unlikely in a merit-driven civil service system that Pilate would have been appointed governor of Judaea without at least five years of administrative experience.

A.D. 26 Pilate becomes governor of Judaea (historical fact). Under the above assumptions, Pilate would have been thirty-five years old when first assuming the position of governor of this lesser province.

A.D. 28 Jesus heals the centurion's servant (documented in the New Testament).

A.D. 29 (Winter) Lazarus dies and is resurrected by Jesus (documented in the New Testament).

A.D. 30 (Winter/early spring) chief priest plots to have Lazarus killed (documented in the New Testament).

A.D. 30 Widely accepted date of Jesus' crucifixion (historical fact). Under the above assumptions, Pilate would have been forty years old at the time of Jesus' death.

A.D. 31 Sejanus, chief administrator of the Roman Empire, suspected of plotting to overthrow the Emperor Tiberius, is executed.

A.D. 36 End of Pilate's term as governor (historical fact). Under the above assumptions, Pilate would have been forty-five years old at the end of his term.

A.D. 69 Manuscript folios written (derived from my analysis of the manuscript). Under the above assumptions, Pilate would have been seventy-eight years old when he began writing the folios.

A.D. 69-70? Pilate's death (manuscript assumption). Based on the physical ailments described in the text, it is unlikely that Pilate lived more than a few months beyond the completion of the document.

A.D. 70 Roman general, Titus, destroys Jerusalem while putting down a

Zealot-led revolt (historical fact). Under the above assumptions, if alive, Pilate would have been eighty years old when Jerusalem and the Jews were crushed by Titus.

A.D. 70-1975 Manuscript preserved by twenty-three identified copyists.

A.D. 1975 A copy of the manuscript escapes the confines of the Eastern Church archives.

A.D. 1998 I receive a copy of the manuscript and begin my research.

Chapter 1
Mac's "Gift"

This is the "Memoir of Pontius Pilate Regarding the Jesus Affair." That is all I can say about it with certainty. A man named Lloyd (who preferred to be called Mac) placed it in my hands with a cryptic explanation of its history. Mac entrusted me with his only copy of this document because of my expressed passion for history and the Holy Bible. He did so after knowing me less than an hour. Why he chose to leave it with me and never reclaim it is as mystifying as the document's content. All of this said, I must confess that it has occupied every spare moment of my life for the past year, and I have come to think of it as my own.

Mac and I met on a weekday afternoon in New York City. As CEO of a software company, and the author of several books on the application of computer technology, I had traveled to New York to deliver speeches in my area of expertise. After completing one speech and having four hours before the next, I took a cab across town to have lunch at a favored restaurant. After my meal, I decided to walk the thirty blocks back to my hotel taking a route that coincidently led me to this book.

The walk back to my hotel included a survey of each cross street for old churches. I have always had an interest in churches, for within their walls is a history of the neighborhood that surrounds them. It is a sad commentary that an increasing number of these archives find it necessary to lock their doors to the outside world. Experience, however, has taught me that a firm knock on one of the side doors often brings both a warm welcome and an informed tour of the facility and its history. On this day, my first and only church investigation required no such side knock, for in spite of its unoccupied visage, its front doors were open to all comers.

The stone mantle above the door identified the tall, thin structure as housing an Eastern Orthodox congregation that had established itself in 1903. A small anteroom led to a dark, deep chapel that was picketed with illuminated icons down each of its long walls. At the far end was a softly lit altar that was perched four feet above the chapel floor. I walked halfway down the aisle and seated myself on an oak pew that had the worn impression of the thousands that had taken the same seat over the past ninety-five years. Bowing my head, I offered a short prayer of protection for my family and a petition for God's blessing upon those who called this their church. I then sat quietly absorbing that which had framed the joys and sorrows of countless funerals, weddings, baptisms, and holidays.

Rising, I decided to begin a more detailed examination of the church from the rear. As I walked back down the aisle, I discovered that another worshiper had joined me. Not wishing to disturb him, I passed quietly, but was instantly called back by his question.

"Excuse me, are you the priest?"

"No," I replied as I turned to address him, "just a visitor. It's my first time here."

The man before me was perhaps seventy, but in the dim light, it was difficult to tell. He continued his questioning. "I'm sorry to bother you, I was interested in speaking to someone who is knowledgeable about the Eastern Church. Are you a member?"

"No, you're barking up the wrong tree. I'm a Lutheran from North Carolina."

He quickly countered, "Your tree may be closer than mine. I'm a Baptist from Alabama!" His gentle, self-deprecating chuckle invited additional conversation, but at that moment two women entered the church.

The matrons were obviously members of the congregation. Both wore loose-fitting scarves on their heads and had the gait of advanced years. I could see that both my companion and I had the same desire to pelt them with questions, but as they walked past us their countenance was unmistakable. The warm smiles welcomed us, but their focused demeanor said that they were here to pray. We waited quietly as they settled into the center of a specifically selected pew and bowed their heads. This no doubt was the pew and position they had worshiped from all their lives, and a spot that would remain empty long after their death.

Standing, my companion leaned toward me and spoke in a soft whisper. "How about letting a fellow Southerner buy you a cup of coffee?"

Not wishing to disturb the parishioners further, I nodded my agreement, and we left the church. Once outside, I could see that my new acquaintance was closer to eighty than seventy, with a full head of white hair that he combed straight back. He was of average height with the posture of a man half his age. Immediately upon reaching the church steps he extended his hand.

"My name is Lloyd, but my friends call me Mac."

I shook his hand and introduced myself while my mind raced to fabricate reasons why I couldn't stay for coffee. Before I could tender my excuse, he caught me off guard with his candor.

"Look, I can see you are all dressed up and probably have important business. Me, I'm retired; I have all the time in the world. If you have something to do, don't feel like you have to be polite and humor an old man." The twinkle of his clear blue eyes and his easy manner offered a guilt-free exit, but that same manner made such an exit unnecessary.

We walked a half block to a corner coffee shop, entered, and without consultation selected a booth that gave us an unobstructed view of the church. With a smile and a small groan, Mac slid into the booth. It was then that I first noticed his battered canvas briefcase.

"Chris, have you ever wondered why old people groan when they get up and down or in and out of a booth?"

"No," I replied.

Mac was still smiling as he leaned against the table. "Neither do I, and I tell myself that I will never do it. But did you hear me? Better watch out because I'm slipping; any moment I may start ragging on today's baseball players or start telling you stories about the big war!" He laughed at himself and was still chuckling when the server brought us our first cups of coffee.

With the skill of an experienced reporter, Mac spent the next twenty minutes having me outline my life, my reason for being in New York, and how I happened to be visiting the church. His curiosity was casually insatiable, but took on a more aggressive tone when I talked about my passion for Biblical history. Even so, had I not made a conscious effort to direct the conversation toward him, I do not believe we would have discussed the manuscript.

I did my best to get Mac to talk about himself, but he seemed more interested in me. It is unfair to say that he was evasive because he directly answered every question. That's it. He answered every question without elaboration or qualification; he directly responded to every query. At the end of thirty minutes, I had only gained a checkerboard view of the man sitting across from me. But that was all I would ever learn, for my schedule forced me to end the conversation. I called for the check.

When the check arrived, I immediately picked it up.

Mac made no protest but quietly reached in his wallet and placed a ten-dollar bill on the table. Then with the same twinkle he smiled at me. "Either I'm buying or I just left one hell of a tip." I conceded the contest and placed the check next to the money on the table. We exchanged pleasantries as we put on our coats and walked to the street.

It was colder outside than I remembered as the afternoon sun was now casting more shadow than warmth. I was reconsidering my decision to walk back to the hotel when Mac extended his hand. "It was a real pleasure, Chris."

I took his hand. "The pleasure was mine," I responded, "and you bought the coffee." Opening my coat I reached into my suit jacket for a business card. "I'm putting my home phone number on the back of my business card. If you get to Raleigh, I want you to give me a call."

He stood for a moment, carefully looking at the card before speaking. "I hear there's some good fishing off the Carolina coast in the fall. I'll call you."

I was buttoning my coat and starting to turn away, but Mac refused to break eye contact. He began to rub his face with his right hand.

"Can I ask you a favor?"

Thinking that he wanted to split a cab, I responded, "Sure."

He opened his briefcase and removed a brown accordion folder about three inches thick. "Would you read this and give me your opinion?"

"What is it?" I asked.

"It's represented to be the journal that Pontius Pilate wrote regarding the Jesus affair."

Knowing that this was going to be more than a brief conversation, I asked if we could cross to the sunny side of the street. As we crossed, Mac continued. "I had a half brother who lived in what used to be Yugoslavia. He was connected to the Eastern Church and was somehow given a Xerox copy of the manuscript in 1975. The journal has thirteen folios, and as he received each one, he gave it to a university professor he knew who was an expert in languages. She identified the text as well-written, first-century Greek that had been transcribed in the hand of an accomplished calligrapher. My brother paid her to translate the document into English. It took them the better part of five years. Anyway, when the wall fell and Eastern Europe opened up, my brother visited me and told me the whole story."

"That is all I knew until three months ago when I received this package along with a note informing me of my brother's death. I came to New York to meet with the professor who translated it. In the early nineties, she accepted a position here in the States, and my brother had written her name and address on the top margin of the first folio. I should have saved my money because she wasn't much help. She admitted to having translated it, in fact to being spellbound by the project, but her career is on a fast track now and she doesn't want to take the risk of being associated with the manuscript."

Looking past Mac I could see the church in the background. "So, did you somehow link the church to the manuscript?"

"No, I hit a dead end with the professor, so I decided to visit an Eastern Church before going back to Alabama. I thought the priest might give me some background information, and you don't find many Eastern Orthodox priests where I come from."

Confused, I pushed the issue. "Why don't you ask the priest to read the manuscript?" Mac momentarily seemed irritated.

"My brother told me that the journal was in conflict with some of the church's beliefs.[ii] That's why it was suppressed all of these years. Look, I know you're a busy man, but I promise you, you've never read anything like this before. It's a quick read and your comments might help me unravel this thing."

I was now dangerously close to being late for my next speech, but Mac had me fully engaged. "But why me?"

His warm smile returned. "Why not? You told me you love history, love to read and study the Bible, and God put you in my life just when I needed you. Take it; let me know what you think. To protect his source my brother long ago destroyed his copy of the Greek manuscript. You hold the only accessible copy of the document." Mac tapped on the folder after placing it in my hands. "You hold what may be the thoughts of the most evil man in history."

Mac's countenance changed again. He put his hands in his pants pockets, looked down at the ground, and then back to me. "I don't want to burden you with this. You're an author and I know you will treat it with respect. But don't do it if it's a burden." Mac went on to dismiss my concerns about holding the only copy of the manuscript. He asked me for another business card and on the back of the card he wrote two numbers. "The top number is where I'm staying in New York. The bottom is my home number in Alabama. I should be here another three or four days." He winked at me and held up the first card I had given him. "I know where to find you."

I accepted the package and agreed to return it along with my comments before the end of the month. The late hour forced an abrupt goodbye and a hurried cab ride back to the hotel for my speech. It would be that evening before I discovered that the local phone number Mac had given me was not valid, and another week before I learned that his home number was also incorrect. In somewhat of a panic, I researched the numbers, trying alternate area codes, possible transposition errors, and alternate exchanges. In the end, having never heard from him since, I am left to conclude that Mac did not want to be contacted.

So, a man named Lloyd, nicknamed Mac, a veteran of World War II, a retired master machinist from Alabama, married fifty plus years to a woman named Gerri, the sire of an undisclosed number of children, having a half brother from Eastern Europe, left me the manuscript. I know part of this to be true because the professor affirmed Mac's story concerning his brother and the translation. But this was another dead end, for she either refused to or could not remember the name of Mac's half brother.

I fear that I have spent too much time on the acquisition of the transcript and on Mac's brief but mysterious appearance, for it is the manuscript and not Mac that has haunted my life for more than a year. I have read it countless times and have documented my observations. I have researched it, spoken to the professor who translated it, and sought the counsel of those whose Biblical knowledge greatly exceeds my own. The results of this effort were interesting, but not nearly as gripping as the text of the manuscript itself.

Upon first reading Mac's treasure, I found myself focused on the plot. Here I discovered a man caught in the whirlwind of history taking one step at a time toward infamy. After completing this reading, I distributed copies to several respected members of the clergy, asking them to identify conflicts between the manuscript and the Holy Scriptures. Specifically, I was looking for dates, places, and chronology that would call its authenticity into question.

The comments I received from my friends in the clergy galvanized my interest. There was a closing paragraph in one letter that succinctly summarized their opinions. "In conclusion, the manuscript covers a great deal of material that is not addressed in the Scriptures. Those events and references that are held in common with the Holy Word are in close harmony. Those persons and events that expand upon a Biblical theme are either logically plausible or are free of direct conflict. The few inaccuracies that were uncovered are minor and could be attributed to the translation or revisions of the manuscript."

Energized, I undertook numerous readings of the text, adding footnotes where appropriate, along with my subjective observations at the conclusion of each folio. These observations, along with the original unedited text, comprise the body of this work. In all cases, I have taken special care to present the journal as the author wrote it. The only two liberties I took with the text are mechanical. First, as the folios present a logical division of the work, I have presented them as chapters with a title that is of my creation. Second, I have not included any of the notes that others had scribbled in the margins.

Some who have read both the original folios and a draft of this book believe that I should have included the margin notes. I deliberated on this matter for some time before concluding that to include the notes would intermingle two stories. I admit to being curious about the origin of the manuscript and the hands that translated, edited, and produced the typed copy. But in the end, I decided that the manuscript must come first, and that including the mysterious margin notes would be a distraction.

My one regret is that I could not get the professor who translated the document to write the forward. She is at a point in her academic career where her employer, a prestigious university, is considering her for a tenured position. When I asked her how I might explain her absence to the readers of this book, she was forceful in her reply. "Tell them it is hard for a woman in certain academic circles and that I have thirty years of my life invested in my career. Tell them I am sorry."

I am also sorry because I believe that she holds a wealth of information that could add to both aspects of the manuscript. Regardless, she has managed to give us a measurable contribution. She informed me that the original document given to her for translation was well-written, first-century Greek, copied in the hand of an accomplished calligrapher, and listed the names of the previous twenty-three copyists of the document.

In addition, she offered the following background regarding the translation effort. "When the document first came to me I was working at a university in Europe. I had acquired a reputation for my abilities in performing English translations of older Greek documents, but I am uncertain as to how your friend's brother found me. He first offered to pay me for translating it, but we instead settled on having two of my better students undertake the effort as a graduate project. Oddly, that never happened. I read the text and was hooked. I ended up translating it not once, but three times. The first time I translated it word for word, the second, thought for thought, and the third was a reconciliation of the first two. I was never paid. I never received anything but his gratitude. He did offer the document to me for publication, but I was being considered for a position in the States and didn't need a potential Hitler Diary[iii] dogging my credentials."

Her answers regarding the manuscript's authenticity and scope were seductively vague. I asked her if she thought the document was real. She squinted and tilted her head to one side. "You mean is it authentic? I can tell you that it was written in first-century Greek, and it is the soul and life experience of someone. That much is authentic." She leaned forward as she continued. "And there is something more than that, we both feel it, or you wouldn't be here." She stood and offered her hand. "Now I have answered what I can. I trust that you will honor my request for anonymity. Should you not, I will sue you and make you a fool. I hope not to see you again."

I left that meeting asking myself the same question that I ask today. "Did Pontius Pilate author this document?" A poignant question, but one that perhaps misses the mark, for what is told here transcends a personage or crime. It is the raw material of the human condition, laid out before us, split open, the cadaver of humanity. The document is an auto accident—tragic, gruesome, but somehow forcing us to look at it.

Someone's soul has been poured upon these pages, and worse, it has flowed over the edges, staining me with its guilt. If Pontius Pilate did not write it, then it is the hand of a master prosecutor, for it presents a convincing case that I am more Pilate than I am Christ. And with this haunting indictment the tragedy draws me to its time and circumstance, asking questions that expose the hypocrisy of my professed values.

Mac no doubt felt the same forces working within him. He attempted to mitigate the document's impact by focusing on its authenticity. But fire, regardless of its source, still burns, and Mac found himself holding something that was too hot to embrace yet too valuable to discard. I am left to conclude that Mac attempted to free himself by giving the manuscript to me. A dubious solution, for our thoughts and feelings are not bound to the pages from which they came. No, all of this will be with Mac until the end, just as it will be with me.

But reason brings no solace to the convicted, so I too pass the manuscript on to a stranger. It is beyond the arithmetic of life. I have been stripped and stand naked in humility. I offer no defense, no explanation, but find only these words of solace:

I understand, Mac. I understand

Chapter 2
Folio 1
An Old Man's Words

I have tasted the dust of Rome's alleys, of her prized coastal jewels and breathed the dirt of those conquered treasures she wished forgotten. I have been a servant and a profiteer, but mostly a simple man looking to make his way in life. I write this knowing that the end is near for me. This I know, not because of advanced age; no, it is the darkness of night that whispers the secret of my impending mortality. The hushed words speak certainty.

"Pontius Pilate, it is your time to fall upon the stone and burst your guts into the consuming fire. It is time, Pilate." That is all that is said, but each night the words greet me with increasing sureness, and each morning I find myself more deeply etched with this fate. Indeed, there is little time left.

Proscribed with this fate, what does a man do? Having settled both personal and financial accounts, I am left to wait. It is this waiting that has caused me to search out the forgotten notes of Simon the scribe, for there remains a handful that care for me, and I will not have their memory of me defined by rumor and speculation. There is no question that I ordered the crucifixion of the one known as Jesus the Christ. I included this fact in the report I sent to Rome[iv] over thirty years ago. As procurator of Jerusalem, I considered death a reasonable lubricant on the axle of peace, and this Jesus would be of no consequence, save the incipient sheep that have labeled him a deity, and me, the spark of their rebellion.

In the sum of my years, I have discovered that all things seem to scatter when spilled. No doubt this will be the fate of this Jesus affair when sprinkled into volumes of Rome. Pilate the fool, Pilate the butcher, Pilate the bungler, if indeed I am mentioned by name. I expect nothing kinder than this.

Now, thirty years beyond the event, I have learned to accept the injustice, but never the means. I shall never be reconciled to having my name crumbled by a race of goat-herding fanatics. It is an inequity that still chastens, and one that I shall not pass on unchallenged. Be it known that there was considered reason behind my actions, reason that was fueled by circumstance and fraud. The details must be understood, for they channeled the outcome before it was conceived. So now it is the how and why of my past that is paramount, for there will be no chiseled stone monument to mark my place. My obelisk is but this fleeting disclosure and the place that it occupies in the memory of those that care for me.

From the moment it was brought to my attention, this Jesus matter had the stench of a sheep pen. Any who have ever governed know the uneasy feeling that one gets in their bowels when presented with a problem that has a snapping head at both ends. In fact, the art of governing might best be defined as avoiding such beasts altogether. Christ Jesus[v] was such a problem. The earliest reports that I received from my informers portended the tragedy of our intersection. I do not know why, but I knew from the beginning that my career was somehow in the hands of this itinerant laborer. It was for this reason that I assigned Simon, my personal secretary, the task of documenting[vi] my activity concerning this man.

Simon was the first Jew I hired after assuming control over Judaea, Samaria, and Idumea. He was average in every respect, save his gift for languages. He could both read and write Aramaic, Latin, Hebrew, and Greek. This, coupled with his ability to remember word for word both conversations and text, made him an ideal personal secretary. Simon's responsibilities included preparing my reports to Rome and Syria and recording the affairs of state. In this position, I required Simon to be by my side during all governing activities. This created some tension with my second in command, Clephus, officer of internal affairs, who believed that I relied too heavily on Simon for counsel. This assumption, of course, was ridiculous as the Roman-born Clephus was my right hand and Simon but a recorder of events.

I should not give you the impression that Simon was without personal distinction, for his common features allowed him to mix freely in the markets without drawing attention. Many times his observations as one of the masses provided the quintessential spice of understanding. Enhancing this ingredient was his detachment from his circumstance. I believe he was the only apolitical Jew I ever met. Simon thought the Sadducees[vii] consumed in politics, the Pharisees[viii] in self-virtue, and the Essenes[ix] in exactitude. As for Rome and myself, he openly referred to us as opportunists. He held himself apart from all these factions, and in so doing, had clarity of thought and observation that allowed him to untangle that which seemed hopelessly knotted.

From the beginning I enlisted Simon's services in documenting what I would later label the "Jesus affair." Simon documented each meeting and every conversation regarding this activity. Further, I did not restrict Simon to mere transcription. I asked him to do his best to accurately describe both the context and actions of the players involved. All of this resulted in the transcript that I have made part of this document. I have copied his unedited words into this text in their entirety.

Of course, Simon did not have the ability or the breeding to fully appreciate the subtleties of governing. Although I have no dispute with the words of his transcript, I do find some of his observations shallow. Accordingly, I have inserted my comments regarding his work as part of this text.

This testimony then is the whole of the Jesus affair. I give this to my family and to those who have the desire and courage to look inside the sack. Always the practical man, I do not expect this text to be any more than a wrapper on my life. It is my hope that these words will see this wrapper clear of the inscription "Pilate the fool," "Pilate the butcher," and "Pilate the bungler."

Note to Mac:

When initially reading the first folio I found myself instantly questioning its authenticity. The voice and words seemed wrong. I read it a second and third time looking for obvious factual errors, but having discovered none was forced to look elsewhere for the source of my skepticism. In the end, I found the root of my skepticism in my own bigotry.

Perhaps it is only I, or it may be the human condition, but I like my heroes smart and my villains dumb. I long for virtue that is pure white and evil that is pitch black. I did not like the voice I heard in the first folio, for it had a humanity about it that was gray. Worse yet, it spoke in a tone of reason and intellect. I was not prepared to accept this villain under such terms, yet that is how he speaks.

It should really come as no surprise that Pontius Pilate might have had such a voice. For during his eleven years of service as governor of Judaea, Roman government was at its apex. During this period, merit was the general rule for positions of responsibility, and with Judaea being a trouble spot, it is unlikely that Rome would send a dullard to manage it. Further evidence of Pilate's abilities can be found in his tenure of service. His eleven years as governor are second only to Valerius Gratus (his immediate predecessor), with the ten succeeding governors averaging less than four years of service.

Pilate's job was to manage this hostile holding with minimal military resources. He was expected to use local authority to manage day-to-day affairs, his soldiers to contain sporadic violence, and the threat of a full Roman reprisal as a means of forestalling an outright rebellion. Within the bounds of such an assignment it is unreasonable to assume that the man who kept such a balance for eleven years lacked the humanity of interpersonal skills.

19

So, grudgingly, I have come to acknowledge my bigotry. I now see that the traits of intellect and humanity are not contrary but, rather, a necessary component of the man who ordered the death of Christ. I must confess that as I study the words and thoughts contained in these folios, an intimacy has formed. I frequently find myself in conversation with the text, in full discourse with a man that I am at ease addressing as Pilate.

Chapter 3
Folio 2
An Uneasy Feeling

My memory is clear on this matter; this Jesus became part of my future when first mentioned in the weekly station reports. I had initiated these reports as one of my first actions as governor for Judaea was ripe for revolt. Today, few remember the severity of the situation as Judaea is soon to be crushed[x], and the Hebrews brought to heel. But in those days, there was no more vulnerable region within the empire.

To say there was an organized plot to overthrow Roman rule would be a clean cut indeed. This was not a surgeon's rebellion; it was the discord of a wild dog tearing at soft flesh. But this too is an understatement for one has a superior chance of defeating a single wild dog; for no matter how large, it must expose itself as it lunges for a lethal grip. Judaea was not like this. It was a pack of smaller dogs incising from all directions, threatening you from the front as it stripped the flesh from your flanks. Such was the territory during my eleven-year tenure, a pack of very aggressive, hungry dogs, snapping at Rome, at me, and at each other.

Referring to the Jews as a pack of dogs, although accurate, is an oversimplification. For a pack implies some commonality of trait, action, and purpose. This group had no such bond as each member of the pack presented a unique threat, as well as a preference for sacrificing one another in their quest to disembowel the empire. This was my lot, to keep the Jews from siphoning scarce Roman troops away from more valued holdings while asserting Roman authority on both friend and foe. All of this was to be accomplished with the most meager resources imaginable. To attain my objective, I initially implemented a plan that focused all of my fortune on controlling the four strongest sects within the territory: the Sadducees, the Pharisees, the Essenes, and the Zealots.[xi] As I soon discovered the Essenes totally absorbed in their rituals, I centered my efforts on the remaining three.

My means of tracking these groups were the aforementioned station reports. Each week I would receive reports from the four geographic commands that detailed the activities of the three groups. Each month the weekly reports would be summarized by group, thus giving me a detailed understanding of political trends across Judaea. It was within one of these reports that the name of Jesus first became significant. As a whole, the report that drew my attention to Jesus was routine except for a specific paragraph that was authored by a reliable infiltrator reporting from the Northwest Sector.

> The Zealot leader, Simon[xii], has become less visible as he has taken up with a group that follows Jesus of Nazareth (JN). Little information is available on JN, but his group appears to be both small and passive. All indications are that Simon the Zealot (SZ) has ceased his open hostility toward Rome. Will continue to track SZ activities as a lower priority as long as he keeps his current company.

Prior to reaching me, the summarized monthly station report passed though the hands of my subordinates responsible for military affairs, domestic programs, and internal surveillance. Generally, by the time I received this document, it was cluttered with notes in the margins and/or addenda referencing specific items. Oddly, there were no notes or references for the paragraph introducing Jesus of Nazareth. It was at this point that I called my secretary, Simon (not to be confused with Simon the Zealot), to begin his transcription of the Jesus affair.

***

The transcription of the Jesus affair:
Day 1,740 of Governor Pilate's administration[xiii]
Prepared by Simon of Emmaus
Present:
Governor Pilate
Clephus, Officer of Internal Affairs
Dalaccus, Officer of Military Affairs
Simon of Emmaus, Secretary to Governor Pilate

Governor Pilate: Where is Janus?

Dalaccus: He left this morning to attend to the matter of the missing soldiers in the Northeast Sector. He is expected to return in two to three days.

Governor Pilate: Does it make sense to review the station report without the officer of internal surveillance?

Dalaccus: The report is of a routine nature, I have...

Governor Pilate: Routine! Routine? When a sheep slays a lion does the shepherd report it as routine? Have you read the report, Dalaccus? And you, Clephus, no comments from you?

Clephus: Governor, if you will tell me which part of the report has you angry, perhaps I could comment.

Governor Pilate: Simon, I want this matter recorded, all of it... This whole Jesus affair, I want it in writing. We shall review it in the future and see just how routine it remains. Make certain Janus is apprised of this matter, Simon. Make certain that you give him a copy of today's meeting. His absence shall not save him from being part of this porridge. I want it all recorded, every word, every gesture. I want their slack jaws and wine-soaked eyes in the transcript, do you understand? Do you understand!

Transcription Note: The above portion of this transcription was prepared from memory as prior to that moment, I was unaware that Governor Pilate required such. As I was not attentive to gestures and details of individuals' movements, I have omitted any description of activity concerning the above discussion. Each evening, as I recopy the day's notes, I shall endeavor to recall and include both physical expressions and settings as part of the transcript.

Simon: I understand, Governor Pilate. And should I produce copies for the officers in addition to yourself?

(The governor is energized and on the hunt. Leaning back, elbows on the arms of his chair, left and right fingers matched and pressed together, he speaks to the others as a man watching his prey fall into a covered hole.)

Governor Pilate: No. I shall hold the only copy, and leave a wide side margin that I might append my thoughts. One never knows when the actions of one's lieutenants may need to be brought before Rome.

(Governor Pilate looks at Dalaccus and Clephus with a small painful smile.)

Do not misunderstand, I consider your appointments by Rome to be a blessing. I myself could not have selected finer counsel. But as we see in this report, there are many muses about, and I would like us tied together.

(Dalaccus steps forward, exposing the governor to wine that seeps from his skin and the redness of his watery gray eyes.)

Dalaccus: With all due respect, Governor, we are very interested in your concerns. And I, for one, am not surprised that your discerning eye has found something that escaped the rest of us.

Governor Pilate: Is that so, Clephus? Is it my keen intellect that has caught you unaware too?

(Clephus does not immediately answer, but rather takes a moment to look at the man asking the question. It is obvious that he is measuring the governor.)

Clephus: I will not contest your intellectual superiority in such matters. This fact has been proven on dozens of occasions when my hide was not being stripped from my bones. In this case, however, my actions concerning the station report may be more accurately ascribed to very fine wine and beautiful women who keep late hours. I confess that I did read the report, but I read it in a somewhat distressed condition.

(Governor Pilate bursts out in laughter.)

Governor Pilate: Did you get that Simon? Flattery, contrition, honesty, and a boast all in one!

(The governor continues laughing while wiping tears of amusement from his eyes.)

Clephus, you are an artist, I swear one day you shall crawl through the bowels of Rome and emerge from her navel claiming to be the very lifeblood of her existence.

(Clephus seems both embarrassed and disoriented by the governor's reaction. He appears much like a man trying to act natural while discovered wearing nothing but a hat and sandals.)

Clephus: (bowing) I am grateful if my response has covered my offense with laughter, but I wish to assure the Governor that I will not make a habit of my errant ways.

(Governor Pilate, turning his head to the right, locks his eyes on Dalaccus and squeezes his words through clenched teeth.)

Governor Pilate: Now if I can just avoid being so brilliant, perhaps in the future we can all give the appearance of some competence.

(Dalaccus shifts his eyes to the floor.)

Dalaccus: You have my apology, Governor.

(The governor stands and looks to the door. Rubbing the back of his neck with his right hand, he looks beyond them both.)

Governor Pilate: Why don't you both go to the bath and then get a few hours sleep? Then perhaps we will cover the business at hand.

(Dalaccus bows, turns, and walks toward the exit. Clephus glances over at me to see if he alone recognizes the opportunity before him.)

Clephus: Governor, may I have a word with you before retiring?

(Dalaccus stops halfway to the door, caught between his own haste to leave and the advantage he has given Clephus. The governor nods assent.)

I shall not find rest without knowing what you discovered in the report. I beg you, allow my trip to slumber to be accompanied by thoughts on this matter.

(Dalaccus, seeing the hopelessness of recovery, leaves the room. Governor Pilate, fingering the pages of the report, smiles at Clephus, and then turns to me.)

Governor Pilate: Simon, I cannot find the passage in question. Would you please take this report... never mind, here it is. Clephus, listen carefully. "The Zealot leader, Simon, has become less visible, as he has taken up with a group that follows Jesus of Nazareth (JN). Little information is available on JN, but his group appears to be both small and passive. All indications are that Simon the Zealot (SZ) has ceased his open hostility toward Rome. Will continue to track SZ activities as a lower priority as long as he keeps his current company." What do you think?

Clephus: Seems rather a sudden turnaround for our friend Simon. He has been identified as one of our most active and potentially dangerous of the Zealot leaders. Do you suspect that it is some form of diversion?

Governor Pilate: What did you just do to your friend Dalaccus? Did you not maneuver him such that you cut him off at the knees? Did you not wait until he had committed himself to the exit before you showed a renewed interest in my concern? Is he not one of your closest friends? What drove you to that?

Clephus: I don't know, mending my relationship with you? Curiosity? A desire to do my job?

(The governor rose from his chair and began to pace. He spoke in a harsh whisper.)

Governor Pilate: Perhaps all of that and more, but at the base of it all is a desire for power. To have it, hold it, increase it, and exercise it.

Clephus: But Simon the Zealot appears to be fleeing power. He had a following, stature, and a stage on which to demonstrate his considerable charisma. It makes no sense.

(Governor Pilate slams his right fist into his left hand.)

Governor Pilate: Exactly! It makes no sense that a man like him can so quickly change his skin. And for whom is he giving up this treasure? An itinerant laborer who appears to share none of his values? I suspect there is more to this Jesus than we know… a great deal more.

Clephus: Perhaps we are questioning a gift of the gods. If one of our most strident enemies is transformed into a harmless follower, are we not the beneficiaries? (Clephus, suddenly animated) Would it not be in our interest to introduce this Jesus to all of the Zealots?

(The governor's face loses all expression as he looks down at the pages spread on the table.)

Governor Pilate: Perhaps. But I know this: men do not shed their skins like snakes. Go get your rest, it shall all be here when you return.

(Clephus bows slightly.)

Clephus: I shall give this matter some thought and return this afternoon.

(The governor, lost in thought, flicks his fingers toward the door and Clephus departs.)

Governor Pilate: And what do you make of this, my young Hebrew?

Simon: It is beyond my scope, Governor. I see it simply; strength only gives way to greater strength. The mighty do not submit to the weak. It has been said that Simon the Zealot is strong, so it follows that the one he submits to must be stronger.

(The governor crosses the room and leans on my table, looking over his shoulder to make eye contact.)

Governor Pilate: It is clear isn't it, Simon, so very clear. Are we to respect the lion more than the one who tames him? I think not. When Janus returns, inform him that I want this Jesus watched.

Simon: Should I schedule a meeting with Dalaccus and Clephus regarding this matter?

Governor Pilate: No, there is no more to ponder. No more on this matter until we learn more about this Jesus, and how he gives lions an appetite for straw…

(Although unaware, I must have smiled, for the governor is again engaged.)

Governor Pilate: Do I amuse you, Simon? You are a boy of little jest, yet you grin. Does my concern about this vagrant amuse you?

Simon: No, Governor, the carry of your words across seven centuries caught me off guard. I meant no disrespect.

(The governor closed his eyes and with a deep sigh pinched the bridge of his nose with his right thumb and index finger. Eyes still closed, he spoke to me as if I was a young child.)

Governor Pilate: Simon, I have had a difficult day and my head is pounding. Do not speak to me in riddles. What are you saying?

Simon: I speak of our writings, Governor. One of our prophets, Isaiah, spoke seven hundred years ago of a time when the lion would eat straw,[xiv] and I thought it curious that you chose the same words.

(Looking directly at me as he closed the distance between us, his tone was one of derision.)

Governor Pilate: Well, perhaps your prophet has an answer; what does he say on the subject?

Simon: I do not recall the exact passage…

(I did not finish before the governor exploded with rage.)

Governor Pilate: I asked you a question! What did he say?

Simon: The prophet Isaiah said that, "The wolf and the lamb shall be together, the lion shall eat straw with the ox, and dust shall be the serpent's meal. They shall not hurt nor destroy in all my holy mountain."[xv] That is the taste of it.

Governor Pilate: (exasperated) Why must you people always speak in riddles? And whom would you ascribe these other animals to represent?

Simon: I meant no harm, I was simply… I thought it odd… I should keep such thoughts to myself.

Governor Pilate: (coldly) Now prepare your report, and bring Janus when he arrives.

(I bowed and was halfway to the door when the governor's call caused me to turn and face him.)

Governor Pilate: (with a broad smile) Simon, did you people ever consider that your prophet's hill might be Rome? Perhaps Rome is your holy mountain![xvi]

Simon: I do not know, for such is the way of prophecy. Each of us may pronounce our own conclusion, but alas, it is the future that cradles the truth.

***

I have no dispute with the above transcription. It is, in both substance and fact, an accurate rendering of that which Simon observed. As I copy Simon's words into this journal, however, I see a picture forming in the reader's mind that paints me as a mercurial academic straining to maintain an emotional set of accounts. Of course, even an exaggerated simplification contains a vein of truth. It would be accurate to say that I am a man of passion. I feel what I live, and I have governed accordingly. I felt my decisions, the opportunities and the dangers. I used this passion as a tool to keep others and myself sharp in a chaotically dangerous environment that at any turn could consume a man and his career.

Simon was accurate in what he had observed, but what he had no knowledge of was the stage on which the players delivered their lines. As was mentioned in the transcript, Janus had gone to the Northeast Sector to investigate the disappearance of fourteen Roman soldiers. These were veteran Roman troops led by an experienced officer, and they disappeared. More than that, they disappeared in one of the most volatile regions of the territory, Jericho, around the same time that this Jesus surfaced.

Within this context, even my most strident critics would find it difficult to think my reaction anything less than rational and measured. But I make no excuse, for all that have ever governed know that such events are the timbers of the stage on which one must perform. Each new day brings its own events and circumstances and forces us to make sense of yesterday's performance while each night brings the realization that our daily efforts are mysteriously carving both our past and our future.

Note to Mac:

There is a fresh reality to this folio that ties it to the present. Pilate's opening comments have a candid, factual tone that one would expect to find in the autobiography of a retired secretary of state. His direct statements, with no qualifications, have a chilling clarity that comes from lived experience.

Of course, there is the obvious question of coincidence. What are the chances that Pilate would select this event as one to be documented? To be certain, it could have been one of many events that he had transcribed, but why have none of the others survived? What are the chances that at the end of his life he would select this event as his defining moment?

The last of these questions, I believe, are definitively answered in the later folios. As for his instinct to document his experience with Jesus, that answer may better be found within the man. There are those who are drawn to positions of responsibility that succeed because they have an inherent sense of what may be important. Typically, such individuals are avid students of history, and are diligent in documenting their actions. Peter the Great (Russia), Winston Churchill (England), and Richard Nixon (United States) are names that immediately come to mind.

Was Pilate such a man? Very little is known about him, but if he had such traits, his actions would be logical. I can find little difference between recording all conversations, such as Nixon's Watergate tapes, and ordering a word-for-word transcript of the "Jesus affair." As for spending the end of his life documenting his actions, we need only look at Winston Churchill's five-volume tome of his decisions to understand that some men are so driven.

All of this brings plausibility to the document's creation, but what of the folios' survival? This answer may be found in the Eastern Church where Pilate and his wife are believed to have become followers of Jesus. If this document fell into the hands of the early Eastern Church, it would have presented the church's leadership with a difficult decision. Should the folios be published or destroyed? Those arguing in favor of publishing the folios would see them as supporting the Scriptures, those arguing for destruction would see them as casting doubt on church doctrine. Again a logical course of action for the church would be to archive, thereby preserving both documents and doctrine.

Some friends have argued that it would be impossible to keep such a document secret in these individualistic times of mass communication. This, however, was not the case. The documents were benignly suspended behind the Soviet Iron Curtain for most of the twentieth century, and when that curtain fell, the folios surfaced. If anything, the timing of the document's appearance lends credibility to its authenticity.

But I have labored too long on the document's pedigree. For me the real treasure in this folio was found in linking the past and present. It reminded me how little our leaders and we have changed. It bolstered my belief that history is more than a subject; it is the quiz of our future. In looking back, we see the multiple choices of our predecessors, and knowing that we hold no greater humanity than they, discover that we also have no greater range of decision. Their desires are our desires, their options are our options, and their fate, if we choose the same course, becomes our fate.

Chapter 4
Folio 3
Military Affairs

In my fourth year as governor of Judaea, I was confronted with the threat of disappearing troops. When first considered, this may seem no more onerous than troops killed in action, desertions, or those lost in capsized boats. But unlike other losses, missing troops can have the residual impact of destabilizing the military and fracturing governmental authority. This is of special consequence to an outpost that is hundreds of miles from meaningful reinforcements. In such isolation, military discipline and effective authority are the great balance against the superior numbers of the populace.

At the heart of all effective government is the bedrock of military action. Strip away the topsoil of a republic's system of justice, wash away the clay of brokered power, and you discover the fear of brute force. And if a stable government is to exist, this force must present itself with a hard, unfractured certainty. The military's ability to address all forms of insurrection with overwhelming force is the granite on which all commerce and domestic tranquility rests. To serve its purpose, the military must be seen as invincible, and believe itself to be the same.

I have bled and killed for Rome. I have carried her sword, slept with her troops, and been consumed with the fever and dysentery of her conquests. I have long since been out of the saddle that was my military post, but even as an old man I count myself a soldier, and hold a martial pulse. I knew then as I do today that a soldier's greatest fear is uncertainty. It is not going into battle that creates anxiety; it is the interminable waiting that stretches the sheath of our courage. It is not the fear of death that haunts the warrior, but the uncertainty of how he will pass that time between wound and mortality. A trained soldier living in certainty is a god! The same man consumed in speculation becomes a blubbering mass of inaction.

The incident of the missing troops had the potential to disrupt this bedrock of strength and all that rested upon it. The disease of uncertainty attacks from within, hollowing out all that defines the greatness of a soldier. Those affected no longer laud the courage of their fallen predecessors, but rather spend their idle moments speculating on the fate of the missing. They no longer search out the enemies of the empire, but avoid places of ambush. These once valiant and courageous troops assume the mantle of wash women gathered around the boiling pot, exchanging speculation and forming fact from rumors.

The other horror of missing troops is more obvious. Fractured authority is the dank moisture of rebellion. Those who would normally distance themselves from subversive activity suddenly discover a taste for sedition. Those who formerly cowered at the mere thought of the military's swift and cruel reprisal are now emboldened by the sneering rejoinder of their leaders: true they may send troops to punish us, that is, unless the troops were to disappear. Here we discover the headwaters of a full-fledged revolt. The first drop haltingly winding its way down the surface, leaving behind enough moisture to lubricate the path for the next, and the next… until a path is worn, and the surface smoothed, and nothing is left to oppose the inevitable.

I have always looked upon this meeting with Janus and the others as a pivotal point in my life, but I have no insight as to why this is so, nor what I would have done differently. But weight is felt, not observed, and the heaviness of this day would tilt my scales for the rest of my service as governor, and as attested by this document, for the rest of my life.

***

The transcription of the Jesus affair:
Day 1,742 of Governor Pilate's administration
Prepared by Simon of Emmaus
Present:
Governor Pilate
Janus, Officer of Internal Surveillance
Clephus, Officer of Internal Affairs – second half of meeting
Dalaccus, Officer of Military Affairs – second half of meeting
Marcus, Centurion – second half of meeting
Simon of Emmaus, Secretary to Governor Pilate

(Governor Pilate had just completed a meeting with the engineers that was a confusion of engineering jargon and technical legalities. Though still early morning, the governor had the look of a man who had worked a full day. He sat before the great desk that a moment earlier had held engineering drawings. Leaning back in the chair, he allowed himself to slide forward on the seat, his head pressed against the back, his hands fully covering and rubbing his face. He spoke to me from behind the motion of his hands.)

Governor Pilate: Simon, has Janus arrived?

Simon: Yes, Governor, he has been here since the cock-crowing watch.[xvii] He is outside your private office.[xviii]

Governor Pilate: Bring him here, lest I chance another meeting with that jar of leaches that masquerade as engineering planners.

(Janus is summoned and enters the room with little discernable motion. I take a moment to describe him, as so much of what he says is communicated through his presence and manner. He is a man well groomed, lean, with an intense gaze that fully captures, but does not alarm. His voice is without distinction and he neither raises nor lowers it during debate. Rather, he uses the movement of his eyes and a mobile countenance to weight his argument. Among all of Governor Pilate's officers, he is the only one that addresses me by my name. He walks to within three paces of the governor and with a closed lip smile, slightly bows at the waist, as he averts his eyes in homage.)

Janus: It is good to see you; you look well. I regret any difficulty my absence may have imposed. I have read the transcript of the meeting that I missed.

Governor Pilate: Simon, you may suspend your transcript as I wish to discuss the matter of the missing troops before addressing the Jesus affair.

Janus: It may be advisable to have Simon continue. This Jesus is not completely insulated from our lost troops.

(Governor Pilate, placing his hands on the arms of the chair, pushes himself back into an erect posture. The weariness of his countenance evaporates as he leans forward drawing closer to Janus.)

Governor Pilate: How so?

Janus: It appears to be incidental, but I am told that you wish a complete chronicle of this matter, and this Jesus and his followers are not without mention.

Governor Pilate: Very well, Simon, continue.

Simon: Does the Governor wish for me to transcribe only the parts that relate to Jesus...

Governor Pilate: (now agitated) All of it!

(Governor Pilate turned his attention to Janus; however, Janus was focused on me. His smile had returned and his manner was one of sincere confusion.)

Janus: Simon, how could you offer to record only the parts that related to this Jesus of Nazareth, unless you knew beforehand how the parts fit together?

(I was startled and felt my face flush. I instinctively looked to the governor, who was looking coldly at Janus. Taking a deep breath, I explained.)

Simon: I am in this job partly because I have the ability to recall conversations. My intent was to listen and then document only those portions that related to this matter.

(Janus said nothing. His smile absent, he stared at me as if he expected me to disappear. I made every effort not to appear uncomfortable, but his frozen manner forced me to speak again.)

Simon: The governor can attest to my skills in this area.

Janus: (crisp and efficient, as if disinterested) Indeed. Quite a gift. Perhaps the governor will allow you to demonstrate your considerable skill at my next gathering.

(Before I could respond, the governor barked an order to the soldier posted at the door.)

Governor Pilate: Send for Clephus.

(To the surprise of everyone, Clephus instantly appeared in the doorway. Acknowledging Janus with a nod, he entered and seated himself at the table. Janus, who to this point had been standing, immediately responded by seeking the equality of a chair.)

Governor Pilate: Out with it Janus. What of the soldiers?

Janus: What we know for certain is that twelve veteran soldiers, a bearer, and a squad officer left Jericho before sunrise for Qumran. They were to stop and assist the engineers at Bethabara, but never arrived. Somewhere in that five-mile journey between Jericho and Bethabara they disappeared.

Clephus: What do you mean disappeared?

Janus: Gone! No men, no supplies, no weapons, no witnesses… nothing.

Governor Pilate: Desertion?

Janus: Very unlikely. They were all veterans of numerous campaigns, and as assignments go in this rectum of the world, theirs was better than most. Also, eight of the men were up for rotation and expected to summer in Rome.

Clephus: Is it possible that they hired a barge and were lost on the river?

Janus: No, the river was out of their way and no funds were drawn for such a purpose. They left before sunrise, and it was only five miles. It was more easily covered on foot.

Governor Pilate: Tell me about the terrain; did you travel the route?

Janus: I traveled it twice, making certain the second time to leave before sunrise.

Governor Pilate: And?

Janus: Mostly open, but there were two spots that would lend themselves to ambush, one where the land fingers into the river. If the troops were drawn to this shoreline, they would have been encircled on three sides by the water. The other, about halfway, is a twenty-foot rock outcrop that would have been an ideal resting point and exposed them to an attack from above.

Clephus: I find it hard to believe that a seasoned squad leader would expose his troops to such peril.

(Governor Pilate and Janus exchanged glances as if to decide which would educate the errant pupil.)

Governor Pilate: (looking at Janus) Do you expect a squad leader to maintain an alert battle posture at all times? Are they to assume that attack is imminent at every moment? Would you expect them to go and protect an innocent from a highwayman? Should they assist a citizen in corralling a stray donkey? Do they seek the shade to eat their meal? You examine this affair backward; that squad leader was marching forward in time.

What of this squad leader, what do we know of him? Who does he serve under?

Janus: (referring to notes) His name is Metellus, but he is known to his peers as Minotaur.[xix]

Governor Pilate: Are the Greeks now part of this mystery as well?

Janus: No, but his Greek mother is responsible for the label. As he is described, Metellus is a man of average stature with a large broad head. His mother endeared him with the label Minotaur.

Clephus: You speak of him as "is." Do you assume him to be alive?

Janus: I am certain he is dead, but as his centurion has not declared such, I respect him as living.

Governor Pilate: Who is his centurion?

Janus: Marcus.

Governor Pilate: What do we know of him?

Janus: (again referring to his notes) Based in Jericho, two-hundred-man contingent, twenty-four years of service, twenty-one campaigns, favored by the locals, scores of citations for bravery, service, etc. Of special note is the fact that he has refused promotion on several occasions, and several years ago had his longtime servant miraculously healed, (looking down as his notes, not really searching, but seeking to capture the governor's attention) by Jesus of Nazareth.

(The governor, animated by the theatrics of Janus, raised and cocked his head as if to signal game afoot.)

Governor Pilate: Jesus assisting Rome's legion? An interesting turn…

(Janus, sensing the governor's new rhythm, sits with his palms and fingers pressed together just below his elevated chin.)

Janus: There is more.

Governor Pilate: No doubt, but I fear we have tread too far down this path without Dalaccus. My stomach sours from hunger. Go have your meal with Dalaccus and apprise him of our discussions. I will meet you here at the second bell.[xx]

(The governor stood, thus dismissing the party. I had begun to gather my things when he motioned me to stay.)

Governor Pilate: (calling to the guard at the door) Summon your commander. Tell your commander that my meetings this afternoon will be held behind closed doors. I wish for all sentries to be posted on the outside, three paces from the entrance.

(The guard acknowledged the governor and retreated. The governor walked to the window and, with his back to me, stared into the courtyard.)

Governor Pilate: What do you know of this Jesus?

Simon: Only what I have learned during these proceedings.

Governor Pilate: Nothing else?

Simon: Nothing.

Governor Pilate: And based on what we know, how do you measure him?

Simon: I know little, but from what we have learned I see a sheep among wolves. He seems to seek no advantage, and has provided useful service to a Roman officer.

Governor Pilate: You call him a sheep, as if he is not to be feared. Tell me, Simon, is it all not relative? Be he considered sheep or a lion, is it not all relative?

Simon: I am sorry, Governor, I do not understand.

Governor Pilate: If you were the grass of the field, Simon, whom would you fear more, a flock of sheep or a pride of lions?

Simon: I would fear the sheep...

Governor Pilate: Why? Because they would consume you blade by blade until they had eaten you to the very ground... leaving your roots to be baked lifeless in the sun.

Simon: I understand; Governor; it is most relative.

Governor Pilate: Eat your meal and return at the second bell.

(I leave the governor in the room, his hands folded behind his back, looking off to the right at the cresting pastures of Jerusalem.)

(Meeting resumes at two bells. Janus and Clephus return and bring Dalaccus. All parties take their previous places, oddly leaving an open seat directly on the governor's right. Dalaccus looks for another place but before finding an alternative, the governor pats the arm of the adjacent chair.)

Governor Pilate: Sit on my right, Dalaccus; we old soldiers must close ranks. The dogs are at our flanks. Have you been briefed?

Dalaccus: I have, Governor. I am grateful that you have allowed me to represent my men.

Clephus: We are here to represent Rome.

Governor Pilate: Well said, and also to find the truth, whomever it may prick.

(Janus, obviously impatient with the exchange, turns to the governor.)

Janus: Dalaccus has been briefed; would you like me to continue my report?

Governor Pilate: Dalaccus, do you have any questions on the matters discussed previously?

(Dalaccus, showing none of the infirmities present during the last meeting, assumes the direct countenance of a soldier.)

Dalaccus: I understand the details, but the target is unclear. Is there a direct tie between this Jesus and the missing soldiers?

Janus: Precisely where we left off. There is no direct tie, but the matter is packaged in a thick cover of circumstance. Marcus, the centurion in charge, has publicly acknowledged that he sought out Jesus to heal his servant. Further, he has claimed that the servant was miraculously healed.

Dalaccus: This took place before or after the disappearance?

Janus: Before.

(Dalaccus' manner began to assume command of the questioning. His tone was one of a commander questioning an ill-prepared junior officer.)

Dalaccus: Hours before? Days before? Weeks before?

(Janus leaned back in his chair and with the confident smile of a surgeon addressed the query.)

Janus: It was two and one-half years ago, while he was serving in Capernaum, that the servant was healed. Marcus has since provided funds to build a temple to their God and has sent the priest of that temple to this Jesus.

Dalaccus: Governor, I am confused. Are we investigating the missing troops, the Hebrew God, or Jesus? If we begin to tie things together with two-and-one-half-year-old tethers, I fear we will entangle the emperor's wife into this folly.

Clephus: A point well made, but a point that stands on some rather foul facts. A Roman centurion, seeking the help of a potential subversive, funding religious practices of the locals, and referring the same back to this very Jesus? Perhaps not a direct link, but certainly a tangle worth investigating.

(At this point, the governor holds up his hand to interrupt. His manner shows no favor to either side, but his question is delivered to Dalaccus.)

Governor Pilate: The clay of assumption and innuendo is easily formed into a snake. We deal with a commander of some record. Send for him, we will suspend this matter until he arrives… he can speak for himself.

Janus: There is no reason to await his arrival. Desiring additional protection on my return from Jericho, I persuaded him to provide himself and a dozen of his men as an escort. He is in the city; I will have him here tomorrow.

(A chill fell over the room, as all parties knew that Janus had encroached upon Dalaccus' command. Further, he had kept secret Marcus' presence within the city. Janus sat with his hands folded on the table; his eyes focused on Dalaccus, awaiting the fury.

Dalaccus appeared to have missed the insult. Governor Pilate, overcoming his surprise, addressed Dalaccus in a formal tone.)

Governor Pilate: Dalaccus, this is your command. Is this what you wish?

Dalaccus: (eyes on Governor Pilate, but shifting his gaze to Janus as he concludes his comment) There is no need to wait until tomorrow; he sits in my office. I can have him here in a moment.

(The governor tried but failed to hide his amusement. The goose had outmaneuvered the fox. Oddly, the irony seemed to amuse Janus the most.)

Governor Pilate: (standing and stretching) My backside is numb and my bladder is full. Summon Marcus and we will resume after I relieve myself.

(When Governor Pilate returned, all parties were seated in their places with the centurion Marcus standing by the door. Before the men could rise from their seats, the governor motioned for the two to stay seated. Instead of joining them, however, he walked over to Marcus. The centurion, a man of average height with a slender yet powerful build, stood at attention as the governor approached. Governor Pilate, his hands clasped behind his back, smiled as he spoke.)

Governor Pilate: You are Marcus, centurion in command at Jericho?

Marcus: Yes, Governor Pilate.

Governor Pilate: Please stand at rest. This is an informal meeting. Will you join us over at the table? I would offer you a seat, but that would encourage us to keep you longer than necessary.

(Marcus follows the governor across the room and assumes an at-rest posture nearest Dalaccus.)

Your record is most impressive, Marcus. Tell me, did you ever serve under mount?

Marcus: I was once in training, but I seemed to have a greater want for the horses than they had for me. It was excellent training on learning how to fall. I am a man who crawled out of my mother with leather on my feet.

Governor Pilate: That is the way of horses. They judge each man either a weight or an appendage. I was deemed the latter and spent my full service mounted.[xxi]

Marcus: It is fine service if you are suited.

Governor Pilate: The same as a foot soldier save one difference: one works leather with his feet, the other works leather with his ass.

(Marcus smiled and some of the tension melted from his at-rest posture. The governor, seeing the centurion eased, placed both of his hands on the table with a light slap and looked up at Marcus.)

I guess we owe you an explanation. We have been carrying on matters of state and a certain Jesus of Nazareth continues to cross affairs of interest. That is not to say that he is driving things in either a good or bad direction, he just seems ever present. Now these soldiers disappear, and we discover that their officer, you, have a familiarity with this same Jesus.

Dalaccus: If I may add...

Governor Pilate: No you may not. I wish to have a conversation with the centurion. When I am finished, you may add what you like.

(Marcus showed little reaction to the governor's comments. If anything, the introduction of Jesus seemed to settle him.)

Governor Pilate: What can you tell me, Marcus?

Marcus: I know Jesus of Nazareth. I do not know of any connection between Jesus and my missing men.

Governor Pilate: Do you believe them missing or dead?

Marcus: I know them to be dead.

Governor Pilate: On what do you base this certainty?

Marcus: These were veteran troops. I considered their officer a friend, and had most of these men under my command for over three years. They would not desert, they would not surrender... they are dead.

Governor Pilate: Then why have you not declared them so?

Marcus: It is a matter of command. It would be demoralizing to give up on them too quickly. Thirty days seems like a respectful time to search and investigate. The men all know in their gut, but it helps that we do not give up too quickly.

Governor Pilate: Most sensible. What have you and your men learned during your search?

Marcus: There is little doubt of what happened. The emperor's image was posted around the Jews' holy places in the area. The Zealots, seeking retribution, set up an ambush somewhere between Jericho and Bethabara and killed the troops.

Governor Pilate: Why there?

Marcus: How do you make fourteen bodies and all of that equipment disappear? They would be discovered in a local grave; you would be at great risk to porter them any distance. No, they were lured to a place near the river and butchered. Their bodies and the scores that they killed in the fight were loaded onto boats and made to disappear. The equipment no doubt is submerged.

(Governor Pilate stands with his hands behind his back and walks toward the centurion.)

Governor Pilate: So you think this whole affair my fault? That in ordering the emperor's image posted in its rightful place I cast these men at the bottom of Asphaltites?[xxii] (The governor's face and neck begin to noticeably redden as his voice rises and the words come more quickly.) Would you have me go to Jericho and serve wine and food to the Zealots that they might leave your men alone? Is that your solution?

(The centurion, although gathering himself to attention, remained unflustered. Maintaining eye contact, he speaks to the governor.)

Marcus: I do not have solutions, I am a foot solider leading foot soldiers. I do not govern, neither do I judge those that assume that burden. I obey orders. I do only three things—I fight, I train, and I observe. I offer only the observations of a foot soldier.

(The governor slowly returns to his seat, taking the opportunity to compose himself. Arms folded across his chest, he stares at Marcus in silence, much as an archer stares at his target. Then, as if the aim were perfect, he presses a smile while addressing the centurion.)

Governor Pilate: Do you suppose if you asked Jesus he would tell you who did this to your men?

Marcus: I know him to be a holy man, a priest, a man of peace. I do not think he would know of this matter. But that was not your question; my opinion is that he would speak the truth.

Governor Pilate: They tell me that you met Jesus. Is that correct?

Marcus: Yes, I met him once. My servant, Caius,[xxiii] was stricken with an illness that left him in an agonizing paralysis. His condition continued to decline and I was desperate to find relief short of death. I have friends among the locals, men I trust and esteem. One of them spoke of a healer named Jesus. He told me of numerous miracles that had been witnessed by hundreds, and he encouraged me to appeal to him on behalf of Caius.

At the time, I was stationed in Capernaum, and Jesus was due to arrive there that morning so I sent several of my men to locate him. When my men found him, they sent word and I immediately followed. What I found surprised me…

Governor Pilate: More important, what did you expect to find?

Marcus: I expected a man dressed in skins, a wild look in his eye, raving at me about the evils of my service to the empire. I expected him to return with me, for a price, and smear the lining of an animal's intestine over Caius' body while mumbling some centuries-old healing incantations.

Governor Pilate: Did you expect a cure?

Marcus: I do not know. I at least expected it to raise Caius' spirits.

Governor Pilate: And when you found Jesus?

Marcus: None of what I expected proved true. As I reached the crowd surrounding Jesus, I feared that I would not be able to identify him. I had no reason to fear. He was taller than the crowd around him, powerfully built, but most striking was his command. He held not only his space, but all of the space occupied by others. When I saw him, I wanted to believe in his powers, and when he looked at me, I felt his command.

(The others in the room sat motionless. Janus' eyes searched every manner of the centurion's delivery for some additional clue that might be missed by the others. Clephus had the appearance of a man deep in distant thought. Dalaccus suffered most as he ingested the questions that ripened on his tongue. The governor's manner shifted to that of a man caught up in a tale, encouraging the storyteller toward the climax.)

Governor Pilate: How large was the crowd… how were you dressed?

Marcus: There was a crowd of several hundred. I was dressed for drills with short sword and dagger and I carried my helmet under my left arm.

Governor Pilate: To the point…I have other business.

(The centurion was clearly confused, he was being asked for details but hurried along. He took a long moment to compose himself and then continued as if delivering a battle report.)

Marcus: The crowd was thick, but Jesus made eye contact with me, creating a clear path between us. I walked to him and asked if he might heal my servant. He nodded and asked me to lead the way. I told him that I believed him to be a man of great authority, that he could command the illness from where we stood, and it would respond. He told me that "as I believed it was so," that "my servant was healed."

When I returned to my quarters my servant was on his feet without pain. That is all.

Governor Pilate: This was how long ago?

Marcus: It has been over two years…[xxiv]

Governor Pilate: And the condition of your servant today?

Marcus: He is in perfect health, providing full service.

(The governor taps his chin with his right index finger, allowing his words to come slowly.)

Governor Pilate: A centurion is a man of some power. Did Jesus or his followers ever seek payment or favor for this kindness?

Marcus: No, Governor. As I said, that is all. I have not seen Jesus since, nor have his followers contacted me.

(The governor's manner eased to one of friendship as he addressed the centurion by name.)

Governor Pilate: Marcus, as you are here, perhaps you can clear up some other details. I am told that you funded a temple for the Jews, and that you attest Jesus to others?

Marcus: I am a man of some means. My family owns the vineyards south of Rome that you may know as Two-Roosters. But I was never bred to be a vinedresser, and my family honored my wish to join the legions.

I came to my Capernaum post a broken man. My wife, a woman whom I married out of love, had recently died after a long illness. I was befriended by one of the locals who proved great comfort to me. Later, when I learned that he struggled to acquire funds to build a place of worship, I obliged by providing a modest sum. It is a one-room dwelling. This same man's daughter later fell ill and I recommended that he seek out Jesus.

Governor Pilate: Was she healed as well?

Marcus: What I know of this matter I have learned from others, but it is said that she died, and Jesus returned her to life.[xxv]

Governor Pilate: Do you believe that so?

Marcus: I believe what I have seen.

Governor Pilate: An answer worthy of Rome's most astute senator. I shall let your ambiguity go unchallenged if you will give me a soldier's assessment of your healer. Should this Jesus be feared?

Marcus: All I know personally, as well as what I have heard from others, has him a man of peace and healing. I believe Rome's resources would be better deployed against the Zealots.

(Governor Pilate looks away from the centurion and around the table at the others.)

Governor Pilate: I believe we have had enough of this matter?

Janus: May I ask but one question?

(Janus appeared to be the only one in the room with an appetite for continuing. His alertness seemed to intrigue the governor.)

Governor Pilate: Very well, but make it brief.

Janus: But a moment, Governor. Centurion, why did you not take your servant to the Temple of Asclepius? Is not a god better able to heal than a wandering Jew?

(Marcus, having considered this matter complete, seemed suddenly fatigued. He drew a deep breath, fixing his eyes on Janus.)

Marcus: If that were so, I would return to Rome this spring and hold the most beautiful woman I have ever known. My wife was treated at the Temple of Asclepius in Rome; I took her there the first time with a light fever. One-hundred-fifty days and one-fifth of my holdings later she was as small as a child, without the strength to walk. I would carry her to the market on my arm with her clutching my neck (the centurion's voice began to shake); at night I would hold her as she coughed up blood. (he stopped and forced out the last sentence as tears formed in his eyes) She died crying, with her arms around my neck.

(The room was still, each man wishing to give the centurion an opportunity to maintain his dignity. Two deep breaths later he continued.)

I had no desire to see a similar outcome for my servant. (the centurion gathered himself, delivering the balance with the certainty of a command) Any result from Jesus seemed more desirable than the cold marble of an impotent god.

Governor Pilate: I have heard enough. You are dismissed.

(As the centurion turned to walk toward the door, the governor whispered to Dalaccus.)

Dalaccus: Centurion, (Marcus stopped and turned at attention) I will require your services here for the next several days. Report to my office.

Marcus: Yes, General.

(Marcus' swift sure steps of departure held the room motionless. As the door closed behind him, Clephus took a deep breath and let out an audible sigh.)

Clephus: Truly a tragedy, a Roman citizen of means grazing with the local sheep... death has taken more than his wife, it has drained Rome from him... the very portrait of Caesar's vessel, but inside filled with local sentiment. He must be relieved. That region is a tinderbox; a man of such confusion cannot see, much less defeat, these fanatics.

Governor Pilate: What will you have me do with him, Clephus?

Clephus: Send him back to Rome to tend his vineyards.

(Governor Pilate, expecting a quick response, looked at Dalaccus who was staring down at the table before him. The governor's voice gained an acidic edge.)

Governor Pilate: Then we will pack him off to Rome dressed in goatskins? Shall we also have him wear a sign that says, "spit on me I have been disgraced?"

Clephus: (picking up on the governor's tone) A better solution than leaving him in his current assignment.

Governor Pilate: (exasperated) Dalaccus, this is your command, yet you sit silent. Do you favor the proposal?

Dalaccus: (looking directly at Clephus, his voice without emotion) It would be illogical to argue the merit of having a commander of forces in place that fraternizes with the locals. I stand by, no, I stridently support my colleague's proposal. Roman authority seduced cannot be counted upon and must be expunged and exposed. Governor, I make myself available to prepare a list of Roman authorities that have fallen into the ways of the locals.

Janus: (laughing) Dalaccus, and they call you a man of no humor.

Clephus: (looking at Janus) You, as officer of internal surveillance, find this amusing?

Janus: A clever prey being snared in a more clever trap? Oh yes, I find it the pinnacle of amusement... Governor, with your permission?

Governor Pilate: (seeming to enjoy the exchange) Be brief with your sport, Janus. I am anxious to conclude this matter.

Janus: Tell me, Clephus, do you know anyone who holds one of the local women in his arms each night? Who has planted his seed in her womb? Who pays the taxes for her family? Who deals with suspicious traders that he might receive delivery of his favorite sweet wine? Do you know a Roman authority of such description?

(Clephus' jaw thrust forward as he leaned toward Janus and spoke in a measured tone.)

Clephus: And do you, Janus, know of an officer who works with locals to export goods back to Rome that...

Janus: My friend, it is not I that have proposed a standard of self-ruin. I merely offer you a hand out of Dalaccus' snare.

Governor Pilate: Enough. I will give Dalaccus the last word on this matter. Dalaccus?

Dalaccus: Jesus, the missing soldiers, healed servants... it is all still a jumble of uncertainty. I do, however, agree that Marcus needs some distance from his current assignment, distance without disgrace. I propose that I keep Marcus working in my office until spring, and then ask that he personally carry an important dispatch back to Rome. I would give him leave for the summer that he might attend to his family's business. When he returns, I will have him assigned to my security detail.

Governor Pilate: (looking at Dalaccus with a broad smile) A solution worthy of his service to Rome, (looking at Clephus) and no one has to forfeit the sweet bosom of their local.

(The governor rose from his chair and stretched. Leaning forward, palms flat on the table, he slowly shook his head in bewilderment.)

All of this and still no soldiers, no suspects, and a Jew healer that embraces both a Zealot and centurion... I have tax matters this afternoon, engineers in the morning. Clephus, you and I will conclude this tomorrow, after my meal with our visiting senators. Janus, push your people to give us a full list of Zealot leaders. Dalaccus, consolidate more of your force in Jerusalem. We will drive matters from here. Simon, Clephus, and I meet tomorrow at the third bell.

Simon: The tax administrators will be the last appointment of the day?

Governor Pilate: (looking past me to the others) Yes. Gentlemen, now I must attend to other matters.

Dalaccus: Governor, may I have a brief, private word with you?

Governor Pilate: It must be brief.

(The others gathered their belongings and left the room. Dalaccus stood, rubbing his hands together, and looked at me.)

Dalaccus: Must he stay and write down what I say?

Governor Pilate: Unless you speak of a state secret, I will have him here. If you like, I shall have him put away his nib. Simon, you need not record this.

(After this meeting, the governor asked me to transcribe the conversation. The balance of the meeting is reconstructed from memory.)

Dalaccus: As you know, Governor, I am married to a woman that is twenty years my junior. She is considered by many to be one of Rome's great beauties… (stopping as if searching for some lost word) I have not been with her for two-hundred days… she has been alone… my brother has written that she is keeping company with another man. I desire leave that I might attend to this issue.

Governor Pilate: Do you know this man? Who is he?

Dalaccus: Yes, I know him, but he is a man of some power and I would prefer to protect you from this matter.

Governor Pilate: A soldier to your very middle, always protecting. I will not pry, but I cannot let you return until we gain control of this situation. The Jews' Passover festival is also approaching. But by summer's end I expect we can have you on your way. I would prevail upon you to serve Rome for the next one-hundred-fifty days and then we shall discuss leave.

Dalaccus: Governor, I… shall do my best to see these issues resolved quickly that I might return home.

Governor Pilate: I share your desire; now I must attend to other matters.

(With a salute, Dalaccus left the room.)

Governor Pilate: Simon, record what you have just heard. I will need it for other reasons. Make a second copy of the conversation regarding his wife that I will include in a dispatch to Sejanus.[xxvi] Let us not take our eye off this matter... it is the small splinter that festers the foot.

Simon: Governor Pilate, I believe you have already seen the opportunity before you? The opportunity to use Marcus to ensure discretion in this matter?

Governor Pilate: Cumbersome tact, Simon... but an excellent idea. The loyal centurion will neither open nor fail to deliver my message to Sejanus. I shall compose the message in my own hand and attach your transcription. You will have the package ready for Marcus to deliver at the first break in the weather.

Simon: I will see it done.

Governor Pilate: I am curious, Simon, how do you see this pieced together?

Simon: It is not my place to reach such conclusions, but as the Governor has requested my assessment on this matter, I surmise an intriguing triangle. The Governor's patron, Sejanus, given free access to the desire of his lust, Dalaccus' wife, via Dalaccus' service in Jerusalem. But I am just a secretary, and not tutored in such matters.

Governor Pilate: (smiling) And not to be tutored, as you have quite enough, any more and you might lose your tongue. You have the gift of seeing matters together, neatly fitting them side to side, top to bottom. And all of this... Jesus, the soldiers, Dalaccus, and the rest, it all pieces together... of this I am certain. But how do they fit? And will we discover the pattern before it gathers itself and overtakes us?

(The governor, rising and moving to the window, spoke in a shallow tone.)

Or perhaps my thoughts create demons that have no life outside of my imagination. For clearly, all of this seems to have fallen neatly in line for me… but do they fall in line because they are all correct, or because they are all flawed? It is before us, the pieces of a mosaic colorfully turned face up, waiting to have us order the image.

(He turned to face me at the table.)

It is all here Simon; can you make it out?

Simon: No, Governor.

Governor Pilate: (voice softening and trailing off) Neither can I… Put your papers away and summon the tax ministers. It will be a relief to deal with affairs that are easily ciphered.

***

I confess that much of the meeting as transcribed by Simon had little direct connection with Jesus. Yet in some odd way everything that came in contact with the Jesus affair became deeper and heavier. No doubt most of what transpired was the predictable result of the human condition. Have not men and women always found their integrity dismissed at the pivot point of their stride? And is it not the nature of mankind to stand on a pillow of their own flaws, in order to reach and pluck the errant feather of another? Do we not find ourselves serving our own plate before passing the bounty? So in all respects this meeting followed the course of our nature.

In reading this again at a thirty-year distance, I still cannot discern the mosaic's pattern. Perchance the pattern is not the treasure. That greater unseen something that bound this meeting may be more fundamental… not the mosaic's image, but rather, that there was a mosaic to be discerned.

We had gathered to discuss affairs of state, yet found ourselves hanging our actions on our flaws and frailties. We had stopped speaking from our rank, and began speaking the whispers that churn within. Lust, loyalties, introspection, these are not things of proper governing! Effective government is laid out in parallel, and modified at ninety-degree angles. The rule is defined and set, it is not subject to mood or motive.

Looking back, it is clear that Jesus had his own unique measure cord, his own standard of construction. It was neither based on Rome's, nor that of the Jewish leaders. Whatever he was building was of different height, of foreign materials, and constructed at odd angles. This oddity prevented it from being pieced or joined to what was around him, be it Roman or Hebrew.

Those not there would see the perfect logic of ignoring the odd structures of his design... I too believe this to be the reasonable course except that all he touched seemed to hold the center space, forcing the rest to either spend their energy razing his structure, or modifying their plans around his design. In either case, Judaea was being bent around the space occupied by a man of no arms, no means, and no apparent agenda.

I have heard the criticism, and have fallen into the pit of obscurity that awaits those overtaken by fate. I no longer defend my actions to those who perfectly govern that which is already known. They judge me while looking into the still, clear pool of history. But the waters of Judaea during my tenure were clouded by the dust of hatred, and continually stirred at the prospect of rebellion. There was no clear line of sight; I picked my way through these matters one step at a time.

So blindfold yourself and run at full speed into the forest. And after you spend eleven years of your life careening into unseen obstacles, you may come and speak to me about governing Judaea. Then you will know and you may make the claim that you understand the choices of Pontius Pilate.

Note to Mac:

Pilate begins this folio with a crisp explanation of the military psyche, yet in concluding the document, we find him lamenting the circumstances that made precise execution impossible. Oddly, the transcript itself is focused on neither the military nor circumstance, but on the politics and the personal ambitions of Pilate's subordinates.

A tumult of desire and deceit are laid before us. Clephus seeks to discredit Marcus. Janus lays an ambush for Clephus. Dalaccus plots his return to Rome. Even Pilate, though attempting to keep an agenda of the missing troops and Jesus, finds himself a participant in the diversions of self-interest. At the conclusion of the folio, the seventy-eight-year-old Pilate laments, "We had gathered to discuss affairs of state, yet found ourselves hanging our actions on our flaws and frailties." It is an observation that is steeped in the wisdom of experience.

At the end of this folio, Pilate correctly identifies the pettiness that persists as part of the human decision-making process. We look back and view our decisions as having been carefully weighed on scales, and then apportioned with discernment. But how many grand decisions have been affected because of a migraine headache or a bout of diarrhea? Does anyone who has been married believe that a fight with a spouse can be insulated from professional responsibilities? We are all human, and so our decisions bend to the frailties of our species.

This folio has no great action or fact base; it is basically the banter of life. Would a forger of such a document think to include such matters? It is a judgement that is best left to the reader. But there is one certainty; there is genuineness to this dialogue that is lost in most historical accounts. It has an odor: the odor of someone's life.

Chapter 5
Folio 4
Setting the Trap

The sum of one's efforts to govern is a long cord. Pull sharply enough on one end and all matters jump in the same direction. Allow loops of slack and smaller tugs create only a local disturbance. But lift it in the middle and both history and the future fall helplessly limp on either side of the present. Truly, one's legacy is the sum of all such actions, but it is those things that we grasp in the middle that define the limits of our greatness. It is only an old man looking back that fully understands this cord of service. For in the power of youth, this twine appears to be a tool of boundless opportunity. The end, however, reveals those careless middle grasps that strangle the life from our aspirations.

My decision to deny Dalaccus' return to Rome was such a middle grasp. It seemed a small, harmless decision that fell neatly into place. It was in the best interest of Rome, advantageous to my patron, and though he might not agree, in Dalaccus' best interest. A small decision, one of hundreds I would make during that critical ten-day period, yet one that would hoist me up and hang me on the hook of destiny.

As I definitively stated in the beginning of this record, I ordered the crucifixion of the one known as Jesus the Christ. I do not back off from this. But in truth, it must be said that the change in Dalaccus' demeanor forced a pace of events that precluded more thoughtful alternatives. Once informed that he would have to remain in Judaea until matters stabilized, Dalaccus and his command became aggressively proactive in the execution of their duties. I should not leave the impression that Dalaccus was any less than a fine commander for he followed orders and did not overstep his authority. His loyalty was unquestioned, and he held no second agenda. But with the disappointment of not returning to Rome, he lost his field of vision, his circumspection, and became a man who viewed his mission through a peephole.

I marveled then, and I marvel today at the soft power of circumspection. A soldier ordered to cross a river is not without choice. He can mount his horse and begin a determined swim to the opposite bank; he can walk the shore in search of shallows that allow him to easily ford the obstacle, or he can seek and find a ferry that would carry him above the waters. In all cases, the soldier executes his orders, but how crucial the terrain of discretion. For if the waters are deep and swift, the swim can be fatal; if the need is urgent, the delay in seeking a ford, irresponsible, or if the ferry fee precious, the decision extravagant. I had ordered Dalaccus bound to Judaea until matters were in hand. His mind fixed on Rome, he drove his mount into the deep swift waters that would yield all to a current beyond our control.

I had saved Dalaccus from the humiliation of confronting the powerful Sejanus; I had honored the desires of my patron, and I had made Rome's best interest my mission. All of this, and Dalaccus cast it all into the current of his loins. How ironic that the beauty of a woman should drive the nails of crucifixion... a beauty that would fade with years, but gain in the consequence of its brief existence.

***

The transcription of the Jesus affair:
Day 1,745 of Governor Pilate's administration
Prepared by Simon of Emmaus
Present:
Governor Pilate
Clephus, Officer of Internal Affairs
Janus, Officer of Internal Surveillance – second half of meeting
Nicodemus, Representative of the Council and a Pharisee – second half of meeting
Simon of Emmaus, Secretary to Governor Pilate

Governor Pilate: Is Clephus here?

Simon: Yes, Governor Pilate.

Governor Pilate: Arrange that Janus and Dalaccus be close by, they may be needed.

(I asked the guard to inform Dalaccus and Janus to be available and returned to my table.)

Simon: Clephus is outside. Shall I summon him?

Governor Pilate: Bring him in.

Clephus: (smiling) It is good to see you, Governor. I trust all went well with the senators?

Governor Pilate: Clephus, I am in no mood for impish wit. I have just seen our illustrious guests on their way to Caesarea Maritima.[xxvii] They wish to spend the balance of their journey in her gardens and baths. Let Herod's court entertain them for a while.

Clephus: Did their unexpected inspection[xxviii] generate any items that require my attention?

Governor Pilate: (obviously losing his patience with the topic) What started out as a simple dinner turned into a three-day geriatric indulgence. They had their nose in every corner of our business, and their hands up every skirt in Jerusalem. If they did discover any items of interest, I doubt they retained them any longer than the flagon of strong wine that was consumed during every waking hour of their tour. As for your attention, you may want to investigate their chamber pots and see if they pissed away their brains before they left... Perhaps we should send them on to Ceasarea... On second thought, I doubt they would miss them.

(Governor Pilate took a deep breath and with eyes closed let out a long sigh) Let us move on to matters of import.

Clephus: Their unexpected stay has not been a total loss. It has given me time to outline a range of alternatives to address the matter of our last meeting.

Governor Pilate: Which matter do you speak of, the missing soldiers or Jesus?

Clephus: They may be one and the same, but I speak of the soldiers.

Governor Pilate: One at a time then. Your first idea?

Clephus: Janus has prepared a list of fourteen Zealot leaders. We seize them and bring them to trial, crucify them and allow their bodies to rot on the cross.

Governor Pilate: Do you know these men to be guilty?

Clephus: Of this crime? Uncertain. But guilty of sedition against Rome, there is no question. Janus' informers have been quite reliable in their information. The Governor need not worry about punishing the innocent.

Governor Pilate: I am not concerned about their innocence. I am concerned about crowning martyrs. Nothing elevates the life of a man higher than his wrongful death. Would you have these filthy, half-starved alley rats become symbols of Roman oppression, a rallying post for everyone that has a grievance against our administration?

Clephus: It is a risk, but a risk that not only serves notice, but also lops the head off of our adversary.

Governor Pilate: It is a poor risk, for sedition is a multi-headed beast. You take one head and another of different strategy assumes control. Crushing the body kills rebellion; the head without a body assumes the mantle of a yammering lunatic.

Other plans?

Clephus: Not a different plan but a variation. We make the Zealot leaders disappear. Like our men, they simply vanish, no trace, no burials, and no martyrs. It sends a direct message, while allowing us the distance of denial.

Governor Pilate: Intriguing. Very, very enticing. We would place them in our position by handing them the other end of the rope. We could leave behind evidence that they are still alive… our message delivered, but their passion doused with hope of their survival?

Clephus: (smiling and rubbing his palms together) I would need the assistance of both Janus and Dalaccus.

Governor Pilate: (with the kind smile of a father) Clephus, your lack of service in the legions is apparent. I mean this as no disrespect, but after you have set strategies and confronted enemies, you attain the habit of knowing what your foe carries in his pack.

Clephus: (without emotion) I am sorry, Governor, your point eludes me.

Governor Pilate: It is simple. The Zealots made fourteen of our men disappear. What did they carry in their pack? They had ten thousand eyes standing watch for them, we only a handful. They went to capture an enemy that was gathered together in isolation. We would have to pluck each from their home. They could choose their time of action. To be effective we must act quickly. They had countless targets. We have but one.

The odds of them executing their plan while going undetected were greatly in their favor. On the other hand, we are like a badger attempting to creep through a village that is rife with dogs. In fourteen attempts, I doubt we would go undetected in half. And once exposed, we would be denounced as thugs and ridiculed as buffoons.

It is tempting, my friend, but I think it best we not play their game.

Clephus: There is another option that, although not producing immediate results, has none of the undesirable collateral of my earlier ideas. It involves gathering a cross section of the Jews and holding them for interrogation.

Governor Pilate: Whom do you propose to interogate?

Clephus: Six leading citizens from Capernaum and six from Qumran. Also six Pharisee leaders, six Sadducee leaders, six of Jesus' followers, and, of course, six from the Zealot list. Add to this six of our informers and you have a most effective mix of possibilities.

Governor Pilate: Six of each for what reason?

Clephus: Three times the fourteen missing, an effective message in itself.

Governor Pilate: And the informers?

Clephus: They would be identified as belonging to one group or another, and when interrogated they would convey matters discussed between those imprisoned. I believe if we select the right individuals that within four weeks we will know a great deal more about our missing troops.

Governor Pilate: You would be holding these men without reason or cause?

Clephus: Janus assures me he will produce witnesses of questionable character that will link each to the disappearance...

Governor Pilate: Questionable character?

Clephus: That is the mission, to split their allegiances and create tension between the factions. They are accused by implausible sources, being held for an indeterminable period while external pressures escalate. That is where I need your help.

Governor Pilate: How so?

Clephus: I want the masses to pay the price for the Zealots' transgression. I want you to order the emperor's image hung on the exterior of the temple and make it known that the same will be done on the interior if the criminals are not produced.

Governor Pilate: You are aware that my decision to post the emperor's image in the temple courtyard caused a minor riot?

Clephus: If this is to succeed, we need pressure from all sides. With enough pressure we can resolve this before their Passover celebration.

Governor Pilate: Let us hope so. We do not have the troops to manage the masses congregating for the festival.[xxix] If it is not resolved, I will be forced to remove the emperor's image and expose our weakness. Such a gamble will require a tightly coordinated plan with both Janus and Dalaccus. Meet with them and outline the specifics. We will gather tomorrow and review the details.

If there is nothing else, I am going to rest. I have promised my wife the theatre this evening.[xxx]

(Clephus rises to leave.)

Simon: May I remind the Governor that there has been a delegate of the Sanhedrin[xxxi] waiting to see him for two days. They come to speak to you on the very matters being discussed.

Governor Pilate: Matters? Who?

Simon: His name is Nicodemus, a Pharisee. He is here to entreat the Governor to remove the banners of Caesar from the courtyard.

Governor Pilate: It is my destiny to nap during the performance. Pray to the gods that my wife is captured in the story. Very well, let us see what he has to say. But I must stretch first… (rising) Simon, you will join me for a short walk. Clephus, get Janus and ask him to join us with whatever information he has on this Nicodemus. I will meet you both here when I return.

Governor Pilate: Come, Simon.

(The governor and I exited the office, and took the stairs to the courtyard. Once outside we walked across the yard to the small gate that placed us on the road to the market. The conversation that took place during the walk with the governor is reconstructed from memory. It was not until we returned that the governor expressed his desire to include our conversation.)

(As we exited the gate) Simon, do you know of this Nicodemus?

Simon: Yes, I know of him.

Governor Pilate: What do you know?

Simon: He is a leader, a teacher, and is respected as a man of God.

Governor Pilate: But he is not the chief priest, nor a known man of power… Why do you suppose that he was chosen to plead their cause?

Simon: There is no way for me to know, but he is a man that belongs to no faction. His reputation is one of being open, fair, and most interested in the will of his God.

Governor Pilate: And what does his God tell him?

Simon: I do not know.

Governor Pilate: You speak of him with some kindness in your voice. Have you met him?

Simon: No, but he is well known. If he were representative of the Pharisees, I would be one myself.

Governor Pilate: High praises indeed. So, do I understand that you suspect a division on how to handle this matter within the Pharisee ranks?

That Nicodemus is the compromise choice to appeal to the detested Pilate?

Simon: For whatever reason, I believe they have chosen wisely.

Governor Pilate: How so?

Simon: Nicodemus is seen by the people as a gentle teacher... He humbles himself to all, and his advanced years have brought him before a large portion of the community. Should you take any rash action against him, the people would respond; yet at the same time, his qualities make it unlikely that he would provoke such an action.

(Governor Pilate said nothing for a hundred paces or more. He walked with his hands clasped behind his back, looking at the ground.)

Governor Pilate: (looking up and over at me) What else can you tell me about the old man?

Simon: It is widely known that he had a meeting with Jesus.

Governor Pilate: When?

Simon: Years ago, but since that time he has been one of the few leaders to avoid denouncing Jesus.

Governor Pilate: What is it about Jesus that draws such hostility?

Simon: The Pharisees seek respect and admiration, the Sadducees control and power. Jesus seems to rob them both of such nourishment. I do not know of Jesus' message, but I know it to be powerful enough to bind oil and water.

Governor Pilate: Oh?

Simon: The Pharisees and the Sadducees have long been enemies. They have found unity in a common loathing of Jesus.

Governor Pilate: A man worth watching... It seems that each time we turn the press, a little more Jesus oil is added to the jar. Add all of this to the transcript, Simon, and leave me to my thoughts.

Simon: Yes, Governor.

(The governor said nothing on the return walk. He kept his eyes fixed on his office window as if filling it with what I had just told him. We entered his office.)

Present:
Governor Pilate
Clephus, Officer of Internal Affairs
Janus, Officer of Internal Surveillance
Nicodemus, Representative of the Council and Pharisee – Later in the meeting
Simon of Emmaus, Secretary to Governor Pilate

Governor Pilate: Sit gentlemen. Janus, I assume you came prepared to brief me on the Pharisee Nicodemus?

Janus: There is not a great deal to tell. He is a moderate among the Pharisees, is highly respected by the common Jew, and has recently fallen out of favor with the leaders of the Sanhedrin. Other information... (referring to his notes) old, well educated, a teacher. That is the full report.

Governor Pilate: No reason for his trouble with the council?

Janus: Only a name, Lazarus of Bethany. I expect a report on Lazarus within the week.

Governor Pilate: I expect you will get your report in a moment. (looking at Janus) Has Clephus briefed you on this morning's meeting?

Janus: (looking at Clephus) No.

Governor Pilate: Then I would ask you to remain silent until you are briefed... (looking at the guard) Send in the Jew.

Janus: I may be more effective if I were to understand...

Governor Pilate: (calling to the guard) Send in the Jew!

(Nicodemus was summoned and entered the room. He wore a robe that touched the floor and covered his head. His hands were clasped in front as if he had captured and held an insect. The watery, gray eyes and wrinkled skin of the old man were in contrast with his erect posture.)

Governor Pilate: You are the Pharisee Nicodemus?

Nicodemus: I am he.

Governor Pilate: You wait two days for an audience. What is it you want, old man?

Nicodemus: I have waited two days to seek a kindness from you, one that will pay a handsome return.

Governor Pilate: What is it you want, old man? I have no time for your marketplace dickering.

Nicodemus: (his voice, losing its lyrical tone and flattening to that of a blade) I ask that you remove the banners of the emperor from the temple courtyard. They are offensive to our faith and disruptive to the tranquility of effective government. You would advantage us both by removing them.

Governor Pilate: Do you know what I want?

(Nicodemus, assuming the question rhetorical, did not answer.)

I said, do you know what I want!

Nicodemus: I am sorry, Governor Pilate; I thought you were going to conclude your question with a thought. Please tell me what you want.

(All in the room braced for the governor's rage, but instead saw the governor tighten his composure.)

Governor Pilate: (with a tight smile) You address me as a student. Are you here to give me a lesson?

Nicodemus: I do not mean to offend, but when attacked I assume my natural demeanor... I am forty years a teacher... I came to speak to you as a man...

Governor Pilate: (raising his eyebrows and relaxing his smile) Then let us speak as men.

It is natural for me to hang the image of the emperor, but I am willing to defer if you could assist me in identifying those who are responsible for the disappearance of my soldiers. You would serve your cause and yourself by helping me…there is great power and prestige in bending to the will of Rome.

Nicodemus: It seems that neither of us has anything to offer. For I know nothing of your soldiers' fate, and as for the tender of power and prestige, you confuse me with a Sadducee.

Governor Pilate: Then perhaps you will learn more when I hang the emperor's image on the temple walls, both inside and out.

Nicodemus: (obviously shaken) That would bring us to mutual destruction, but it would give me no knowledge of your soldiers. I know nothing of your men; perhaps that is why I was chosen to speak.

You are a man of intellect, you must know that hanging the emperor's image upon the temple would cause a full-scale riot. You are aware that you do not have the troops to successfully contain the Passover crowd, yet I do not see a man before me that bluffs… What advantage would such an action bring?

Governor Pilate: You stop your analysis of the consequence before discovering my advantage. I am a soldier in an outpost. My job is to bring Roman authority to this place, but should I fail, to fail with great noise, dying to the last man. Then the legions of Rome will come and crown us martyrs. There will be no mercy; you shall feel the hellfire of retribution: your fields plowed with salt, your women enslaved, and every stone of your temple tumbled.[xxxii] That is my advantage, the certainty of you in Idumea…[xxxiii] yours the fate of Teman.[xxxiv] That, is Roman victory. Surely you do not expect to defeat all of Rome?

Nicodemus: (pausing and showing an uneasiness at the reference to Teman) No, we shall not, but we are the people of a righteous and just God. A God who has raised His arm in battle and defeated the mighty enemies confronting His children. It was Israel that was the crushing hand of God. This is our hope, our reserve.

Governor Pilate: It is difficult to reason with a man who argues the power of a deity. But since you speak of your God as righteous and just, I am curious. Do you know the mission of the fourteen soldiers that disappeared?

Nicodemus: I know nothing of the matter.

Governor Pilate: They were on their way to Qumran[xxxv] to provide protection for those making the pilgrimage to Jerusalem… to the Passover feast. My men were to stop in Bethabara to assist the engineers in completing an aqueduct that would bring fresh water to the homes of your people.[xxxvi] Do you think your just and righteous God finds this reason to bring his wrath down on Rome? Does not innocent blood, be it Roman or Jew, stain the conscience of a righteous deity? The murderous acts of your people will be the whip of your scourging; will your God not know this?

(Leaning toward Nicodemus) Help me correct this injustice; help me to bring peace to your temple; allow me to lift up the name of Nicodemus and of all Pharisees. Tell me, who killed these men?

Nicodemus: (momentarily confused) You have created a great mixture of things. You mix the mortal with the eternal, the splinter with the cedar, and honor with expedience. I cannot answer these things together, for three profound but separate questions have been struck. As you have suggested, let us speak as men; and if I am imprisoned, let me be sentenced by the integrity of my comments.

First, you presume the mind of God. God himself spoke of this through the prophet Isaiah when He said, "His thoughts are not our thoughts, our ways are not His ways."[xxxvii] I do not know the economies of God, but I know them to be righteous, and I know of His covenant with the nation of Israel.[xxxviii] I do not fear Rome. He may allow you to plow us into the earth, but only that you might sow a greater harvest for His people.

As for the splinter of men you identified as helping my people, they came from a mighty cedar log that has tumbled down from the hills of Rome, crushing countless innocents in its path. It is most difficult to consider the splinter while fleeing the log. Still, I acknowledge that Roman women cry for their loss with tears no less wet, and wails no less pitiful. I regret the spilled blood of the righteous, be it Jew or Roman.

Finally, if I knew the identity of those you seek, I would either tell you because I believed them guilty, or I would refuse because I believe you wrong. In either case, I would not hide my knowledge of them. As for your offer of esteem for my brethren and myself... you suggest that I would discover their names simply because it would bring me power and honor. It is juxtaposition; power and honor are conceived from truth, they do not give it life. Your bargain is better tendered to the Sadducees.[xxxix]

(Gathering himself) You asked that we speak as men. I have given you the full of it. And should my words carry me to the depths of your prison, then I should descend on the steps of integrity, for I have spoken without deceit.

Governor Pilate: (maintaining direct eye contact with Nicodemus) Your candor will bring you no harm here, though I suspect it is not as well received with your council. But as you are their representative, I ask that you deliver my message. Either I am given the names of the murderous leaders, or in two days your temple will become a gallery for the emperor's portrait.

Nicodemus: (showing no emotion) I will deliver your message.

Governor Pilate: Tell those seeking an audience with me to say that they are sent by you. (Governor Pilate noticing the discomfort generated by his last remark, smiled at Nicodemus) Better, have them say that the council sent them.

Nicodemus: It shall be done as you say. Now I beg your leave.

Governor Pilate: I would ask you to stay but another moment and teach me. What might you tell me about Lazarus of Bethany?

(Nicodemus looked around the room, not searching or reading postures, but making certain that he commanded full attention. He addressed us as a group.)

Nicodemus: I do not know Lazarus of Bethany, but know of him. Men of high regard whom I trust have reported this man to be a miracle. Lazarus of Bethany died; this is well known by all in Bethany. His body was prepared, wrapped in grave cloth, and sealed in a tomb. Three days later Jesus arrived, had the tomb opened, and called out a living Lazarus.[xl]

Governor Pilate: This is not the first I have heard of Jesus. I assume you speak of Jesus of Nazareth? (Nicodemus nodded agreement) You and I both know that the raising of the dead has been the sport of deceivers for centuries. What makes you think your Jesus is not just another clever magician?

Nicodemus: That is not my belief, but you may make of it what you wish. Lazarus was dead; now he is alive. A large crowd witnessed the event. There is nothing hidden.

Governor Pilate: How is it that this man placed you at odds with the council?

Nicodemus: Your spies serve you well, but they bring you facts without reason. No matter, it is well known. The rulers of the council are Sadducees. They do not believe in the resurrection of the dead. I am a Pharisee, I do. The evidence of Lazarus has brought our conflict to the forefront.

Governor Pilate: Lazarus of Bethany or Jesus of Nazareth? It is hard to believe that words written are more loathed than their author.

Nicodemus: You seem to have a keen interest in Jesus; may I tell of him?

Governor Pilate: You may answer my question. Which has brought you in conflict, Jesus or Lazarus?

Nicodemus: In truth, neither has endeared me to the council, for it is common grit that seasons the porridge. Jesus' raising Lazarus from the dead grinds both the beliefs of the Sadducees and the authority of the Pharisees. As you say, one is the author and the other his works. Are they not equally dangerous to those that fear?[xli]

Governor Pilate: Fear what? All I have heard of Jesus identifies him as a man of peace and good works. Will he topple the Jews?

Nicodemus: Not topple, but rule. The fear is that he brings teachings of the Spirit. He calls men to open themselves to God's Spirit… to be judged and forgiven. There is no place in his ministry for those who would seek position or prestige for themselves.

Governor Pilate: (smiling) Coarse grit for those who seek the syrup of honor and power.

Nicodemus: Again, I cannot help but notice that you have a keen interest in Jesus...

Governor Pilate: I have a keen interest in all that would subvert Roman authority, including a new ruler of the Jews. Tell me Nicodemus, do you see sedition in this man?

Nicodemus: Against the emperor? No, I believe he has no such agenda.

Governor Pilate: You speak with authority on the matter. Are you a follower? Have you met him?

Nicodemus: I am a follower of the God of Israel. I have met Jesus, yes, and I have given you what he revealed to my heart.[xlii] I am certain that you would find him most engaging. Perhaps you should summon him?

Governor Pilate: Why do you seek to trap me, old man?

Nicodemus: Trap you?

Governor Pilate: You suggest that I bring forth and esteem the common enemy of the council just weeks before the Passover turbulence... You would have the Pharisees, Sadducees, and Passover pilgrims tearing me in odd directions... Is this the plan you use to tumble my office?

Nicodemus: You misjudge me. I am an old man with no hidden motives. My only desire was to bring you the knowledge that you sought.

Governor Pilate: No. I shall avoid your internal squabbles for now... There will be time to address this matter once rid of the Passover crowds. I will not be drawn in.

Nicodemus: I fear I have occupied the Governor too long. I again beg your leave.

Governor Pilate: (smiling) Nicodemus, I believe you are not enjoying our conversation nearly as much as I am... I will detain you no longer.

Deliver my message to the Sanhedrin, and tell your friend Jesus that we shall talk after the Passover crowd has disbursed.

Nicodemus: You suppose him my friend... I would be flattered to be considered such, but I do not see him as belonging to any man. He is a teacher, a prophet, and more.

Governor Pilate: (agitated) More?

Nicodemus: He speaks with authority about matters that reach beyond what we know. You will understand once you meet him.

Governor Pilate: You speak of more. More to accomplish what end? What do you know of this?

Nicodemus: I have followed his ministry.

Governor Pilate: And what did you discover?

Nicodemus: A man sent by God that we might be saved from our sins. I believe him the fulfillment of prophecy. Our prophets spoke of him in ancient times when they called out the one who would bring about miraculous things.

Governor Pilate: What things?

Nicodemus: The blind receive sight, the lame walk, those who have leprosy are cured, the deaf hear, the dead are raised, and good news is preached to the poor.[xliii]

Governor Pilate: (smiling) Then I will be most entertained when we meet, for I will have him perform for me.

Nicodemus: You would be well advised to consider him a holy man, a man of God. There is a power in him that is not found in others; a man such as yourself would see this immed...

Governor Pilate: (his voice rising in mock astonishment as he leaned across the table) Power! Power? Perhaps, but unless he can identify those that murdered my troops, such an indulgence will have to wait. In two days my troops will begin hanging the banners on the temple. If I hear nothing from your leaders, they will be responsible for any blood that flows.

Nicodemus: (moving for the first time, taking a small step toward the governor) Your message is clear, but what of yesterday's casualties? What of the children? Should their blood not be assigned to a responsible party?

(The governor stared at Nicodemus in search of further explanation, but he offered none.)

Governor Pilate: Are we now speaking of children? (growing impatient) Spit it out, old man, what are you talking about?

Nicodemus: (speaking quickly, with an edge to his voice) The actions of your troops that were hanging banners in the temple courtyard. They ran down three children and smashed their heads with the hilt of their swords. One child is dead, the others near death. Who shall wear the stain of their blood?

Governor Pilate: Are you telling me that Roman troops bludgeoned three children without provocation?

Nicodemus: No, the children were throwing manure at those hanging the banners.

Governor Pilate: Then you may place the blood on the children's hands or on the hands of their parents.

(Nicodemus' face lost all expression, and for the first time his voice took on a hard edge.)

Nicodemus: The dead child had just turned six, the two clinging to life are five years old. Your men chased them down and now carry their blood and the hair from their scalps on Roman weapons. Is this Roman valor?

(Janus and Clephus exchanged glances as they saw the blood drain from the governor's face. The governor took a deep breath.)

Governor Pilate: No, that is not Roman valor; it is a tragedy. Such actions are in neither of our interests.

Nicodemus: Some believe otherwise, including those smashing the tiny skulls and those who watched and offered no reprimand.

Governor Pilate: I have expressed my regret, but you continue to goad me. I have enjoyed our conversation and I shall overlook your words of grief. Just deliver the message...

Nicodemus: I go now to pray for the children. I will keep you informed.

(Nicodemus, with a slight nod, turned and left the room.)

Governor Pilate: (looking at Clephus) Talk to Dalaccus. Find out what provoked his troops. Tell him to visit the children's families and deliver concern and support.

(The governor stood and walked to the water stand. Pouring himself a cup of water in his left hand, he rubbed the back of his neck with his right. He said nothing as he stared at the door Nicodemus had just exited.)

Janus: The loss of a child is always regrettable, but the whirlwind of violence is blind to age and innocence. It regards only the passion of the moment. I...

Governor Pilate: (lost deep in thought, suddenly seems irritated to be brought back into the moment) What? What is it you prattle about?

Janus: I was sharing your regret concerning the children. I was going to say that the blood of a child brings the deepest remorse...

Governor Pilate: (visibly irritated) Do you suppose that I grieve the spilled blood of these children? Three young Jews? These people breed like goats; before they even fell to the ground a dozen had been conceived to replace them. I have no taste for innocent blood, but these were hardly innocent. Moreover, their fate may yet serve Rome if it brings caution to the rest.

Tell me, Simon, how many brothers and sisters do you have?

Simon: I am the sixth of seven children.

Governor Pilate: You see, Janus, there will be no shortage of Jews. But there may be a shortage of troops if we do not take decisive action. Better to open the doors of our armory to the Zealots than attack children so close to the festival.

There is fire in the spilled blood of children. Such actions clothe the rhetoric of the Zealots in plausibility. Their ranting will no longer have the edge of farce, but the palpability of evidence. This mindless retribution, if not immediately addressed, will make the meek bold and the bold violent.

Clephus: I will pass on your instructions to Dalaccus. Your ordered kindness will go a long way in settling the matter.

Governor Pilate: (leaning on the table, looking down into his cup) The expressed kindness will buy us but a few days. (looking up) The hunger of hate is not satiated with kindness; it demands the raw meat of retribution.

(Looking up at Clephus) Imprison the soldiers involved, bring them to trial and have them publicly flogged. See that they are sentenced to live chained in the galleys. Publicly shackle them and march them to the coast. Let them see these men chained in the belly of a ship with oars strapped to their wrists.

Clephus: Some would argue that we are punishing these men for serving Rome...

Governor Pilate: Then use light leather in your whip and release them once you clear the coast. I seek no punishment, just a few stripes, a trickle of blood, and a show of justice. Send orders with them to have them reassigned, but keep them clear of Judaea... I want Dalaccus at the forefront of this folly.

Clephus: I will inform him.

Governor Pilate: Oh yes, do not inform the condemned of their true fate until they are clear of the coast. Soldiers are rarely convincing actors, but Jews are most astute in reading a man.

Janus: If we are finished with this matter, I am anxious to learn of the plan that you and Clephus alluded to at the beginning of this meeting.

Clephus: We are going to arrest six each—Pharisees, Zealots ...

Governor Pilate: (holding up his hand) My guess is that the good Nicodemus will obviate our little scheme. We will let matters rest as they are for now. The old man will deliver the message, and we will wait a few days to see what slithers its way to our door.

Now if you will excuse me, I must meet an angry woman. Simon, schedule a meeting late tomorrow to resume our discussions on this matter.

Simon: The same parties?

Governor Pilate: Clephus, Janus, myself, and of course whoever comes forth with the prize.

(Governor Pilate rose and walked toward the door.)

Clephus: (calling after the governor) I shall triple security for tomorrow's meeting.

Governor Pilate: (speaking while neither breaking stride nor looking back) Hold your dogs, Clephus; tomorrow we are trapping, not hunting.

***

Though the course seemed so clear at the time, now, as an old man, I read these pages and see beyond the actions and reactions. Traps, plots, and responsibilities, these are things of the present; while motives, suspicions, and fear are transient within the individual. But all of this, all of life, rises and falls on the tidal sea of destiny. And what are its elements, salt and water? No, this tide rises and falls on a mixture of time and power. It swells and recedes in an ever-changing mixture that is indiscernible to those caught in the clutch of the moment. Yet each day we are lifted and descended, awaiting our fate... events unbalancing us until we are capsized. Then, at that moment, we discover the power of destiny, for those that fall while in the tide's ebb find themselves standing safely in the shallows, the less fortunate, in the crushing deep of tragedy.

Today, I see both time and power at play in this portion of the transcript, each equally carrying my fate, but time the more obvious. For it was I who chose to postpone the meeting with Jesus until after the Passover festival. Would my fate have drifted in a less perilous direction had I met him prior to him being the center of events? What would we have discussed? Some will think my musings senile, for I had several direct conversations with Jesus. This is true, but true with a twist, for events had overtaken us both by the time of our encounters. By then I had lost the chance of free choice and there would be no post-Passover meeting. At Passover I would order Jesus crucified.

And power? Power is equally evident in this encounter, albeit camouflaged in the form of an old man. He was magnificent! Simon does me a disservice in portraying me as condescending toward Nicodemus. "Old man" is what the transcript has me call him, but in a tone that one uses with a revered elder; the transcript is mute to inflection. In my service to Rome, I never met a more powerful man than Nicodemus. At that time in Judaea, he was more cogent than either the Sanhedrin or myself.

Of course, then we did not consider ourselves eclipsed by Nicodemus, for we operated within the formula of grasp. The more you held, the greater your power. But in wisdom, I discovered those economies reversed, and Nicodemus the more mighty. For grasp requires that we hold onto what has been accumulated, weighing us down with yesterday and encumbering us with what might be lost. Nicodemus held only his belief, or better stated, was held by his belief. He did not speak or act out of fear, for there was nothing to be lost. He knew in the very marrow of his bones the great something of his life, and he lived knowing that it was beyond the reach of both man and Rome.

Looking back, I see him as a great rock unmoved by the raging waters, watching both men and circumstance stream past on the current of events. He was prescient, seeing through the mists to the future. It was all clear to him, observed with certainty… He knew, and we did not; he may have said… but no one was listening.

Note to Mac:

There is a complexity evidenced in this folio that is mind-numbing. Within these few pages, Pilate instantly recognizes the spilled blood of children as a powerful weapon, chillingly rationalizes their conceived replacements, and then in retrospect warmly memorializes Nicodemus.

What kind of man, when reflecting upon past events, omits any remorse over the death of small children while expounding upon the flow of time and power? I first sought an explanation by looking in the folio. Eventually I discovered the answer in the daily newspaper.

I recently read about an errant missile that was targeted to hit a terrorist camp. Through some human or technological error it missed the intended target and killed a dozen innocent civilians, including multiple children. The leader of the country sending the missile immediately acknowledged the error and just as quickly assigned blame for the tragedy to the terrorists. His logic was that the actions of the terrorists had precipitated the reprisals; therefore, any unintended consequences of such reprisals were the responsibility of the terrorists.

I do not hold myself above such logic, as I supported the attack and admire the man who ordered it. It is the way of history that the small tragedies are washed clean and forgotten by the detergent of purpose and mission. But there may be a more basic answer to Pilate's recollections that is found within us as individuals.

We view and live our lives through various filters. Some filters elongate, some compress, others color. We snap combinations of these filters on our perceptions and use them as we record our histories. These filters I speak of are not devices of the weak, but requisite survival gear for all of humanity. For how else could we endure the abject horror and disheartening tragedy that accompanies our survival?

Chapter 6
Folio 5
A Casualty of War

There is no warmth in old age. You either feel the cold reality of death or the white-hot passion of lost chances; there is nothing in between. So it is with my decision to include this portion of Simon's transcript. I attested that I would include the whole matter unedited, and I have met this obligation to the extreme.

The reader may wonder why this interchange was originally recorded, as it holds Simon at its center and only mentions Jesus in passing. I must confess that I have read it over several times and see no milestone within its words. In fact, it may best be described as a lesson between mentor and student. All of this said, I am an old man and the dim sight of age brings a greater appreciation for items of clear contrast. It is all here, the Jesus matter, not just the parts that seem important… all of it.

***

The transcription of the Jesus affair:
Day 1,746 of Governor Pilate's administration
Prepared by Simon of Emmaus
Present:
Governor Pilate
Simon of Emmaus, Secretary to Governor Pilate

(Recorded from memory, as Governor Pilate did not indicate a desire for a transcription until later in the meeting.)

Governor Pilate: (rested and energetic) What do we have scheduled today, Simon?

Simon: The meeting you requested yesterday evening. I have Dalaccus, Clephus, and Janus available, messages from Nicodemus and Annas, and a report from Janus. Apart from yesterday's discussion, the chief engineer has requested an audience as he requires additional funding. The report is back concerning the grain stores, and the dispute over port entry fees requires your attention.[xliv]

Governor Pilate: (seeming pleased with the light schedule) What of the grain stores, Simon?

Simon: The report is not favorable. The recent bad weather breached the roof and dampened the grain.

Governor Pilate: Can it be saved?

Simon: The report has it a total loss. The grain is moldy, top to bottom.

Governor Pilate: What do you know of goats and sheep, Simon?

Simon: I come from a family of merchants.

Governor Pilate: Cattle can eat moldy grain, Simon. I wonder if the same can be said of goats and sheep? There may be a denarius[xlv] to salvage from this yet.

Simon: I will investigate and have an answer tomorrow.

Governor Pilate: On second thought, send my instruction to have it burned. There is no way to keep this grain from finding its way back to our stables. Horses cannot tolerate the mold.

Simon: I will see it done.

Governor Pilate: Summon the others. I am anxious to see this matter concluded.

Simon: Does the Governor wish to review the messages and report before summoning the others? I believe the matters are of some relevance.

Governor Pilate: Covering what topics?

Simon: The children, Jesus, the council, and the missing soldiers.

Governor Pilate: Very well, we will review the correspondence first. Include this meeting in the record.

Simon: From the beginning?

Governor Pilate: (somewhat irritated) Fine.

Simon: First received was the message from Nicodemus; it came during the cockcrowing watch.[xlvi] His message is short. "I promised to keep you informed. Here is my report. Both of the injured children died last night. One quietly in his sleep, the other while suffering great pain." The message is signed "Nicodemus."

(The governor rose and walked to warm himself before the small fire. He spoke with his back to me.)

Governor Pilate: There is a chill in the room. Children… such a tragedy.

Simon: Have not a dozen already replaced them?

(Governor Pilate turned toward me, his back to the fire and his full attention on my face.)

Governor Pilate: Your tone and your words speak offence. Tell me, Simon, did my comments yesterday about the lives of these children offend you?

Simon: It is not for me to be assuaged or offended. I am here in service. Should I fail in this service there are a dozen others to replace me.

Governor Pilate: You see, I have offended you… I did not speak as a man yesterday, but as governor, as a soldier. Do you not see the difference? As governor, I view these people as a shepherd views a flock, so much meat and wool. There is no room for sentiment. It is all numbers.

Simon: It is good to know that the governor I have loyally served for the past four years has numbered my family and myself. It is good to know that we are tick marks in your ledger.

Governor Pilate: You are young, Simon, and correct in stating that you have provided faithful service to this office. I would dismiss you for impertinence, but you hold a greater place than secretary. You have become part of my household, a repository in which to place the wisdom of my experience. We have no dispute; it is ignorance that has created this misunderstanding.

(The governor moved toward me speaking in a soft tone.)

Put your nib down for a moment and listen, you may catch up later.

(The balance of the conversation was reconstructed from memory.)

Men of the past, present, and future carry a quixotic capacity within them. They possess the ability to hate a race of people while loving them as individuals. Field commanders have long understood this fine balance and are careful to respect its authority. A soldier ordered into the fray of the masses has the capacity to indiscriminately slay men, women, and children by the scores. However, that same man will defer from slaying a lone woman standing before him... Even under the shame of refusing a direct order, he will dishonor himself before lifting his sword to her.

You see the group holds no life, no aspirations, and has no face. It is a mob, a beast that is either contained or destroyed. To contain or crush the enemy, Simon, you must keep them huddled together as a mob or your troops will begin to distinguish them as individuals. This is the key to being a shepherd and to governing a people.

Simon: And what of my brothers and sisters? You have not seen their faces. Are they not part of the mob? Would you not slay them with the masses, never knowing until it is too late that you have destroyed all that is dear to me?

Governor Pilate: I would go out of my way to protect your family, but yes, they might well become casualties. But you proclaim this fault as if it is exclusively mine or Rome's. Do you think your people exempt from such instinct? Do you honestly believe that the Zealots or the Pharisees, given the upper hand, would behave differently? What we speak of is not in government or politics, Simon; it is within the condition of mankind.

Simon: I cannot find fault in your observation, but I lament what we are. So much is lost with the life of a child, of a loved one. Perhaps this is the appeal that Jesus has to the people...

Governor Pilate: You have heard Jesus speak then?

Simon: No, my duties prohibit such activity, but his words seem to ripple through the streets. In an odd way you both use the same vessel to carry different matters. He speaks of shepherds and the masses also.

Governor Pilate: Does he?

Simon: Yes, but it is a different message. He calls himself the "good shepherd"[xlvii] saying that he is willing to give his life for his sheep, and other sheep[xlviii] that are not of this fold;[xlix] he says he will bring them together, as they respond to his voice. All of this he claims will result in one flock with one shepherd.

Governor Pilate: A grand thought, but one of ignorance. He may indeed gather these sheep together, but their common purpose will be his demise. Now is this matter settled, Simon? Do you understand that one must govern within the bounds of the human condition? That my esteem for you or any individual must be held apart from my duties and opinions as governor?

Simon: I appreciate your time and care in putting this matter to rest. I understand, but it is a bitter drink to swallow.

Governor Pilate: Bitter for us all, Simon… bitter for us all. Now summon Clephus and Janus. We will meet after my meal. You may tell Dalaccus that he will not be needed today.

(The governor walked toward the door, turning to deliver a final message.)

And, Simon, when you record this, make a copy of our conversation for yourself. It is a bit of wisdom that will make a good companion for your future.

***

This would be the last time Simon and I addressed the expendability of children. He resumed his former demeanor in all respects, demonstrating a full trust and willingness for all aspects of his duties. It was as if no breach had occurred, except for a quiet reserve that he now held apart. We never spoke of this almost invisible span, but both of us knew it was there. I came to imagine it as the thinnest of threads that he had tied to his roots, a thread that he would carefully extend each time his duties beckoned him deeper into the ways of Rome. It was the flimsiest of lifelines, but it served its purpose, for Simon believed that its careful retrieval would lead him safely back home.

I had always envisioned Simon returning to Rome with me. I would sponsor him for Roman citizenship, adopt him,[1] and thought us likely partners in a successful trading venture. But whenever I spoke of him returning with me, Simon, although showing immense gratitude, expressed a will to stay in Judaea. I needed no explanation... Rome was too far, the thread not long enough.

And, so from a simple comment was spun the finest of threads that bound the son of my choice to a land apart from my future. A double portion of tragedy, mine the lesser for having to live a future bereft of an heir, Simon's the greater for vesting his hope with the flesh-hungry dogs of Judaea. All of this a sad tale that some would label ill fortune, or catastrophe of circumstance. But such labels are ascribed by women and those who have never known the callus and blister of the short sword. The soldier knows better. The loss of Simon 'twas not fate or circumstance. He was simply a casualty of war.

Note to Mac:

Although the aged Pilate dismisses its relevance, reading this folio lifted Pilate off the flat pages of the manuscript, giving him a human dimension. Specifically, his sensitivity and parental concern for Simon forced Pilate to soften and qualify his previously expressed opinions.

Pilate's affection for Simon is apparent even to the most casual reader. This affection is evident in both Pilate the young man (as recorded in Simon's transcript) and Pilate speaking at the end of his life (commentary on the transcript). How can this be? Simon was a Jew and Pilate had an obvious hatred of the Jews. But here, and with Nicodemus, we discover a man who has sensitivity to the individual that is not transferable to the masses.

In many ways, I am reminded of something a Southerner told me when I was fourteen years old. It was 1965 and we were watching the news footage of the race riots on television. As the news commentator at that time continued to speak of race relations as a "Southern problem," my friend could no longer contain himself. Rising, he wagged his finger at me and pronounced, "You know what, it's too damned easy to blame this on the South. This whole country hates the coloreds in their own way. In the South we hate them as a race and love them as individuals; in the North they hate them as individuals but love them as a race. This isn't a Southern problem, it's a country problem!"

Of course my friend proved to be correct, as the duality of hatred found its way North, just as today it timelessly seeps into my reading of this folio. It empties me to know that my culture and Pilate's exercise a duplicitous value system. We have the ability to dispassionately dismiss the headlines of a starving nation, but cannot bear the sight of a single child in want of food. We disparage differences in other cultures, but find the same differences fascinating in the individual. Our judgements are quick and sweeping when applied to a group, but thoughtful and deliberate when applied to a person.

How disquieting it is to discover a value shared with Pilate. My instinct is to run, set these pages aside, for they hold before me an ugly mirror. But there is no running from a reflection, for no matter how far you flee, the image is forever attached to your soul.

Chapter 7
Folio 6
Baiting the Trap

Is life not a game? Is it not comprised of moves, rules, strategies, and penalties? Are there not time limits, winners, losers, and protests? Are we not continually keeping score of our life and counting our pieces? It is not by choice that we play, for we are born into this struggle, and we often die never knowing the final result. And if there are varying degrees of difficulty within this competition, then I can think of no more difficult field of play than Judaea. It was the master's field, for it brought together the worthiest opponents, highest stakes, and the blind serendipity of chance.

More than anything, my service in Judaea made me aware of my participation in this labyrinth of competition, and the complexities of playing. Do not misjudge me, for I do not believe there is anything profound in citing the parallels between mortal existence and our inventions of entertainment. Centuries-dead philosophers waxing on such similarities have long been fodder for schoolboys. It was not the rules or gamesmanship that Judaea taught me; it was the disconnection between the players that was to be my education.

At the heart of each game that we construct for our entertainment is its finish. Be it an end line, a filled hole, an amount of money, or a simple count; all players vie for its capture. And to make certain that each player has an equal chance to attain the objective we define rules that force all playing to engage in a proscribed manner. These are the games we invent, not at all like the game we must live. For the rules of our existence engage players with divergent objectives playing on a field of their choice. Life's players do not move in turn or stop and start together, but choose a pace that complements their purpose. Yet in all this chaos they are held together, for each must dodge, outwit, and maneuver past the others. Each seeking their own end… an end that long ago may have been precluded by the unknown actions of an opponent.

***

The transcription of the Jesus affair:
Day 1,746 of Governor Pilate's administration
Prepared by Simon of Emmaus
Present:
Governor Pilate

Clephus, Officer of Internal Affairs
Janus, Officer of Internal Surveillance
Annas, Former High Priest
Simon of Emmaus, Secretary to Governor Pilate

(The governor returned to his office after his meal. As he entered his office, he asked the guard to summon Clephus and Janus and have them wait outside.)

Simon: I trust your meal was satisfactory, Governor. Shall this meeting be part of the transcript?

Governor Pilate: Include it all. Where were we, Simon?

Simon: We had reviewed your schedule, and I had just read you the correspondence from Nicodemus...

Governor Pilate: (not seeming to hear my response) I took my meal with the chief engineer. I told him his funding requests were obscene. He droned on about the cost of materials, labor, and the weather... and then do you know what he said? (The governor's tone became playful.)

Simon: What, Governor?

Governor Pilate: That if he were in Rome, he could complete the project for half the cost. Agreeing with him, I said that familiarity with the area and its resources were no doubt of great advantage. He concurred. So I asked him to give me a copy of his specifications and I would investigate having the locals manage the project.

(The governor was consumed in a fit of laughter, forcing out his next comments in gasps.)

I thought he was going to piss himself; I really thought he was going to piss himself. (beginning to regain his composure) It seems our chief engineer had a sudden awakening of economy, for he is going to rework his estimates before requesting additional funds.[li] (wiping his eyes) In any case, you can take him off of today's schedule.

(The governor, still amused, motioned to the papers before me.)

Are those the messages from Janus and Annas?

Simon: They are. May I read them to you? (The governor nodded.)

First received was the message from Annas. It reads, "At your request the council is willing to send a representative to discuss the removal of the banners from the temple courtyard, Jesus of Nazareth, and associated matters. We will make every effort to accommodate your schedule." It is signed, "Annas."

(As I read the message, the governor's good humor was transformed to controlled anger.)

Governor Pilate: Willing? Did the message say willing? I did not seek a discussion of Jesus… a representative to discuss what? I want to know who murdered my soldiers… that is what I want! Address the following message to Annas.

Simon: Do you wish this correspondence included in the transcript?

Governor Pilate: (exasperated) Please stop asking me that question. Include what you like. We can strike out the extraneous later.

Simon: Very well, the message to Annas?

Governor Pilate: Governor Pilate is willing to hear your petitions regarding his plans to hang the emperor's image inside the temple.[lii] Your failure to appear before him immediately will be deemed your consent in this matter.

Your personal presence is required; no representatives will be received. Absent your appearance, please make the temple ready to receive an engineering contingent.

Simon: Do you wish to sign the message?

Governor Pilate: No, put the seal of office on it and have it delivered by a local.
(I had the guard summon a carrier and gave him instructions for delivery.)

Simon: The message is on its way.

Governor Pilate: (leaning back in his chair, fingering a medallion in his right hand) Have you ever seen a crocodile,[liii] Simon?

Simon: No, Governor.

Governor Pilate: They are an interesting study. They lay openly in the waters near the shore, entirely submerged except for their eyes, nostrils, and a few vertebras. They sit motionless for hours waiting for careless prey to wander into the shallows. Admirers see crocodiles as noble predators that neither stalk nor hide, using only patience and quickness in their kill. Others who have lost an arm or a foot see them as silent assassins, using the water for cover that they might pierce death into an unsuspecting innocent.

Simon: And your opinion, Governor?

Governor Pilate: They are neither, they are what they are… crocodiles. You either avoid them or eat them, but always with deference… for they see no choice in you. You are their next meal.

Simon: I hope to one day see them myself.

(The governor stood and stretched and walked to my table. Looking down at what I had written, he smiled.)

Governor Pilate: You should not have to wait that long. I expect Annas will be joining us this morning.

(Our discussion was interrupted by the captain of the security detail. A large quantity of food stores was reported missing, and informers had identified two soldiers as attempting to sell the goods on the black market. After a lengthy discussion, the governor had the matter assigned to Dalaccus and asked me to summon Janus and Clephus.)

Janus: (entering the office) Good day, Governor. I trust that my report was satisfactory?

Clephus: (entering the office and taking a seat to the left of Janus directly across from the governor) Citizens…

Governor Pilate: (looking at Janus) I have yet to read your report. In fact, I have yet to read this month's station summary. That is tonight's reading.

Janus: Perhaps I can be of service, for the report on Lazarus is lengthy, but its content holds only two matters of topical interest. A brief summary may relieve the Governor of wading through yet another document, while providing useful insight into today's agenda.

Governor Pilate: What do you have?

Janus: The report contains a great deal of background information on Lazarus, but most interesting is the fact that he, his two sisters, and Jesus are close friends.[liv] Further, Jesus was informed of Lazarus' failing health days before his death. Appeals were made to Jesus to quickly come and heal his friend. It seems that Jesus made no effort to reach Lazarus before he died.[lv] His death appears beyond dispute. It was witnessed by scores who prepared the body and buried him. Even a larger number claim to have seen Jesus call him out of the grave.[lvi]

Governor Pilate: (raising his eyebrows in an incredulous tone) Are you saying that you believe Jesus has raised the dead?

Janus: No, only that he has convinced others of his ability to do so.

Governor Pilate: Do you see this a threat to Rome?

Janus: In an odd way it is a service. For it has solidified the Sadducees' hatred of Jesus and driven them toward an alliance with the Pharisees. This new alliance schemes to enjoin Rome in a plan to destroy Jesus.[lvii] It is all very tidy; we could end up with a formidable union that we could use to crush the Zealots.

Governor Pilate: I shall not attempt to hide my confusion. It was my understanding that the Pharisees and the Sadducees' contempt for one another centered on the raising of the dead, and now you tell me that this issue has brought them together and they seek cooperation with Rome?

Janus: Forgive me. In my effort to be brief, I have omitted several key facts. The Pharisees' leadership has developed a profound hatred of Jesus because he brings them before the people as hypocrites.[lviii] Jesus has been no less harsh with the Sadducees, but it took the Lazarus incident to forge a tight alliance with their contentious brethren. They have simply found their common hatred of Jesus greater than their disdain for one another.

Governor Pilate: And for their common hatred of Rome?

Janus: They have designed a perfect trap. There is no way for Jesus to escape as long as we play our part.

Clephus: Our part being?

Janus: They plan to publicly confront Jesus and ask him if it is lawful to pay taxes to Caesar.[lix] If he says yes, he will lose his populist following because he will be seen as aligned with Rome. If he says no, we will serve their bidding because he will be arrested for sedition. Either way, their common enemy loses his stature. Of course this assumes that we play our part in their little drama.

Governor Pilate: It seems that we are trapped as well, for we can hardly allow a man of influence to advocate a tax rebellion. But they do not know that we view him as a man of influence, do they…

(The governor slowly tapped his fingers on top of the unread report while never losing eye contact with Janus.)

This is very good work Janus. You are correct. This all may prove to be of great service. (looking at me) Have we heard from Annas?

Clephus: He was waiting in the outer office when I arrived.

Governor Pilate: We must not keep the high priest waiting. Simon, have the guards bring him in.

(The guards were so instructed, and shortly Annas entered the room. The long tassels of his robe[lx] reached the floor, the shawl covering his head nearly reached his waist, but all of this did nothing to hide a calculating demeanor. His movement was slow and deliberate, his hidden feet never raised far from the ground, and he appeared to measure and weigh both man and object as he encountered them.)

Annas: Governor Pilate, I am an old man. My legs are no longer my willing companions. May I sit at the table?

(The governor motioned to a chair across and at the far end of the table. Annas took his seat and leaned back in a comfortable pose.)

I thank you. Now, as we have private matters of common interest to discuss, may I suggest that you dismiss your spy, your lackey, and that mongrel pup in order that we might have a more candid discussion?

(Annas targeted his words of derision with a flick of his fingers. Each of us stiffened as we received his barb. The governor seemed unaffected, directing his full attention and a smile toward Annas.)

Governor Pilate: Does the High Priest expect to draw me into the water so easily? Now look what you have done; you have insulted my council, yet I am still balanced and no closer to your grasp. What is your next trick?

(Annas' eyes widened in astonishment; his tone and manner appeared wounded.)

Annas: If I have offended, I must apologize. I addressed them in the language of the people. I meant no offense, my apologies to all... I come as a common man to provide a service for others. I no longer hold the position of high priest;[lxi] the Governor knows this as Rome removed me from office in favor of my son-in-law. Why does the Governor seek my audience and then mock me?

Governor Pilate: My father used to tell me, "You may pluck the tail feathers from a rooster, but he will still rule the hens, perhaps with less swagger, but he will rule." In removing you from office, Rome never expected to take anything but your swagger... and in fact that is all that you lost.

Now as much as I have enjoyed this repartee, I have other pressing matters. This meeting is over.

(Turning to Janus) Arrange for the engineers to outfit the temple. Simon, have the guard escort Annas to the courtyard.

(Annas did not move or appear shaken. He waited for an opening, and without acknowledging his dismissal, spoke with confidence.)

Annas: So how is the transaction to be accomplished?

Governor Pilate: (shifting his weight to one hip and leaning toward Annas) You tell me who murdered my soldiers, and I remove the banners from the courtyard and promise to keep them out of the temple. The former is never associated with you; the latter is seen as Rome's deference to the power and influence of the Sadducees. You see, it is not so complicated.

Annas: The result is acceptable, but the means holds the risk. How do you propose to keep all parties clear of culpability?

Governor Pilate: Before leaving, you will give me the complete details of what happened to my soldiers. At the conclusion of this meeting, my engineers will accompany you to the temple courtyard, and under your instruction, remove all offensive material. I had a local summon you here; no doubt you have a waiting audience.

Annas: Will not the people make the association, Zealots for favors? Such an association would bring disdain, not glory. You view the men you seek as murderers. I see them as obstacles to the common good. But to the masses they are heroes.

Governor Pilate: I will take no action against the Zealots for ten days, and then have them arrested as part of a larger group on an unrelated charge. This is my business; you may be assured that I understand the mutual need to keep these matters apart.

Annas: I fear that my risk is the greater, yet I place the execution of these matters in your hands. I...

Governor Pilate: Passover is but three weeks away. To destabilize your rule over the people at such a time would be catastrophic. I do not have half the men that I would need to manage such chaos. I believe our risks equally measured.

Annas: I am sure that the Governor understands my reluctance in this matter. Would it be acceptable to tender my part as your representations unfold?

Governor Pilate: What do you propose?

Annas: That I give you the name of the Zealot leader responsible, and my limited knowledge of what happened. After you successfully apprehend this leader under the guise of another charge, I will give the names of the other six.

Governor Pilate: Do we not increase our risk of exposure by gathering the guilty under two separate efforts? Would it not be safer to gather both the leader and his executioners at the same instant?

Annas: I believe that my way creates a better story for both of us. The leader is taken, several days pass, and then the others are arrested.

Governor Pilate: A very clever misdirection of betrayal. And the name of this leader?

Annas: Barabbas of Bethabara,[lxii] he now lives outside Bethany.

Governor Pilate: So this day the banners come down, raising your esteem. In ten days, we successfully arrest Barabbas on other charges, and you turn over the names of the others. Is that your proposition?

Annas: Essentially. I would add that several days should pass between the arrest of Barabbas and the arrest of his men. Without such a delay, Barabbas' betrayal of his men would hardly be obvious.

(The governor said nothing for a hundred count, never losing eye contact with Annas.)

Clephus: We would be foolish…

Governor Pilate: (holding up his hand) I accept your plan as outlined with one small request. Before you leave you will go to Simon's table and write on a scrap of paper the following words, "Barabbas is the man you seek," and suffix your name and mark.

Annas: May I ask the purpose of your request?

Governor Pilate: When you give me the additional names, I will give you the scrap of paper. Fail to give me the names, and after Passover I will deliver the paper to your friends, the Pharisees. It is an ugly thought for both of us, but it keeps us bound together by self-interest.

Annas: Both of us being men of integrity, I find your lack of trust impertinent.

Governor Pilate: Then, as men of integrity, you may give me the names of the others and avoid my request. But you will not, for this whole matter has the putrid stench of dead flesh. There is no integrity in murder or in the twists of our plan. Sign the paper and let us get on with business. You are beyond walking away from this transaction.

(Annas stood and came to my table. In careful script, he wrote out the required phrase, placing his name and mark beneath it. The task complete, he returned to his seat at the governor's table.)

Annas: (using a tone of intimacy) I would join you in celebrating our success in bringing justice to Barabbas' mob, but there are other issues that assault the tranquility we seek. There…

Governor Pilate: You speak of Jesus of Nazareth?

(Annas appeared to have the wind knocked out of him. Unable to inhale, he nodded, using the time to regain his composure.)

Annas: (taking a deep breath) It does not surprise me that you are aware of this movement. It is a sore that festers against the common good. It must be cut out lest it consume the whole body.

Governor Pilate: (in a spirited manner) You call him a sore, but the reports I receive label him a healer, a man who has raised the dead! You see this as a disease affecting our people?

Annas: Our… people are easily misled. By the time they discover their mistake, they will find themselves hopelessly in conflict with Rome. This is in neither of our interests.

Governor Pilate: Is this not a Jewish matter? Why seek to entwine me in your internal struggles?[lxiii]

Annas: I do not seek to encumber Rome with our internal matters. My desire is to preserve a tranquility that is mutually beneficial, not to invite Roman interference in our affairs.

Governor Pilate: And so you and your Sadducees have joined the Pharisees to snare your common enemy?

Annas: (less surprised and becoming irritated) Your enemy as well! Our risk is that Jesus turns some against our beliefs; your risk is that he turns all against your taxes. (appearing to relax) But if this is of no concern, I will drop the matter. I do not wish to impose upon your office.

Governor Pilate: I believe you have baited me into asking what my part might be in this plan. Very well, what would you have me do?

Annas: You are obviously well informed of our plan to expose Jesus. The Pharisees will confront him regarding his alliance to Rome, and we shall expose his apostasy. You may expect his answers to be of interest, for they will either advocate rebellion or create civil unrest. Your men only need to be present and act in Rome's best interest to serve our purpose.

Governor Pilate: Purposes vary. You propose an alliance of adversaries, and yet what of my allies? Do I join you in facing Jesus only to strike the Herodians[lxiv] from behind? I should speak with them before considering your scheme.

Annas: Most prudent, but you will find that the Herodians share a common interest.[lxv] You see, we all seek a common good.

Governor Pilate: Janus, confirm the Herodian position regarding Jesus.

(Turing toward Annas) I do not seek a common good, but you may be certain that I will protect Rome's interests.

And where and when is this confrontation to take place?

Annas: Jesus will be in Jerusalem for Passover, sometime early that week, away from the temple.

Governor Pilate: If it is as you say, and the Herodians are part of your plan, I will have my men discreetly blend with your Herodian brethren.

Annas: That is all I ask.

Governor Pilate: I have indulged you on this Jesus matter. Now the balance of our bargain. What happened to my men?

Annas: I know few details, but I will share with you what I have heard. The plans of your troops were well-known to the Zealots days before their departure. Your troops' planned route was to travel east on the highway that leads to the Jordan River and then about halfway to the river turn south on a trail that would take them directly to Qumran.

Governor Pilate: Do you know anything of their planned detour to assist the engineers at Bethabara?

Annas: I know nothing of Bethabara. Bethabara is not far, but my information does not include such a detour. Perhaps they were going to stop on the return trip? In any case, it was at the fork where the highway and trail meet that your soldiers first met their fate. The Zealots had two old men and a woman approach your men at the fork and beg their assistance. They told your men that they were ferrying jars of oil down the river when their barge lodged in the shallows and was near capsizing. They offered the soldiers an attractive payment to help them retrieve their goods before they were lost to the river.

It was calculated that although the detour would delay your men a few hours, the route to Qumran via the river was an easier journey. This, coupled with the reward, was certain to draw your men into the trap. As it turned out, your men were most accommodating. The officer in charge refused to accept any payment and ordered his men to double their pace to the river.

Upon arriving at the river they discovered the barge that had been precariously perched on a sand bar by the Zealots. The commander ordered half of his men to remove their weapons and armor and wade out to assist in righting the barge. The others were to gather wood and build a fire. Once the men reached the barge, the Zealots emerged from under cover and hacked them with their short swords. Before the men gathering wood could react, Zealots that had been concealed in the brush attacked them. It was not without a price, for even at this disadvantage your men maintained discipline and fought to the last man.

All of your men died at the river, five Zealots were killed, two seriously wounded. Those two would be dead within days.

Governor Pilate: What of their bodies and armament?

Annas: They were weighted with rocks and loaded onto barges. The bodies of both Zealots and Romans were then ferried to Lake Asphaltites[lxvi] and thrown overboard.

Governor Pilate: (squinting his eyes and leveling his voice) Barges? I thought you began your story with a single barge?

Annas: I was told there were other barges at hand, but only one was used in the deception. I do not know how many, but I suspect more than two, as it is not easy to conceal twenty bodies.

Governor Pilate: How many Zealots were involved in the attack?

Annas: Fourteen including Barabbas.

Governor Pilate: Including the two old men and the woman?

Annas: I am told that they were innocents, but I know nothing more of them.

Governor Pilate: Can you get me their names?

Annas: I am not prepared to turn over old men and a woman who merely perform for a fee. Besides, inquiring about such matters would raise suspicion.

Governor Pilate: (leaning toward Annas, his voice rising and gaining a shrill edge) Tell me, Annas, are you proud of your people? Do you take pride in butchering men who provide assistance at no price? Who wade into the cold waters to salvage your people's livelihood? Is this your badge of honor?

Annas: (showing no emotion) If these were my people, I would not be here, and as for honor, it is in the color of your allegiance. Is it not a Roman tactic to kill innocents in order to secure a strategic position?

Governor Pilate: (suddenly rising from his chair) Are you here to give me a lesson on Roman military tactics?

Annas: (showing no reaction) No, Governor, such an endeavor would be as foolish as you lecturing me on the morality of a people…

Governor Pilate: We have our bargain. (looking at Janus) Arrange for the engineers to accompany Annas. (looking toward Annas) We will arrest Barabbas in ten days, his conspirators several days hence. I believe this concludes our squalid little treaty.

Annas: I believe you failed to mention your support of our plan against Jesus?

Governor Pilate: Yes, yes, my men will be among the Herodians.

(The governor stopped and smiled as if digesting an amusing thought.)

You know, Annas, you seem to have a greater fear of Jesus than you do Rome. Perhaps I should dismiss my troops and employ Jesus?

Annas: (smiling) Your jest is well tendered, but do not take lightly the danger that Jesus presents to us both. He is a dangerous man, and our plan is critical to our mutual success.

Governor Pilate: (looking past Annas at an empty wall) Have you considered the enemy?

Annas: The enemy?

Governor Pilate: (his eyes locking on to Annas') The enemy—Jesus. You plan a strategy, acquire allies, choose your battlefield, and yet never consider the generalship of your foe? What do you expect from Jesus?

Annas: He is worthy of no consideration. A dangerous animal that must be trapped… nothing more.

Governor Pilate: (as if suddenly distracted from the topic) Forgive me, I deal in matters in which I am apparently not needed. Clephus, will you see that the engineers join Annas? Janus, I would like some background information on Barabbas. Get back to me as soon as you have it. Simon, you will remain to conclude today's schedule.

(After the others left the room, the governor asked the guard to post outside and instructed me to close the office door.)

Governor Pilate: What remains of today's activities?

Simon: Except for the reports, which you can read at your leisure, there are no other pressing matters. There are several hours of light remaining. I could have your horse readied?

Governor Pilate: Yes, and have them pack a small meal. If the weather holds, I will stay out until dusk.

(I summoned the guard and passed on the governor's instructions.)

Simon: The guard will return when all is ready.

Governor Pilate: You must learn to ride, Simon. There is a freedom on the back of a horse that is unique. You are in control of something that is far more powerful than you are, and yet the control is gained only by bending yourself to the animal's force. And, as you acquire skill, you soon discover that the line between horse and rider has disappeared, that a common function and thought has grown, and at once, the animal has your intellect and you his power. It is the wine of gods, Simon; we must have you trained.

Simon: I have little experience with animals, but I have longed to have such skill.

Governor Pilate: I shall speak to the stable master today. If we begin your instruction soon, you can practice your new skills when we return to Caesarea Maritima.[lxvii]

So what did you think of Annas, Simon?

Simon: You were correct, Governor; one need not leave Jerusalem to experience a crocodile.

Governor Pilate: Do his loyalties disappoint you, Simon?

Simon: As I had no expectation of loyalty, I cannot say that I am disappointed.

Governor Pilate: It is a lesson to remember. Crocodiles are loyal to their next meal… that is why we had him sign the paper. Anything else surprise you?

Simon: That he refused your help.

Governor Pilate: Help?

Simon: When you attempted to instruct him on anticipating the actions and reactions of Jesus.

Governor Pilate: (smiling) Annas is blinded to all but his desires. It is a condition that exists within each of us. When we discover our lives tumbling out of control, we not only grasp at precarious footholds, but disdain those who label them such.

Annas has seen a path to the destruction of Jesus. He has blinded himself to anything that might steal that victory from him. He is a man at peace, at least until the battle is engaged.

Simon: Do you think him a fool in this matter?

Governor Pilate: Not a fool, but foolish, for it is never wise to ignore your enemy. In this case it is especially so, for while Annas attends to the smallest detail of the Barabbas bargain, he ignores an enemy that is purported to have raised the dead. Does that seem balanced to you, Simon?

Simon: No.

Governor Pilate: We have little certain knowledge of Jesus, but all that we have learned esteems him a man of power. If he were easily defeated, he would not have survived. But Annas leaves port oblivious to the weather; we shall keep our distance lest the clutter of his wreckage scuttles us. If his plan works, we shall join him in victory; if not, he shall cling to the wreckage alone.

(The guard knocked and announced the governor's mount ready.)

A beautiful afternoon, and I shall spend the balance with my horse. I look forward to the day when you will join me.

Simon: I look forward to that day as well, Governor.

Governor Pilate: (leaving the room) Leave the reports and other correspondence in my private quarters. I will spend the evening with them.

***

It is all clear at a distance of thirty years: the participants: the goals, and the various fields of play. I sought tranquility as a means of furthering my career. Annas played a shorter game, one of immediate power and prestige. Jesus, however, played a game that was invisible to us both, for its span exceeded our vision. He was after neither power nor promotion, but the ethos of his followers... his field of play held time a bystander.

Thirty years later, my service to Rome is forgotten; Annas' power has leached from the wormholes in his bones, but Rome and Judaea both continue to contend with Jesus. An ironic juxtaposition... the high priest and governor dead and awaiting death, their competition of no consequence... while a crucified itinerant laborer fully engages the Roman Empire.

Note to Mac:

At the risk of hearing my words twisted by those who may read this, I confess that I like the Pilate that is contained in this folio. It seems bizarre to make such an admission, and I feel compelled to underscore that I have no admiration for the man who ordered the crucifixion of Christ. But isolated within these few pages, I find a man to admire.

This folio contains the actions and thoughts of someone who demonstrated introspection, focus, and a playful humor. His firm manner with Annas and offer to tutor Simon further speaks of a man to be admired. Within the folio's context of events I found nothing to loathe, no great evil stamped upon him; as I have said, this folio alone would find me liking the man.

I do not like Pilate, however, for both my education and the preceding folios demand enmity. For I have read the value he placed upon children's lives, and know him to be more concerned with ambition than justice. These things balance my view and allow me to see the man in the totality of history. But what if my only encounter with Pilate had been limited to the events contained in this folio? With such a narrow view, would I not esteem the man and find charges against him to be implausible?

It is unsettling to realize that friendships are so formed. We esteem or shun others based on a limited set of transactions that are bound within the

100

context of specific circumstance. The leaders for whom we vote, the friends we hold near, the partners we choose, all are drawn close by some finite set of encounters. What different companions might be chosen if we could view them within the totality of their history? What pallor might be discovered if we stripped them naked like Pilate, and read the pages of their current actions along with the folios of both their past and future.

There is no such vision for us. We have no perfect knowledge of others' pasts, nor a vision of their future. We must weigh our relationships on the scales of today. Our task is to examine the residue of character that sticks to us as we touch others, to consider both the space and vacuum of their presence in our lives. We must ever be alert for those sticky points of character that are found between actions and neglect, for it is within such subtleties that we discover the true value of our companions.

Such consideration leads me toward disliking the Pilate of this folio, for he presents life as a game, neglecting any mention of divine purpose or higher mission. He exhibits humor, but at the expense of another. He is insightful and firm with Annas, but to what end? He is self-reflective, but it seems more motivated by vanity than truth. Upon close examination we find that even the attractive confines of this folio cannot hide a quiet darkness that exists within the man. It is a murkiness that warns the wise person to run, but I continue to find myself drawn near. I see within the pages of this folio a humanity that continues to speak to me, or is it my darkness calling to his? It would seem a matter of perspective, but it is not. It is a matter of character.

Chapter 8
Folio 7
Forewarned

The arrogance of man is as boundless as his ignorance. In youth we see nothing beyond the reach of our power; in middle age we imagine our experience greater than any risk encountered; and in old age we fabricate the greatness of our past. It is only with the certainty of death that we allow ourselves to dismount from the wild horse of pride, and once off, discover the scattered, discarded wisdom that was the map to our aspirations.

Such a dark tone concerning a man's destiny would raise the question of eminence, for some men do stand above others and are remembered. What sets them apart? What allowed them to climb while the masses loll in folly? One element is that of circumstance. I do not believe that Augustus[lxviii] himself, serving in Judaea, could have risen above its din of cross-purposes. But circumstance is only a portion of the equation, for the gods hand some men the small slip of paper,[lxix] the whispered confidence, or the unintended observation that advantages their entire life.

This serendipity, gift of the gods, whatever you may call it, has the appearance of unearned fortune. But fortuity is realized only by those who, while experiencing the apex of events, let go of their prideful arrogance that they might grasp these fragile treasures of wisdom. It is a lesson that we learn as children in the fields for the butterfly lands on those who stop to receive it. And while our halted motion does not guarantee the colorful treasure, our continued thoughtless striving assures the opportunity lost.

None of this portion of Simon's transcript was part of my memory. As I read it almost thirty years later, it seemed like new evidence that I had never encountered. But I have no doubt of its accuracy. Simon properly identified the butterflies, but I, racing toward conclusion, had forfeited any chance to receive them.

***

The transcription of the Jesus affair:
Day 1,749 of Governor Pilate's administration
Prepared by Simon of Emmaus
Present:
Governor Pilate
Clephus, Officer of Internal Affairs
Janus, Officer of Internal Surveillance

Dalaccus, Officer of Military Affairs
Simon of Emmaus, Secretary to Governor Pilate

(The governor, having spent the previous three days refining his Tax Revenue Summary[lxx] for Rome, had called a meeting of his council to review Passover preparations. Clephus, Janus, and Dalaccus had already arrived and taken their customary seats when the governor entered.)

Governor Pilate: Good morning, I trust we have all come prepared. Has Dalaccus been briefed on my conversation with Annas?

Clephus: I briefed him shortly after the meeting.

Governor Pilate: Simon, any other pressing matters?

Simon: No, Governor. You wished to discuss the disposition of the troops, you had Janus prepare a report on Barabbas, and there is a message from Nicodemus.

Governor Pilate: Dalaccus, have the troops arrived from Caesarea Maritima?

Dalaccus: They are expected the day after tomorrow.

Governor Pilate: Cutting it close, the pilgrims[lxxi] have already started to arrive. How many men are you bringing over?

Dalaccus: I have left only three-hundred[lxxii] behind. The rest, including the entire equestrian corps, will be stationed in Jerusalem through Passover. Is the Governor expecting trouble? If so, I can send word to bring the men on a forced march.

Governor Pilate: Just the usual Passover tensions. But I think we should instruct our officers to avoid confrontation, lest we bring on more trouble than we can manage.

Dalaccus: As you wish, Governor, but I do not think this is the time we should show weakness. We will soon have the murderer, Barabbas, in hand, and I believe we should waste no time in hanging him before the crowds.

Governor Pilate: Your personal interests aside, Dalaccus, I am in no hurry to stir up trouble. There will be time to deal with Barabbas after the Passover crowds have disbursed and before our soldiers return to Caesarea Maritima. I think it prudent to be bold with more favorable numbers.[lxxiii]

(Dalaccus got up from his chair and walked to the window. As he walked, he appeared to be speaking to himself, but his words were not audible. Once reaching the window he turned and addressed the governor in a clipped tone.)

Dalaccus: You would know best, Governor Pilate… but I was not thinking of my personal situation when recommending a firm hand. It has been my experience that an early, decisive display of authority can weaken the liver of a crowd; with our numerical inferiority such an advantage may prove invaluable.

(The governor sat silent, responding with neither word nor gesture. Soon the silence forced Dalaccus to continue his thought.) Perhaps a better strategy would be…

(The governor exploded in rage. His voice screamed in a rasp, his hand slamming down repeatedly on the table.)

Governor Pilate: Perhaps you should obey orders. Perhaps you should spend less time lecturing me on military tactics. Perhaps you should excuse yourself and instruct your men on the orders that you have been given… There will be no dead children, no rotting Barabbas corpse, and no provocation! Do you understand your orders, Dalaccus?

Dalaccus: (with a controlled military bearing) You have made yourself clear. I excuse myself that I might inform my subordinates.

(The governor, motioning to the empty chair, addressed Dalaccus in a composed, almost warm tone.)

Governor Pilate: Sit down my friend, these matters require your experience.

You are, of course, right; a firm hand is always preferred, but if required, such a hand must make an effective fist... Anything greater than a small riot and we will be on the receiving end of the whip. The numbers do not favor chance... Is a holding action not called for?

Dalaccus: (appearing genuinely persuaded) I am afraid my anger has clouded my judgement. The numbers speak for themselves. I will instruct my men to maintain the peace. I must apologize...

Governor Pilate: (holding up his hand) A difference of opinion, nothing more. Janus, you have a report on Barabbas?

Janus: I must say, our murderer is a man of some repute. He is hated, feared, revered, and ostracized... by different people, but with equal passion.

To begin with, everyone who does business with him hates him. He is a man who suspects a dishonest scale on every transaction. This, coupled with a violent temper, makes him a rather unattractive trading partner. Merchants go out of their way to avoid taking his money.

His temper, coupled with an irrational jealousy regarding the chastity of his wife, has him rumored to have killed several men.

Governor Pilate: He was not held accountable for these offenses?

Janus: Rumored to have killed, for the men simply disappeared within a week of their argument with him. It seems one day he accuses you of stuffing his wife, and within the week you disappear. Such coincidence engenders a certain fear, which is advantageous to his cause.

Governor Pilate: Does he have reason to question the fidelity of his wife?

Janus: If having a wife that is reputed to be one of the most beautiful women in Judaea is reason for jealous rage, then yes, he has reason. All sources, however, speak of her as a woman devoted to him and their marriage.

Governor Pilate: So how does such a fellow earn reverence?

Janus: He is fearless; his affection for the homeless an affectation. At great risk to himself he shields the weak from harm. This has led to his crusade against Rome. He is a Zealot with a core of followers that would willingly die for him.

Governor Pilate: And so they shall... and his enemies?

Janus: The merchants who despise his abuse, the religious leaders who abhor the trouble he creates with the Roman authorities, and any man who happens to gaze upon his wife.

Governor Pilate: I need him placed under arrest for an offence not related to the murder of our soldiers... something that would cause him to be brought before this office.

Clephus: Taxes, assaulting a tax official?[lxxiv]

Governor Pilate: Can it be arranged?

Janus: When do you want him arrested?

Governor Pilate: Within the next four to six days, no sooner.

Janus: A simple task. Are there any other considerations?

Governor Pilate: Yes, the arrest must be made in public and appear to be justified. These conditions are essential to our success. And, oh yes, make certain that Barabbas is not harmed; there will be no broken bones or stripes, am I clear on this matter?

Janus: Quite clear. It is easily arranged. But I see that your young secretary is not in full accord. This whole Barabbas issue seems to cause him concern. I am curious, Simon, what has you sitting on a thorn?

(Up until that moment I had been unaware of my countenance. Once made conscious of my posture, I discovered myself leaning forward on the table with my jaw clenched. I did not respond to Janus, but looked to the governor for direction.)

Governor Pilate: (looking at me) Do you have something to say on this matter?

Simon: Not an opinion, Governor, but a concern.

Clephus: (in a mocking tone) Well, let us not close the issue without the counsel of a young Jew. In fact, it may be wise to have him review all matters of state.

(Clephus and Dalaccus burst into laughter that brought a smile to the governor's face. Janus, however, continued to focus his attention on me, showing no trace of amusement.)

Janus: (factually) I know of no one in this room closer to issues and dangers we face. I, for one, would like to hear the boy's concern.

(The governor held up his hand, silencing the merriment.)

Governor Pilate: (turning his smile toward me) And what has you concerned, Simon?

Simon: Annas. He does not like Rome, Jesus, or Barabbas; yet he trades in their fate with equal alacrity... I am confused. I know he serves himself, but for whose fate does he trade, and for what purpose?

Clephus: He trades Barabbas for prestige and Jesus to secure his power. I think his bargains are obvious.

(I did not immediately answer, but looked to the governor.)

Governor Pilate: Go ahead, Simon, finish your thought.

Simon: It is true that Annas trades Barabbas for prestige and Jesus to secure his power... but we did not ask for Jesus. Annas made him part of the bargain. I am concerned that there is a link among Annas' interests, Jesus, and Barabbas. Annas agreed to turn over some of his own people to Roman authority in return for removing the banners? Even his enemies consider him shrewd. Could he not have secured the banners' removal by guaranteeing a peaceful Passover?

Clephus: The governor had threatened more. Annas did not wish to lose control or take the risk of further empowering his rivals.

Simon: But this is my concern, he did not bargain to advantage himself against the Pharisees or Herodians, his rivals... His interest was in castrating Jesus. More specifically, having Rome castrate Jesus.

Governor Pilate: And your speculation?

Simon: I have none, only a concern. Annas is using Barabbas to draw us in, but to what end I do not know.

Governor Pilate: Janus, do we know of any ties among Jesus, Annas, and Barabbas?

Janus: No, but we have not focused on such ties. I will put my men on alert.

Governor Pilate: For now, we have what we want; we will see what develops.

Janus: Governor, your young protege shows promise. Perhaps one day you can persuade him to join my service?

Governor Pilate: Perhaps, if that is his choice.

(Looking at me) Simon, the other items on today's agenda?

Simon: You are scheduled to accompany Dalaccus in the inspection of the security posts. With luck you may have the opportunity for a quick meal, and then you are scheduled to adjudicate this afternoon and all day tomorrow.

Governor Pilate: Then let us finish up matters here, and perhaps I can hold court with a full belly.

Simon: The only matter not covered is the message from Nicodemus. It is sealed; do you wish me to open it and read it?

Governor Pilate: If it is not too long, we can cover it now; if it is, put it with my night reading.

(I broke the seal on the scroll, and spread it on the table.)

Simon: It is a short message written in Greek. It reads:

Governor Pilate:
I have learned that you have been made a part of a plan against Jesus of
Nazareth. He is a man of no malice, and I urge you to treat this as a
Jewish matter. The Sanhedrin has adequate authority to judge any
accusations brought against Jesus of Nazareth, and should he be found
guilty, to punish him accordingly.[lxxv]
Your entanglement in this affair is of no benefit to Rome, and introduces
quantifiable risks. I know you to be a man of reason, and I ask that you
give consideration to my request.
I seek only justice.

(Signed)
Nicodemus

Governor Pilate: Is there more?

Simon: No.

Governor Pilate: I wonder if Annas told Nicodemus of our role in the plot
to trap Jesus?

(The governor stopped and looked beyond me toward the window. With
his elbow on the arms of his chair and his left fist captured in his right
hand, he directed his comments to me in a soft deliberate tone.)

Send a short message back to Nicodemus. Write the following:
My only interest is in protecting Rome. I do not view Jesus as an
adversary, but should he present himself as such, he will be subject to
Roman justice.

I will sign it in my own hand.

Clephus: Do you think it wise to correspond with those that oppose
Annas? The alliance is new and fragile.

Governor Pilate: (animated, directing his comments to Clephus) Oppose?
Do I hear any of us, including Annas, stand and pronounce opposition to
justice? Nicodemus has chosen his words carefully so as to not impale us
upon them. Both Annas and Nicodemus will be mollified by my message.

Of course, they will read it differently… there is indeed an artist's touch to governing.

As for our alliance, it stops and starts with our respective best interests. Oh yes, we both seek the common good, but as we define it. Nicodemus is the only one seeking true justice, and in doing so he makes himself a bystander.

Janus: It may be prudent to devote more resources to keeping track of Annas' activities.

Governor Pilate: No need, he is predictably self-serving. Keep your resources focused on the Zealots for they have weapons, passion, and a taste for Roman blood. I wager any serious trouble will come from them.

Now we squander my mealtime. (standing and stretching) Let us move on to the inspections.

Simon: Governor, will you need my services during the inspections?

Governor Pilate: No. I will need you here to coordinate the trial docket.

***

Now having read this portion of the transcript a second time, I have a vague recollection of these matters. But this vagueness of memory does not lessen the relevance of the encounter; rather it serves as a pedestal on which to display the abject stupidity of my actions. It was all before me to clearly discern. Annas wanted to be free of Jesus and he wanted me to dispose of him…the rest was all smoke. I was focused on Passover, Barabbas, and the execution of the plan. Annas served it to me as a fine meal, and I, with the hunger of immediacy, willingly consumed each course.

I offer this explanation not as an excuse, for cross-motives and intrigue were part of the natural rhythm of Judaea. At that time, I considered myself experienced beyond such trickery. Ignoring the expressed concerns of Simon, Janus, and Nicodemus, I stumbled into the snare placed by the Sanhedrin. Was it the skill of Annas, the paltriness of Jesus, or my own arrogance that entangled me? A fair judge would probably not ascribe my mistake to any of these. It is most likely that I failed because I was human.

I knew then, as I know today, the three components of judgement: actions, words, and mission. Each transaction with both ally and foe must be considered within the totality of these three elements. I was too busy, too certain, and too anxious to stop and pose a simple question: Is there a confluence of words, actions, and mission in Annas' bargain? But I was running hard and never stopped to ask that question... blindly running toward a fate of obscurity and derision.

I fault myself not too greatly for my mistake, for all of mankind yokes progress to motion. We believe that great men never break stride, moving ever forward through all pain and circumstance. But those that have reached the summit know this to be folly. For like butterflies, the small treasures of difference that lift our fate, land only upon those who pause to receive them.

Note to Mac:

As I read the old man's opening and closing commentary for this folio, I discovered a detached wisdom that disoriented me. The origin of my confusion was not due to a lack of clarity in word or thought, but its source. Pontius Pilate is not a man whom I wish to embrace or quote, and yet the old man's reflections bring a fresh perspective. What am I to do with this revelation? Can pure wisdom be poured from a corrupt vessel?

Can sagacity be separated from its source? Are there worthy morsels to be found in vomit? Western culture inseparably attaches thoughts to the morality of the author. We do not teach our children the espoused wisdom of Hitler, Stalin, or Pol Pot, yet mixed within their twisted intellects are no doubt shards of wisdom. "Shards of wisdom," these words themselves may hold the collective understanding of our culture, for shards are the sharp splintered pieces of something broken. And as we clear the wreckage of despots, we should handle the sharp edges of their intellect with great care, for these remnants too have the power to harm.

But this argument supposes Pilate to be a despot on the order of Hitler, Stalin, and Pol Pot. Does he deserve such a label, or was he a man caught in the destiny of circumstance? In answering this question, we make the last two paragraphs of the folio either lamented wisdom or an intellectual disease. The matter rests in the dusk of subjectivity, but still it must be considered, for the butterflies of wisdom land only upon those who pause to receive them.

Chapter 9
Folio 8
An Illusion of Reality

It has been almost forty years since death took my friend and mentor Sejanus.[lxxvi] I have never held anyone in greater esteem, for he attained greatness, yet through all my struggles continued to affirm our friendship.[lxxvii] Sejanus taught me the ways of power and government and was in no small measure responsible for my appointment to Judaea. Yet among the litany of wisdom which he unselfishly poured into me, one insight stands paramount.

I had just completed ten years of service in the legions when he first approached me about pursuing a career in government service.[lxxviii] Having risen rapidly through the ranks, I had always assumed the legion to be my destiny. When I expressed this predisposition, he nodded and asked me if I had ever walked in the emperor's gardens. I indicated that men of my rank were not granted such privilege. He smiled, placed his hands on my shoulders, and said, "Then you must go, for the first lesson of your new career is painted across her landscape."

The next day we entered the gardens through the courtyard gate. Before us was an enormous bath with steam rising and drifting down its length. At the far end of the bath was a seating area that could easily accommodate several hundred bathers. As we walked the length of the bathing pool, I counted my paces. It was nearly thirty paces long and almost as wide. When we reached the end Sejanus, motioned for me to sit in a chair next to him with our backs to the bathing pool. Before us was a natural pond four to five times larger than the bath, filled with water lilies. A line of willows, which perfectly framed its beauty, lined the lily pond on either side.

"As you can see, this garden was constructed at some elevation. If you look straight ahead you will notice there are no willows at the end, that is so you can gaze at the splendor of Rome and its surrounding hills," Sejanus said. I had not noticed earlier, but it was a perfectly composed picture. Beyond the lily pond was an expanse of manicured garden, then a well-kept lawn, and finally the vista of the city cast about the hills. "A perfect picture is it not?" I admitted that it was indeed magnificent. "Let us walk on to the lawn, and I will give you your first and perhaps most important lesson about governing."

As we walked the length of the garden, Sejanus said nothing, his hands behind his back with his full attention focused on the vista before him. "Is it not perfect, Pontius?" I readily agreed, as the vista of the city sprinkled across the distant hills seemed the very definition of perfection. "Come, let us walk further that we might gaze more closely upon Rome's splendor." We walked another hundred paces and a slight disharmony of color appeared across the horizon. My curiosity must have been apparent, for Sejanus stopped. "What is it my friend? Has your view been disturbed?" I indicated that I was trying to make out the jagged line of color that scraped across the horizon. "That is no jagged line; it is your lesson. Come let us have a closer look."

With another thirty paces the mystery was exposed. At the end of the lawn there was a stone wall that was sloped upward from its base at a forty- five-degree angle toward the city. The wall spanned the length of the willows like an elongated triangle of stone that had toppled over, exposing its long side toward the garden. As we approached, further details of the edifice were apparent. The visible portion of the structure had an uneven top with its elongated side plastered to a semi-smooth surface. An artist had painted the face of the fence to perfectly blend into the backdrop of the distant hills. "Quite an illusion, is it not?" I agreed as my mind raced to rationalize the two-pace[lxxix] fence. Sejanus, reading my bewilderment, continued, "It is simple, Pontius. The hovels of the slums are in the foreground of the distant hills; it is simpler and less expensive to build, paint, and maintain the wall than correct the eyesore."

Sejanus went on to explain that artists touched up the wall several times a year to keep it in harmony with the seasons. It seemed farcical, and I expressed my dismay, but Sejanus pressed the issue with a series of simple questions.

"And the purpose of the garden?" he asked.

"To entertain visitors and present the beauty of Rome," I replied.

"And those visitors are?"

"Men of power and influence."

"And from the pools and garden does it present a desirable picture?"

"Yes."

"Then why are you puzzled?" he concluded.

We spent several hours in the garden that day discussing the expedience of the wall and its relevance to governing. Sejanus brought nuance and depth to the discussion that my memory and pen fail to capture, but his message was straightforward. In the realm of governing, perception is as relevant as fact, and oftentimes comes at a more attractive price. It is a lesson that I used often and effectively in my career, and one that made Barabbas a quintessential, albeit unintended, instrument of Rome.

***

The transcription of the Jesus affair:
Day 1,757 of Governor Pilate's administration
Prepared by Simon of Emmaus
Present:
Governor Pilate
Clephus, Officer of Internal Affairs
Janus, Officer of Internal Surveillance
Dalaccus, Officer of Military Affairs
Simon of Emmaus, Secretary to Governor Pilate
Barabbas of Bethabara, Prisoner
Contingent of Guards, Responsible for the prisoner

(The governor had returned late yesterday from a four-day annual inspection of eastern forts surrounding Jericho. I had left the weekly station reports in his quarters. The governor had called an early morning meeting.)

Governor Pilate: Where is everyone?

Simon: Clephus and Dalaccus are waiting in the outer office. Janus sent word that he is meeting with his men and will join us shortly.

Governor Pilate: I have waited a long time to deal with Barabbas. Call in the others.

Simon: Before the others join us may I request a few moments with the Governor to address administrative matters? Your seal and approval is required on several dozen documents, many of which are in need of your immediate attention.

Governor Pilate: I have only been gone four days… What matters?

Simon: The final tax report to Rome, the allocation of grain stores, promotion orders for…

Governor Pilate: Very well, you made your point. The tax report first.

(The governor spent the next hour reviewing the documents that I had prepared and executed them with only minor modifications.)

Simon: Thank you, Governor. I shall have these recorded and distributed. I will summon the others.

Governor Pilate: Simon, if you ever choose to work for Janus, he shall have to give me a small cadre to replace you. Have you considered Janus' suggestion that you work for him?

Simon: I think I am better suited to the administration of the affairs of state. I will leave the affairs of men to others.

Governor Pilate: Are they not the same, Simon? But I agree that your greater service is here.

Now dispose of your documents and call the others.

(Janus, Clephus, and Dalaccus entered the room and took their customary positions around the table. All exchanged amenities with the governor; only Janus acknowledged my presence.)

Governor Pilate: No doubt all have read the weekly station report… do we have any other details on the capture of Barabbas?

Janus: I received a detailed report this morning from men that were present during the arrest. The plan was executed to perfection with only minor collateral damage.

Governor Pilate: What was he arrested for?

Janus: For assaulting a tax collector. It seems that he was asked to pay the same tax twice. When the collector denied collecting it the first time, Barabbas went into a rage. He beat the man severely and cut him across the face with a knife.

Governor Pilate: Was the collector a Roman or a Jew?

Janus: Jew.

Governor Pilate: And the collateral damage?

Janus: There was a large crowd present and during the arrest, a half-dozen locals were injured.

Governor Pilate: By whom?

Janus: By those making the arrest. The good news is that they were not offering support to Barabbas. They merely got in the way of the soldiers.

Governor Pilate: They were your men, Dalaccus?

Dalaccus: Yes.

Governor Pilate: (obviously irritated) Is there a reason that your men seem to be continually subverting the policy of this administration?

Janus: I do not believe any serious harm was done. The tax collector that assisted us was of good reputation in the region, and all reports indicate that the crowd was supportive of the arrest.

Governor Pilate: (looking at Dalaccus) I want a full report prepared by the officer in charge. Deliver it tomorrow afternoon.

Dalaccus: (looking first at the governor and then at Janus) Yes, Governor.

Governor Pilate: So where is our friend Barabbas now?

Clephus: He was in the prison, but I had him chained and brought to the guardroom on the first level. I thought you might have an interest in speaking to him.

Governor Pilate: Let us not keep Barabbas waiting. You three go ahead; I will join you in a moment.

(The others left the room.)

I am curious, Simon; why have you decided to transcribe this meeting when it has nothing to do with Jesus?

Simon: You gave me orders to transcribe matters that I deemed relevant, and I am still of the opinion that Annas has these matters tied together. Perhaps I am foolish. Do you wish for me to exclude Barabbas from the transcript?

Governor Pilate: (smiling) No, Simon, there is no harm. I was curious. If it is irrelevant, we can strike it later.

You and Janus see shadows and hear creaks around every corner. I cannot say I envy your neurotic state, but I am grateful to be surrounded by such watchmen.

(The governor pushed his chair back, and we adjourned to the guardroom on the first level.)

Governor Pilate: (entering the guardroom) So this is the fierce Barabbas.

(The room was large with a single long table running its length. Barabbas was seated on the right side at the far end, his hands chained behind his back. Governor Pilate walked down the left side of the table and stood across from the seated Barabbas.)

Clephus: So far he has little to say.

Governor Pilate: (looking at Barabbas) I am Governor Pilate; do you know why you are here?

(Barabbas did not immediately respond but was attentive. I judged him to be a man of forty, with dark, uneven hair, appearing to have a body made of leather and bone. The governor refused further comment and awaited a reply.)

Barabbas: (snapping his head up, looking directly at the governor) I kicked one of your dogs that attempted to rob me.

Governor Pilate: (in a tone of derision) I do not think you understand. I did not ask you why you were arrested; I asked you if you knew why you were here.

You are here because you are responsible for murdering fourteen of my men, and I want to know who helped you.

(Barabbas composed himself, smiled, and leaned his head back as if searching for something on the ceiling, then throwing his body forward, spit in the governor's face. The guards grabbed Barabbas by the hair and prepared to strike him.)

(Flushed with rage, thick spittle hanging on his forehead over his right eye) No! Leave him alone!

Simon: (I took the corner of my cloak and went to wipe the spittle which had now begun to crawl down the governor's face.) Governor...

Governor Pilate: (pushing me aside) Leave me be!

(The governor looking at Barabbas) What do you expect from me? To have you flogged...[lxxx] to spit into your face? No, I will not trade with you in your currency; you will answer me on my terms.

(The spittle, having traced the governor's right eyebrow, now slide down his right cheek.)

Tomorrow afternoon we shall have another meeting and we will settle matters.

Clephus, clear a storage room with no windows. I want him in this building, chained and under constant guard. If any harm comes to him either from himself or others, I shall hold you responsible.

Dalaccus, you will make your best legionnaires available for the guard detail. You see that nothing! Nothing! happens to this man. Do you understand?

Dalaccus: I shall select the men myself.

(Clephus nodded agreement.)

Governor Pilate: I want this man served from my own table with wine from my own stores. Let the kitchen staff know who the food is going to, but let no one other than the hand-picked Roman guards have contact with the prisoner. Understood?

Clephus: Yes, Governor.

Dalaccus: Yes, Governor.

Governor Pilate: (the governor turned to Barabbas, who made eye contact with a self-assured smile) Now for your part... Tomorrow morning you will awaken at dawn and beg, I said beg your guards to take you out into my courtyard where my personal guard will be mustered with full bladders. You will then lie upon the ground, face up, and beg them to piss on you. When they are done you will thank all thirty individually for the pleasure of bathing in Roman piss.

(The governor's face reddened, his words clipped and controlled) You will then return here tomorrow afternoon and apologize to me for your actions today and for killing my men. Do you understand?

(Barabbas said nothing, maintaining a mocking sneer. Then leaning forward as if to reply, he again spit at the governor, with his spittle this time gracing the front of the governor's tunic. The guards again crashed down on the prisoner, but before they could strike him the governor held up his hand.)

Dalaccus: (moving toward Barabbas) This insubordination must be punished! Have your way with him, Governor, but first let him be flogged.

Governor Pilate: No, Dalaccus, such men must come to terms within themselves; we cannot beat contrition into them. He does not understand the burden that comes with this office. If I could only explain to him…

(The governor, still standing across from Barabbas, looked directly at the prisoner) Did you know that I just completed an inspection of the remote fortresses near Jericho?[lxxxi] The men of that fortress, men away from Rome, away from their wives and families… are left to care for themselves… It is difficult to look at them and not long to make their life easier.

I cannot help but think how much relief these eighty Romans might receive from a little female companionship, you know, cleaning, milling the grain… pounding the meat. But there are so few women worthy of these men. They deserve only the very best that Judaea has to offer.
I understand that your wife is a woman of such beauty. But I could never take another man's wife for such service without his permission… so let us strike an agreement. If you conform to my earlier wishes, I will consider it your expressed desire not to send your wife into the service of Rome. Should you not comply with my requests, you shall have the

119

comfort of knowing that eighty men are most grateful for your disobedience.

Oh yes, I will view any attempt at escape, including suicide, as your permission to also send your budding eleven-year-old daughter along to comfort my troops. Or you may indicate your desire to include her at this time by again spitting in my face.

(The governor leaned across the table. Barabbas, jaw clenched, sat motionless.)

I give you an easy target; are you dry or thinking of your daughter? I hear she takes after her mother...You have much to think about, and you have added a bath to my schedule. We will talk again tomorrow.

(The governor leaned back and walked toward the door.)

I will bathe, take my noon meal, and then spend the balance of the day on correspondence. Simon, if you would set some priority to matters, I will join you in my office after my meal. (looking back at the others) I will have Simon notify your offices of our meeting schedule.

Barabbas: (directing his comments toward the door) Even if I let your guards piss on me and I grovel before you... how do I know you will leave my family alone?

Governor Pilate: So now you seek my counsel?

Barabbas: I seek an answer.

Governor Pilate: There is no certainty in life or death, but I would encourage you to consider two facts. First, you have fought against my administration for what, five years? And what have you called me, a murderer, a thief, a tyrant? But have you ever called me a liar? Am I known to have betrayed a treaty? Withdrawn from a bargain? No, I have kept my word to both friend and foe... it is a matter of necessity.

But consider this, even if I may be a scoundrel, what other choice do you have? Resist me and your family's fate is certain, submit and there is a chance that they might be spared.

I am still damp with your spew, yet you see me as the source of your anathema. You have placed yourself in this press.[lxxxii] I turn it only for the pleasure of seeing you broken to my will. It is your choice. Betray your pride, or betray your family… It matters not to me, for in either case I shall see you broken.

(The governor left the room before Barabbas had the opportunity to respond.)

The transcription of the Jesus affair:
Day 1,757 of Governor Pilate's administration
(Same day, after the noon meal)
Prepared by Simon of Emmaus
Present:
Governor Pilate
Simon of Emmaus, Secretary to Governor Pilate

(The governor entered his office.)

Governor Pilate: Are you ready for business, Simon?

Simon: The matters are on your desk in order of importance. I suggest that you give the first three the majority of your time.

Governor Pilate: (looking though the stack of documents) What did you think of Barabbas?

Simon: I thought he was stupid.

Governor Pilate: How so?

Simon: He put himself and his family at great risk, but for what purpose? It was a shallow show of strength, one that you turned to foolishness.

Governor Pilate: Oddly, he risked nothing, Simon, for he has no fate but crucifixion. As for his family, women and children are not part of my arsenal. His wife and child have nothing to fear from me.

Simon: Then he has no reason to submit?

Governor Pilate: No, he believes there is a risk, therefore he has every reason to submit. It is the fate of most men to live their life around what they perceive, and in so doing, vacillate between false glory and imagined fear.

Simon: But…do we not all live what we perceive?

Governor Pilate: Perhaps… but had Barabbas looked within or behind, he would have charted a more advantageous course. Looking behind at the past, he would have discovered that my administration has never used women and children as weapons. Had he looked within himself, he would have found the quiet peace of his convictions and avoided the rage of fear…

(With a deep sigh) We spend most of our lives struggling to learn these lessons, Simon, but practice them infrequently. Men can learn, and those that claim this wisdom before being overtaken by old age thrust fate to the rest. I do not think Barabbas such a man, but we will know soon enough.

The transcription of the Jesus affair:
Day 1,758 of Governor Pilate's administration
(Next day)
Prepared by Simon of Emmaus
Present:
Governor Pilate
Clephus, Officer of Internal Affairs
Janus, Officer of Internal Surveillance
Dalaccus, Officer of Military Affairs
Simon of Emmaus, Secretary to Governor Pilate
Barabbas of Bethabara, Prisoner
Contingent of Guards, Responsible for the prisoner

(The governor had spent the previous afternoon and all morning on administrative affairs. After his noon meal he instructed me to summon Janus, Dalaccus, and Clephus. All were present in the governor's office when he returned from a walk.)

Governor Pilate: (entering his office) So which of you were up at dawn to see the show? (No one in the room responded.)

Your loss…He entered the courtyard slouched over, already broken… lay down on the ground and let the entire morning guard piss on him. I could not hear from where I watched, but the captain of the guards tells me that our prisoner dutifully thanked each man for his participation.

(Looking at Dalaccus) Where is the prisoner now?

Dalaccus: I have had him brought to the guardroom… where we were yesterday.

Governor Pilate: Have your men bring him here. (Dalaccus, without getting up, motioned to the guard standing at the door) Have you prepared the order, Simon?

Simon: Yes, Governor.

Governor Pilate: Give it to me.

(I took the order from my desk and handed it to the governor.)

Governor Pilate: Janus, what is the word on the street regarding Barabbas' arrest?

Janus: In general there is a sense of relief, but his cadre is making noises of retaliation. I am not sure that it is serious, but we have men assigned to it.

Governor Pilate: Arrest his six accomplices tomorrow. If all goes as planned, the only cries of retaliation will be against Barabbas.

(Janus and the governor smiled as if sharing a private joke.)

(Looking at Clephus and Dalaccus) It will become clear in a moment…ah, the guest of honor has arrived.

(Barabbas stood at the door. His hair was matted, and he had dirt caked to his clothes and skin. The governor looked at those guarding Barabbas.)

Governor Pilate: Bring him before me.

(Barabbas was led to the governor's table. The governor remained seated with the table separating the two.)

It seems that we have reversed roles. I sit, you stand, and now it is you that is in need of a bath. Do you have something to say?

(The prisoner continued to look down at his feet. His tone of contrition was belied by the ridged posture of his body.)

Barabbas: My apologies to the Governor for my actions yesterday, and for taking the lives of your soldiers.

Governor Pilate: Was that so difficult?

(The prisoner did not respond with word or gesture.)

Can you read?

Barabbas: I can read.

Governor Pilate: No doubt you have spent much of the time since our last meeting speculating as to why I did not make the names of your accomplices part of my conditions. Now that we have settled our differences, I see no reason not to satisfy your curiosity.

You see, I suspected that a man of your makeup would never bend to sacrifice those that trusted him. Equally strong would be your desire to protect those you love. As I very much wanted to see you humiliated, I did not give you a bargain that had you frozen in indecision, but rather a bargain that you could accept.
As for the names of your men, I had them before we met. (the governor placed the arrest and crucifixion order on the table before Barabbas) As you can see, your accomplices are clearly identified.

(The prisoner paled, looked briefly at the paper, but said nothing.)

Did you notice that your name is missing from the order? Have you wondered why you share my building, eat my food, and drink my wine? It is all a matter of perception… within these walls you are a filthy piss-soaked murderer, but on the outside you appear to be a traitor. Why else would you receive this special treatment? Your special care is known among the kitchen staff who no doubt report it to your friends on the streets. Why else would all be sentenced but you?

It is a tidy package, don't you agree? You and I meet, you are given special consideration, and your friends are identified. I believe that by tomorrow evening you will be the most hated man in Jerusalem. And you know what? When I kill your friends they will hate you, not me.

(Barabbas looked up, his eyes locking on to the governor's.)

Barabbas: They will not believe you.

Governor Pilate: They believe what they see.

Did I mention how I plan to complete the picture? After your friends are arrested, I will have the local tax collector deliver fifty denarii to your wife.

(Looking at the guard) Get this man a bath and proper Roman attire. Get him a mattress, table and chair, and a lamp for his room. Provide him scrolls if he likes, but no outside contact.

Barabbas: (agitated, straining at the chains on his hands) I do not want your consideration and neither does my family... return me to the prison!

Governor Pilate: I thought we were past this... It is not about what you want, but what I want. And I want you to eat, drink, and enjoy my hospitality or your wife and daughters will become Roman whores. And even if you were willing to sacrifice them, your fate would not change. You would still be seen as a traitor. So enjoy your life, what is left, and think of those you love... You have my word, if you behave, they will not be harmed.

(Barabbas appeared to be a man ready to burst. The bulging veins across his forehead and clenched jaw all gave warning of wrath that could no longer be contained. Yet he said nothing, turning toward the door as if dismissed.)

Are you in such a hurry to resume your life in a closet? I thought you might answer a few questions, and depending on your answers, help your six friends...

Barabbas: (snapping his head around to make eye contact with the governor) Your games wear thin, Governor.

Governor Pilate: I am offering to spare your friends the agony of crucifixion… grant them a more noble and less painful death… perhaps even poison.

Barabbas: In return for what?

Governor Pilate: Useful information regarding your relationship with Annas and Jesus of Nazareth.

Barabbas: (squinting his eyes, as if straining to see the meaning of the governor's request) Your spies have no doubt kept you informed of my relationship with Annas. He and his bastard son-in-law[lxxxiii] wear the robes of piety while they trade with the enemy. Our relationship is fear… He fears me so he sends his Roman dogs to bring me down.

(The guard reached to strike Barabbas, but the governor held up his hand. Barabbas did not flinch or break eye contact with the governor.)

As for Jesus of Nazareth, he is a sheep. His miracles gather the masses, teaching them the ways of submission. Some call him a messiah, but he is no different than the other imposters.[lxxxiv] The crowd's interest will fade with their curiosity… and then they will find a new messiah.

It is just as you and Annas have planned it, Governor. Annas keeps the people's heads pinned to the ground so you can pick their bones.

Governor Pilate: So, if you were keeping score, who would you say is winning… Rome, Jesus, Annas, or you and your followers?

Barabbas: It is not who is winning, but who is losing. Annas is losing the attention of the people; he lashes out at Jesus, but it is of no use. As I said, there will always be another.

Governor Pilate: What you tell me is common knowledge. If you have something to offer, bring it forward or your friends shall hang on the cross.

Barabbas: (smiling) Here is something that others will not tell you... the people will win. It is they that have superior numbers; they fight on their own soil, and have nothing to lose. You are a solider, Governor; is the outcome not certain?

Governor Pilate: (sighing) Very well, your friends shall be crucified, and you shall be known to betray them.

(Looking at the guards) Care for this man as I have instructed.

(Barabbas was led out of the room.)

Clephus: The six will be arrested tomorrow, with a trial to follow within a week?

Dalaccus: (seemingly indifferent, yet fully focused on Clephus) It is clearly not my place to make decisions on such matters, but I would prefer we not make the arrests tomorrow. It is the Hebrew Sabbath, and I am not anxious to kindle any religious fervor during the week of Passover.[lxxxv]

Governor Pilate: The arrests can wait, but keep watch over them. I will not have them escape. As for a trial, they have had their trial, and I have signed the order.

Janus: Should we send word to Annas?

Governor Pilate: From this point forward nothing is to be said about Barabbas. I want him to disappear. Except for the kitchen staff's food orders, he is to be a mystery. The illusion is best achieved if there are no facts obstructing the view.

(The balance of the meeting addressed a trade dispute and the arrival of troops. The meeting ended at the sixth bell, but Governor Pilate and I worked late into the evening responding to accumulated correspondence.)

***

During my career I had many occasions to return to the emperor's garden, and each time I found myself searching the horizon for the false line of reality. Once, early in my new career, I was standing at the furthest point near the front of the bath when Sejanus approached me.

"Can you make out the line?" Sejanus asked. I nodded. "But before you had to walk halfway to the wall to discover the deception. What changed?"

"Now I know that the wall is there and I look for it," I replied.

"Enlightenment, Pontius, it rules both mind and heart. Once you are enlightened, both innocence and deception peel and crumble, with no amount of maintenance overcoming the harsh light of truth. It is truth that allows us to effectively govern, but perception that allows us to rule. The trick, my young friend, is to keep them apart within us, while keeping others at an optimal distance."

My bewilderment must have been apparent for Sejanus continued, "Perception and truth, you may manipulate the one by touching it up to blend with the seasons, but the other is immutable. Beware of men, Pontius, that scan the horizon seeking only the line, ignoring the picture that you place before them. These men wield something more powerful than themselves; they grasp truth… It is a commodity that cannot be bought, sold, or overcome by force. Your only hope is to paint it too, giving it the many hued facets of subjectivity. This is how you fight reality, but act quickly, for time soon blisters the paint, and the white light of truth bleeds through."

Note to Mac:

There is much to be observed in this folio: controlled power, strategy, deceit, and brutality. Any one of these is worthy of comment, but somehow I find myself captured by Sejanus' admonishment to Pilate. "It is truth that allows us to effectively govern, but perception that allows us to rule. The trick, my young friend, is to keep them apart within us, while keeping others at an optimal distance."

Today, as a society, we find ourselves steeped in cynicism. We no longer trust our elected representatives, have lost faith in the press, and fully discount the representations made by advertisers. Sejanus' seemingly noble statement that, "it is truth that allows us to effectively govern," is in reality a hideous spin of morality that has infected our culture. Here he proposes truth, not as an answer, but as a platform on which one must stand in order to craft a desired deception. It is this misuse of truth that has us isolated and sneering at the very values for which we hunger.

Sejanus also saw the danger of using truth in deception, for he warned Pilate to "keep them apart within us." Sejanus understood that should the two become indiscriminately intermingled, those governing and those being governed would soon develop a banality of self-interest. I fear we have reached that point, as we now dispute all we encounter and find comfort in only what we can grasp.

But what of this white light of truth that Sejanus laments "bleeds through?" For me it is found in the Bible. Each morning as I read it, I discover the searing light of truth that cannot be contained, a truth delivered to me by a Creator and Savior who is uncorrupted by carnal desires. It is only within the Scriptures that I find the cradle of certainty. And within this quiet place of acceptance, we discover that Sejanus was indeed correct; the truth is immutable.

Chapter 10
Folio 9
Missteps

I am tired. My limbs no longer carry me, each breath is a labor, and binding these matters together becomes more difficult each day. What began as vindication, now has the pallor of a decomposed corpse. I was something, I was in the center of these events. But now seeing the corpse of my past before me, I know that I shall never be able to stitch it together in a fashion that gives it life. The reader of these pages knows the end, and with such foreknowledge, feels none of the immediacy and rhythm of my journey.

The reader stands on the summit, already having an opinion of Pontius Pilate. You effortlessly reached the top, following a path worn by my known struggle in Judaea. You look down and clearly see the missteps, errant ways, and the dead ends of my journey. How easy it is for you to fabricate the motives and reasons that weave this matter together into a garment of your choosing.

I do not have the energy for such foolery. There were thousands of decisions, some made, some ignored, and some forgotten. Pick them apart if you like; I lived them one at a time, unable to see the interplay of their consequence. Those reading this portion of Simon's transcript no doubt will exclaim, "He should have read, he should have noticed, he should have acted," but let this be your warning. At this moment in your own life, what have you failed to read? What have you ignored? What have you not acted upon? Your life too is determined by the decisions you make this day, seemingly insignificant, yet profound in their hidden consequence.

I piss blood and spend my days tending the oozing boils punched into my flesh by my bed. Such a schedule encourages little sympathy for the arrogance of your supposition. Read it and make what you will out of these meetings. I shall find my comfort in knowing that others shall treat your life with equal disdain.

***

The transcription of the Jesus affair:
Day 1,762 of Governor Pilate's administration
Prepared by Simon of Emmaus
Present:
Governor Pilate

Janus, Officer of Internal Surveillance
Simon of Emmaus, Secretary to Governor Pilate

(The governor and I had spent most of the morning reviewing trade[lxxxvi] and station reports. The morning session had left me with an assignment of several dozen time-critical items that needed further attention. The governor had agreed to let me stay behind while he inspected the construction of the newest aqueduct. I was gathering my scrolls when the guard announced that Janus was in the outer office requesting an audience with Governor Pilate.)

Governor Pilate: (responding to the guard's announcement) Tell him I will be a moment.

(The guard saluted and left the room. The governor walked toward the window.)

Simon, we have spent all morning on reports from various stations and departments. Did you notice anything missing?

Simon: No, Governor.

Governor Pilate: (turning toward me, with increased intensity) Jesus, Simon, Jesus… there is no mention of the man. Just a moment ago he seemed to be our companion at every turn, now… nothing.

Simon: Perhaps there is nothing to report, or other matters may have had a higher…

Governor Pilate: …Or perhaps he has been forgotten, or worse, wishes to be forgotten. There is still much of a field commander in me; I like my enemies before me.

Simon: Do you now see Jesus as an enemy?

Governor Pilate: I do not see him at all… and should he prove to be such, invisibility would make him most dangerous. But we do not know, and in such ignorance it is prudent to imagine ghosts to be fortresses. It is information that grants discernment…

(The governor's eyes narrowed as his gaze focused on the floor. Inviting no conversation, he walked slowly to the door and opened it.)
Send in Janus.

Janus: (entering the room) It is good to see you, Governor. Forgive my intrusion on your schedule, but I thought the matter sufficiently urgent...

Governor Pilate: (raising his voice) Has Jesus of Nazareth and his tribe disbursed to Macedonia? Is there nothing worth noting about them in your reports?

Janus: If the Governor wishes, I have recent news concerning the activities of Jesus, but I came in regard to Barabbas' followers. Two are dead, the others are in chains.

(Governor Pilate's entire countenance stiffened as he slammed his hand down on the table.)

Governor Pilate: (in a harsh scream) Summon Dalaccus!

Janus: (composed) Not his men, Governor, but mine. We had all six under surveillance, and at first light this morning they attempted to flee in unison. I had my men under orders to take whatever measures were required to prevent their escape. While being pursued one was trampled by a horse. Another, when cornered, took his own life. The other four were captured with only minor incident.

(The governor looked away from Janus then back to me.)

Simon: Do you want me to summon Dalaccus?

Governor Pilate: (again looking at Janus) What is the mood in the street?

Janus: Amazingly good. The murderers did us a great service by cursing Barabbas during the struggle. It seems that we will hang them, but Barabbas will be deemed the executioner.

Governor Pilate: Where are they now?

Janus: On the way to the prison, here.

Governor Pilate: When they arrive have them isolated. I want no word of their capture, trial, or sentence until after the Passover crowds disperse. Issue your orders. I will wait.

(Janus got up and summoned the guard. Soon another soldier appeared and was given the governor's orders. Janus returned to his seat.)

Janus: I have sent word and I will personally check on matters when we are finished.

Governor Pilate: We cannot let this get out of hand. (the governor paused, looking toward the door then back to Janus) See to it that another payment is made to Barabbas' wife.

Janus: Where shall I draw the funds?

Governor Pilate: Clephus will see to the funds.

(Janus nodded.)

Simon: I am sorry, Governor, but did you wish me to summon Dalaccus?

Governor Pilate: No.

Janus: If there are no other matters, Governor, I will allow you to resume your schedule.

Governor Pilate: (sarcastically) Before you leave, would you be kind enough to enlighten me on the activities of Jesus? It seems that my copies of the station reports have nothing to say on the topic. Tell me, have Jesus and his followers relocated?

Janus: As earlier reports indicted, Jesus seems to have been occupied with educating his followers in his passive doctrine. As nothing had changed, the most recent station reports made no mention of him. It was not until this week, with his entry into the city and the confrontation with Annas' minions, that Jesus once again became significant.

Governor Pilate: (in a mocking tone) Significant, significant? So significant that you failed to inform me?

(Janus seemed confused. He looked at me as if I might have an answer, but before he could respond, the governor continued with his voice rising in anger.)

You keep me in the dark on the activity of a potential threat during the Passover festival? Is that your idea of effective surveillance?

Janus: Governor, I sent you two dispatches under my own seal. They were delivered to Simon for your review.

Governor Pilate: (snapping his questions) Did we receive these dispatches, Simon?

Simon: Yes, Governor.

Governor Pilate: Why did you not pass them to me?

Simon: As you know, Governor, the flow of work has been exceedingly heavy the past two weeks. I must have set them aside and forgotten to give them to you.

Governor Pilate: (agitated) You forgot to give me two sealed dispatches? Does Janus' seal on a document mean nothing to you? You incompetent fool, I should have you flogged.

Simon: My apologies, Governor. You know my dedication to this service, it will not happen again.

Governor Pilate: Perhaps a few stripes from the whip will help your organizational skills. How many stripes do you think it will take?

Simon: I do not know, Governor. I will accept your judgement.

Governor Pilate: So you shall. Now get me those dispatches.

Simon: I am not sure…

Janus: …There is no need, I have the material committed to memory.

(The governor composed himself and directed his attention to Janus.)

Governor Pilate: Go on.

Janus: As I said, we have seen little activity from Jesus, but recently he drew quite a crowd when he entered the city.

Governor Pilate: When, how many?

Janus: Three, no four days ago.[lxxxvii] Estimates of the crowd vary, but there were thousands.

Governor Pilate: And the crowd was friendly?

Janus: More than friendly, they threw their garments on the road before him, allowing his donkey to tread upon them.

Governor Pilate: He rode a donkey[lxxxviii] into the city? Did troops or men at arms accompany him?

Janus: No, he rode on the lone donkey accompanied by his usual band of followers. It was somewhat chaotic, the crowd was reported to be enthralled; they shouted praises to him.

Governor Pilate: (eyebrows raised) As some form of king or prince?

Janus: No, they called him a great prophet.

Governor Pilate: And his reply?

Janus: He said little of note.

Governor Pilate: Where did he go once he was in the city?

Janus: Directly to the temple, but he didn't stay long. He looked around, then left the city, and spent the night in Bethany.[lxxxix] Oddly, he returned to the temple the next day and caused a near riot.[xc]

Governor Pilate: How so?

Janus: He went in and overturned the tables of the moneychangers[xci] and of those selling sacrifices, he called them thieves. I am surprised that he escaped with his life.

Governor Pilate: How did he make his escape?

Janus: He just walked out. Everyone seemed to be afraid.

Governor Pilate: (leaning back in his chair) It seems that our prophet is a man of some power. Men do not easily see their livelihood threatened and not respond. Annas may be more right than wrong about this Jesus, and if we are not prudent, we may find him toppling Rome's treasury.

Janus: I think Annas has more to fear than Rome. Do you remember the trap that Annas was to spring on Jesus? The one where he intended to ask Jesus in front of his followers whether it is lawful to pay taxes to Rome?

Governor Pilate: I remember well; the old fox had Jesus shunned if he said yes and arrested if he said no. A clever play...

Janus: Not clever enough. As planned, they gathered a crowd and asked Jesus whether it was lawful, that is according to their law, to pay taxes to Caesar. Our Herodian friends report that he called them all hypocrites and asked them to produce a denarius. Looking at the coin, Jesus asked them, "Whose image and inscription is on the coin?" They replied, "Caesar's." He then told them to "render to Caesar that which is Caesar's and to God the things that are God's."[xcii]

Governor Pilate: And their reply?

Janus: They had no reply. I am told that Jesus stood his ground and began searching their faces one at a time, seeking a response. Embarrassed, they broke up quickly.

Governor Pilate: How is Annas taking all of this?

Janus: He continues to pressure the Herodians to label Jesus a threat to Rome, but they refuse to consider the matter. I think they really enjoy seeing the old man flop about.

Governor Pilate: As do I, but what do we do about Jesus? A man of power who has the skill to outmaneuver Annas must be considered.

Janus: We could arrest him, but I fear that he holds more influence with the crowds than Annas and his followers. Arresting him may create unrest that we cannot contain.

Governor Pilate: No, the time to safely arrest him has passed. When he first entered the city, maybe, during his outburst at the temple, perhaps, but now? Now he has shown himself to be a man of the people and no threat to Rome…

Do you see the irony, Janus? You, Jesus, and I agree. We all consider Annas and his brood to be hypocrites; we all believe that Rome should be paid its due tribute. And, which of us has ever known a moneychanger that was not a thief?

Still, he could be dangerous, but my incompetent secretary has obviated any strategy other than status quo. For now we will have to live with him until the Passover is complete and the city returns to normal. Then we shall hang the murderers and rein in the Nazarene.[xciii,xciv]

Janus: If there is nothing else, I will return to my duties.

Governor Pilate: We are finished.

Janus: If it pleases the Governor, I could produce another copy of the dispatches and have them sent to you?

Governor Pilate: (looking at me) Can you produce the dispatches?

Simon: Not readily, Governor.

Governor Pilate: (angry, looking at Janus) It seems that I must accept your offer.

(Janus, with a slight bow, left the room. The governor's tone became stern but controlled.)

You disappoint me, Simon, and I find disciplining you distasteful, but your actions are inexcusable. Your incompetence has compromised both this office and its mission. Do you understand what I am saying?

Simon: Governor, I gave you those reports the days that they were received. As they were closed with Janus' seal, I did not review them, but passed them directly to you. In both cases, you assigned them to your evening reading. I am certain that if you check your quarters, you will find them.

Governor Pilate: (after a long pause and in a subdued tone) Why did you not speak up and defend yourself?

Simon: I thought it better to be the fool than to expose you to criticism.

Governor Pilate: (drawing himself up in his chair while looking down at the table) What remains of today's calendar?

Simon: The engineers wait to accompany you on an inspection of the new aqueduct. I can postpone the inspection until after Passover if you prefer. Except for the inspection, there are no other appointments.

Governor Pilate: (making eye contact and smiling) As you have said, I must adjourn to my quarters and catch up on my reading. Enjoy the rest of the day, Simon; I will not need you until tomorrow morning.

(The governor rose and moved toward the door.)

Simon: Thank you, Governor, but I must stay and complete my work, there are several items…

Governor Pilate: (still smiling as he rose and moved toward the door) I said I would not need you until tomorrow morning.

Simon: Thank you, Governor.

(Stopping halfway to the door, the governor turned to face me.)

Governor Pilate: My boy, you…(taking a deep breath) you… are a very rare sort.

(The governor left the room without further comment.)

***

There is a bitterness that accompanies old age. It is something that causes us to pull away from others, view kindness with suspicion and sentiment with disdain. There is no single ingredient that delivers this brackishness; it is the recipe of life. One part disappointment, one part pain, and one part self-recrimination, all baked together for a life span.

I do not just speak of myself. Go sit near the aged and listen. You will hear their common refrain, "I should have," "it wasn't fair," "I will never forgive them for..." This is the glue of old-age introspection, binding together those haunting memories that retain life's passion. These raw, unhealed recollections, trapped in bodies that have long since failed us, are all that remains to occupy our last days. It is, however, a most just prison, for it is a dungeon of our own making.

As I struggle to scratch out this testament, I fear that my life will be hung on a single hook. I did more, much more, than crucify Jesus of Nazareth. Someone needs to know that I laughed and held others as they cried. Someone needs to know that my wife truly loved me, and that I loved the empire. I need it known that my favorite food was figs, and that I hated meal cakes. Does it matter that I lost two toes to frostbite on a forced march through snow that was up to my waist? Is it important that I can still feel pain in those toes sixty years after I left them in a forgotten mountain pass? To an old man it matters, for that is all that remains. What you were becomes what you are.

I sit and listen to the incipient bitterness of the old as they vomit the tragedy of their lives upon the still vibrant, and I tell myself that I shall not give in to the past. This too is an old man's foolishness, for though I do not sing my dirge to others, these silent lamentations poison still. Each day, each pain, each labored breath groans the same refrain, I should have had... a son like Simon. It wasn't fair... that Simon was taken from me, and I shall never forgive them... for what they did to my boy.

Note to Mac:

This folio is a study in contrast. The young Pilate of these pages is at the pinnacle of his life. He is successfully maneuvering through a maze of complexities and has the sacrificial loyalty of a young man whom he considers a son. In contrast, the old Pilate laments that he has nothing but the bitterness of a failed body and accumulated tragic memories.

What was the journey between this white and black? Was it a sudden turn or a slow graying? I would give this little consideration if I believed the dichotomy unique to Pilate, but as I look around, I see so many living the same existence that I find it impossible to leave the matter unexamined.

My first endeavor to solve this puzzle resulted in a predilection for the graying hypothesis. My reasoning was that life slowly chips away our illusions until all that is left is the remorse of what we have lost. For is not life a slow decline from one summit after another? Do we not, upon reaching the bottom of each of our achievements, lament each missed step? But I came to realize that there must be something else, for everyone's life is punctuated with tragedies, but not everyone succumbs to the despondency of Pilate.

Confronted with this conundrum, I turned my attention to the sudden-turn theory. I reasoned that each of us is forced to deal with varying degrees and types of tragedy while simultaneously having varying capacities to absorb such punishment. Using this logic, it was easy to reason that some individuals reach their "tragedy capacity" and tip toward the dark perspective of the old Pilate, while others die before reaching their limits. But this theory too falls short, for though presenting a perfect explanation of the split between light and dark, it fails to explain the process. For we do not observe people flipping from white to black in an instant, but rather the transformation is accomplished at a glacier's pace that is indiscernible.

What then is the dividing rod? Is it within our capacity to direct our lives white or black? Can we will ourselves to see life as a journey rather than a tragedy? Specifically, is it possible to step back from what we live to direct how we live? All of this, I determined, was beyond my intellectual grasp as I see life and life's direction as inseparably mated. If there were a simple answer to be found, I reasoned, it must be outside of ourselves.

It was not long after I abandoned my life-centered theories that a simple answer presented itself. It is not what we live that determines our view of life, but where we look. Those who focus on themselves are destined to paddle about in their own swill, while those who focus on something beyond themselves make the past a step toward something larger.

All this should not have come as a surprise, for experience has taught me that it is only when I focus on God that I find true joy and peace in my life. If this is the answer, then why would a loving God not make such a focus an intrinsic part of our character? To be certain, it is within God's power to hardwire a God-centered focus into each of us, but in doing so He would make us his pets. No, it is God's way to seek our love through choice. And as I choose to focus on the gift of salvation offered through Jesus, I am able to make both this life and world a part of my journey to eternity.

It is all so simple, yet elusive. We are creatures of faith. Pilate's faith was in his career and persons, and once they had expired, there was nothing to look to but his past. This is the dividing point: do we have faith in a God that is all around us, but cannot be grasped, or do we focus on what we can touch, abandoning our old age to lamentation?

It has been said that faith is the chariot to our future, and no doubt it is a quintessential element of our fate. But within this folio are the lamentations of a man who forgot that this chariot is able to carry in many different directions. We must be ever mindful that faith is but a dutiful servant, it asks us for a destination, and then gallops us to our destiny.

Chapter 11
Folio 10
First Encounter

It has been over thirty years since I left Judaea.[xcv] The empire has discovered the tenacity of this mongrel race, and has finally begun to marshal the resources required to forever crush the rebellion.[xcvi] Had they given me one-sixth of what they now commit, I could have defeated the rebels in less than a year. But those were different times, before the Jews had discovered the vulnerability of our isolation, and before Jesus.

The empire will soon crush Judaea as it has so many other of its vassal states; that is not questioned. What remains undetermined is whether Rome can control the followers of Jesus that have fingered out into the furthest reaches of the empire. "The Way"[xcvii] they call themselves. We count them, persecute them, and banish them, but they persist. Rome itself is infected, with each day bringing new reports of the Jews stirred up by Christ-centered public disturbances. But these Jews are not just part of the Jewish race. They are Roman blood, citizens who abandon the corruption of gods,[xcviii] temples, and priests in favor of the itinerant laborer that I hung on the cross.

I will not live to know the final disposition of The Way, but I feel its effect. The moon does not cycle that I do not receive visitors. They seek me out, wanting to know of Jesus, that I describe him, and recall his words. I lure them near with the small voice of an old man, and then I strike out with my staff. They are sheep treading behind a ghost that holds more notoriety in death than he knew in life. I do them a favor, for what I have to say regarding Jesus is not what they hunger to hear.

Still they come, labeling him the "great teacher, good shepherd, and beautiful father." That is not the man I knew. He was neither teacher nor shepherd, nor was he beautiful. He was a large, powerful man, of average favor, hardly a god. Yet the fact that he possessed a unique quality is undeniable. When he entered a room he filled it. And when his black eyes caught you, you knew that he was in control. Such power is a noticeable quality in any man, but especially so in one who is brought to you bound and beaten.

Annas had good reason to fear him, for Jesus showed an abject disinterest in all but his mission. But that is the core of what all seek to know: what was his mission? As I said earlier, Jesus sought the ethos of his followers, but for what purpose? Looking back, I believe that it was within his power to incite a rebellion, to rule Jerusalem. He was before me, and I placed him before Jerusalem. He could have called to marshal his followers, offer a defense, or lash out at his accusers, but he did nothing. Having searched his eyes, I am left to conclude that nothing was part of his plan.

Simon's transcript is characteristically accurate, but fails to fully speak of the atmosphere that accompanied the day. It is fair to say that it was a hostile circus of activity. The streets were full of vendors shouting their calls, crowds of partisans, holy men, thieves, and the soldiers keeping them from riot. The Praetorium[xcix] was awash with the noise of the crowd. When I entered the Hall of Justice, you could not be heard in a normal voice; when I stepped upon the south porch of the hall, the crowd noise swelled to a din that made it impossible to communicate at any level.

That was the atmosphere in which Jesus was condemned. The crowd that called for his death packed the yard and streets from the south porch to the temple, bounded by the walls on either side. I had but a garrison of six hundred men within the Praetorium, hardly sufficient to control an angry crowd of such magnitude. This was Judaea, Jerusalem at Passover, and the crossroads of my fate.

***

The transcription of the Jesus affair:
Day 1,763 of Governor Pilate's administration
Prepared by Simon of Emmaus
Present:
Governor Pilate
Clephus, Officer of Internal Affairs
Dalaccus, Officer of Military Affairs
Curio, Captain of the Guards
Simon of Emmaus, Secretary to Governor Pilate
Jesus of Nazareth
Annas, Former High Priest
Caiaphas, High Priest and son-in-law of Annas

(I arrived at the governor's office at first light. Immediately upon entering, I passed two of Dalaccus' chief lieutenants who were leaving the office. The office was well lit and the arrangement of the papers and furniture indicated that it had seen activity for several hours.)

Governor Pilate: (looking up from a map of the city that was spread before him) Have the guard tell Clephus that I am ready.

Simon: My apologies, Governor, I was unaware that your day had started…

Governor Pilate: I need Clephus.

(I gave the guard the governor's instructions as he again returned to the map.)

I have been up for some time… Janus reported a disturbance here. (the governor pointed to the south end of the city map) Dalaccus is down there now. He just sent a report that a crowd of several thousand has gathered; we have about four hundred men here (pointing at the map), and three hundred in reserve south of the palace.

(Looking up at me) It seems that Annas and his band have arrested Jesus[c] and are bringing him before the council. He has sent word that he has a prisoner he wants to bring before the Seat of Judgement. I believe…

(Clephus entered the room unannounced by the guard. He was noticeably out of breath.)

Clephus: You were correct, Governor, the crowds are beginning to gather north of the temple. Dalaccus has sent word that he believes it is best to maintain a strong presence in the south sector as conditions are hostile and it will allow us to control the crowd from three sides.

Governor Pilate: (looking at the map and tracing the plan with his finger) Dalaccus would be using the east wall to funnel the crowd into the palace area. If the crowd can be contained there, we need only control the south porch, Sheep Gate, and Horse Gate.

Simon, take down and seal this message for Dalaccus.

Dalaccus,
I assume that you intend to funnel the crowd toward the east wall, giving them the opportunity to gather in the palace area. If this can be accomplished without incident, I will secure the south porch and Ephraim Gate with the Praetorium garrison. You must control the Sheep and Horse Gates. Obviously, a crowd outside the Gate of Ephraim will place the plan in jeopardy. Direct all unassigned forces to that area.
Be aware that they intend to lead a prisoner (Jesus) to the Hall of Justice.

An eastern route to the hall will advantage me in maintaining control of Ephraim (gate). Under no circumstance are you to provide any form of protection to the prisoner or to those transporting the prisoner. We need to treat this as a Jewish matter.

You have full command of forces outside the Praetorium.
Governor Pilate

Clephus: Might it be prudent to reinforce the Praetorium?

(The guard enters and places a message on the table before the governor. Without looking at the document, the governor slides the message in my direction.)

Governor Pilate: (both relaxed and exhilarated) If it comes to a confrontation, Clephus, I think we are better off having a viable force surrounding our adversary. Not that it will make a difference... the numbers forecast but a single outcome... little difference whether we are overrun in one hour or in three.

We position ourselves to make such a victory seem both costly and uncertain. This is a mob, not an army; they do not know their numbers alone bring them victory. We will only win by defeating their will.

(The governor looking at me) The message?

Simon: It is from the captain, do you wish me to read it? (the governor nodded)

A crowd has assembled below the south porch. I estimate it to be between two to three thousand, but it is growing rapidly. I have deployed two-hudnred men at the base of the porch with short swords and shield; thirty lancers are stationed on either side of the porch. The oil is in place, should a fire defense be required. The full garrison has been recalled to duty and is on alert. Please advise.

(Signed)
Captain of the Guards

Governor Pilate: The deployment is fine. Tell Curio that he is to instruct his men to treat the crowd with courtesy... It is easier to control a

145

thousand pets than a thousand belligerents... strict discipline, no retaliation or self-defense unless commanded. Absent a direct order to the contrary, his men are to be peacekeepers.

(I rose to inform the guard when the governor stopped me.)

(Looking at Clephus) No, I want Clephus to deliver the message.

Clephus: Yes, Governor.

Governor Pilate: I want to have a look at the crowd myself. Clephus, I will meet you back here shortly. Come, Simon; you are with me.

(We climbed the stairs and walked the long hall that led to the armory. The room was long and narrow with each wall neatly ordered with weapons. At the far end was a small, narrow window that looked down on the palace west wall rampart, with a left view of the assembled crowd.)

Governor Pilate: We see them, but they do not notice us. There is no sense in exciting them any sooner than necessary. Your thoughts, Simon?

Simon: The crowd is larger than I expected, but they seem orderly.

Governor Pilate: You tell me what Simon, but why? Why have they gathered? I have no announcement, and there is nothing of special interest that the temple should draw such a crowd. Yet here they are, orderly and purposeful. I believe that Annas has assigned us roles in his little drama and has assembled us an audience.

Simon: For what purpose?

Governor Pilate: No doubt to solve his Jesus problem. (the governor stepped back from the window and smiled) But all dramas have surprises, and before this is over we shall deliver a few to our robed crocodilian.

We keep Clephus waiting.

(The governor retraced his steps back to his office, stopping only to ask that four portions of meat and figs be brought to his office.)

Clephus: (as we entered the office) I delivered your message to Curio. He will keep you advised.

Governor Pilate: (looking at both Clephus and myself) I have ordered a meal of figs and meat. Partake of it as you can, we may not have the opportunity to eat the rest of the day.

(The meal arrived and was served on four plates. The governor took his plate and placed it within reach, then returned to studying the map.)

Governor Pilate: Eat gentlemen, we cannot have you faint when the party begins.

(We took a plate and watched the governor study the map. He seemed to be focusing most of his attention on the area southwest of the Praetorium.)

Governor Pilate: (tapping his finger on the map) No crowds here yet, that is good news.

(Curio, after being announced by the guard, enters.)

Curio: Governor, the Jews are bringing the prisoner here through the Horse Gate. There is a large crowd that is following.

Governor Pilate: Let them come. Any sign of Annas?

Curio: There is a large contingent of officials with the prisoner, but they were too far away… I could not distinguish individuals.

Governor Pilate: (taking a deep breath) Annas is there, for how often does one have the opportunity to dispose of one's adversary while twisting the tail of another?

When they arrive, escort the prisoner and a dozen leaders of their choosing to the Hall of Justice. Take them in through the south porch; I want the crowd to clearly see the faces of their chosen representatives. And, oh yes, make certain that Annas and Caiaphas are among the twelve.

(Upon hearing this, I attempted to capture the governor's attention by setting down my writing implement and making eye contact. The governor immediately responded.)

Governor Pilate: Do you have something, Simon?

Simon: Only that Annas and the others will not enter the hall. In so doing they would be defiled and unable to continue the celebration of Passover.[ci]

Governor Pilate: (exasperated but under control) Do they allow themselves to stand on the porch, the steps?

Simon: To do so would make them unclean, they are not permitted to enter the house of a gentile.[cii]

Governor Pilate: (looking at Curio) When the prisoner arrives take him into the hall. Inform the others that I will address them from the south porch.

(Curio, having acknowledged his orders with a salute, left the room.)

Now is not the time for a test of wills. Annas brings Jesus to the Roman Hall of Justice, but has managed to detach the council from the proceeding... And a full portion of justice they shall receive... Roman justice.

(The governor looked up as the guard entered the room) Yes?

Guard: The captain sends word that the prisoner has arrived and is in the hall. The captain thought it prudent to remain with the prisoner until the governor's arrival.

Governor Pilate: Tell him I will be there directly.

(Saluting, the guard left the room.)

(Looking around the room with a quick smile) He tames the lion, raises the dead, and outfoxes the fox. Let us finally meet this Jesus of Nazareth.

(The governor rose and at a brisk pace led the party to the Hall of Justice.)

Governor Pilate: (to the entrance guards at the Hall of Justice) Announce me.

(As the large bronze doors were opened, the crowd noise washed over us. The doors to the south porch opposite us had been opened, bringing in both light and the audible presence of the crowd outside the hall.)

Guard: Hail all, Pontius Pilate, Prefect of Judea, Prefect of Samaria, Prefect of Idumea, hail Pontius Pilate.[ciii],[civ]

(We entered the hall, discovering only the captain and eight of his guards present. The governor climbed the one step to take his place on the Seat of Judgement. Clephus sat to the right of the governor, just off of the platform; I took my place at the scribe's table on the left.)

Governor Pilate: (to Curio) Bring in the prisoner.

(Curio motioned to two guards that were standing in front of the holding room door. They entered the holding room, shortly returning with two additional guards and the prisoner.)

Governor Pilate: (nearly screaming to be heard above the crowd noise) Bring him before me.

(The guards brought the prisoner before the governor, the customary five paces from the platform.)

Governor Pilate: Close those doors, and bring him to the platform.

(The guards closed the porch doors, and the prisoner was brought forward.)

Bring the lamps forward, I cannot see the man.

(The two large lamps on the back of the platform were brought forward and placed to the right and left of the governor, just behind his seat. The two smaller lamps on either side of the room were placed at the right and left of the platform between the governor and the prisoner.)

Is this man so dangerous that he must be bound and held?

Curio: It is as we received him.

Governor Pilate: Step back, let him stand on his own.

Curio: (to the guards holding the prisoner) At attention three paces back.

(The guards responded to their orders.)

Governor Pilate: (in a commanding tone) I am Governor Pilate, I am told that you are Jesus of Nazareth. Why are you here; what are the charges against you?

(The prisoner, hands bound in front of him, head bowed, did not respond.)

(Looking at Curio) Do we have charges?

Curio: These were delivered with the prisoner.

(Curio approached the platform and handed the governor a small scroll.)

Governor Pilate: (opening and reading the scroll half audibly) Public disorder, insurrection, attacks, (inaudible) King of the Jews...

(The governor extended the scroll in my direction. I collected it from him.)

Are you the King of the Jews?

(The prisoner's posture suddenly changed, he gathered himself and lifted his head. This face was swollen as if he had been beaten. He stared at the governor for a five-count before responding.)

Jesus: (clearly and without passion) As you say.

Governor Pilate: And these other charges, have you heard them? Have you nothing to say of these?

(Jesus, showing no emotion, continued to look directly at the governor.[cv] The governor rose and walked to the edge of the platform, toward Jesus. Looking down at the prisoner, the governor appeared to be searching for something.)

Open the doors, I will speak to those who bring these charges.

Curio: (to the guards standing before the doors that led to the south porch) Alert those outside and then open the doors.

(One of the guards opened the door enough to slide out and returned a short time later.)

Guard: (to Curio) The centurion believes that the situation is stable.

Governor Pilate: (exasperated, looking at Curio) Open the doors!

(The guard looked to Curio who motioned for the doors to be opened. The noise from the crowd rushed into the room as the doors swung open and increased to a roar when the governor appeared at the threshold.)

Governor Pilate: (shouting into Clephus' ear in an effort to be heard above the crowd noise) Instruct the council leaders that… (this portion of the governor's comments inaudible because of crowd noise) …We will wait.

Clephus: (looking at the governor and nodding agreement while shouting his reply) You should be ready… (this portion of Clephus' comments inaudible because of crowd noise) the danger is on our left.

(Clephus descended the steps and met with the gathered council members, including Annas. Clephus appeared to be making a request and was forced to shout directly into the ear of a council member in order to be heard above the noise. Several exchanges took place before Clephus returned up the steps.)

Clephus: (upon reaching the governor, still shouting) Done.
(The governor nodded and both he and Clephus looked to the base of the steps. Soon a cart was pulled through the crowd and placed near the council. Caiaphas climbed onto the cart and faced the crowd. Raising his arms above his head, he brought still louder roars. Finally, in apparent frustration, he made fists with both hands and crossed his arms above his head. The crowd gradually fell silent.)

Governor Pilate: Clephus, Simon, you will accompany me.

Curio: Governor, I believe that I should…

Governor Pilate: You will have a better vantage point from up here. I need your head, not your sword.

(The governor descended the steps with Clephus, and I was a step behind. Reaching the council, the governor spoke in a commanding tone.)

Governor Pilate: You bring me charges but no facts. What factual accusations do you bring against this man?[cvi]

Caiaphas: (now down from the cart) Would we deliver him to you were he not guilty?

Governor Pilate: Then take him and judge him according to your law.

Caiaphas: (in a louder voice that can be heard by the crowd surrounding him) His crimes deserve death. It is not lawful for us to put anyone to death. He has stirred up the people, teaching his sedition from Galilee to Jerusalem; we bring him to you for justice.[cvii]

(A roar began to ripple through the crowd, starting at the gathering of the council and soon reaching those near the temple. Visibly angry, the governor climbed the stairs and returned to the hall.)

Governor Pilate: (taking the Seat of Judgement and addressing Jesus) They would hang you for sedition. Consider carefully, are you the King of the Jews?

Jesus: (assuming the tone of reason, looking directly at the governor) Are you asking for yourself, or have others said this of me?[cviii]

Governor Pilate: (leaning forward, hands apart) Am I a Jew? Your own people and chief priests bring you to me. What have you done?

Jesus: (in a quiet, direct tone) I do not rule this place. If I did, my servants would fight so that I would not be delivered and accused. But my kingdom is not here.[cix]

Governor Pilate: (thoughtfully) You speak of a kingdom, are you then a king?

Jesus: (head raised, with a slight smile) You speak rightly that I am King. For this I was born, and for this I came into the world… that I should bear witness to the truth.

(The smile no longer evident) Everyone who is of the truth hears me.

Governor Pilate: (sitting back in his chair, hands cupped before him in a quiet tone) Truth? What is truth?[cx]

(The governor stared at Jesus for a ten-count and then rose from his chair, briskly walking toward the porch door.)

(Looking at the door guards) Open the doors!

(Without instruction, the governor descended the steps toward the council. Before he reached them, a council member had already mounted the cart to quiet the crowd.)

Annas: Governor, we await your ruling.

Governor Pilate: (clearly irritated by Annas' impertinence) I find no fault with him at all…

Annas: (in a loud voice) Then you mock…

Governor Pilate: But have you not identified the sedition as having its source in Galilee? Is this man not a Galilean? Herod[cxi] is in Jerusalem; he is of Herod's jurisdiction. Should Herod not be the first to pass judgement?

Annas: (clearly surprised) Then take him before Herod now.[cxii] I will send word…

Governor Pilate: (sternly) No! I will send Clephus ahead. This is your prisoner, and you have the responsibility for his care. I am done with this matter until I hear from Herod.

(The governor turned and began to walk up the porch steps. Once at a safe distance from the council, he addressed Clephus)

Tell Curio to turn the prisoner over to Annas. Then go immediately to Herod and, in your most diplomatic tone, tell the moron that we seek his council on this matter. Be swift, I want you there before Annas.

(The governor turned to me) Simon, send word to Dalaccus. Have him turn the field command over to one of his lieutenants; I need him here.

(The governor returned to his office.)

***

This was the Jesus that I knew, a prisoner who spoke few words and offered no defense. His questions were riddles and his statements were questions. I am not disputing that he had an aspect of command. He held his space with an ease that brought Sejanus' admonition to mind. "Beware of men that trade in truth, and of its power to overcome our deceptions." But truth does not wear an insignia, and Sejanus' lesson fell short on teaching me how to identify the commodity.

Sejanus had said, "The white-hot light of truth blisters away the paints of deception that others and we liberally apply to both mean and profound matters." What he failed to say was that this blistering is not instantaneous, that truth is revealed only after time has cracked and flaked away the cover of circumstance and deception. This was the burden of governing that day. I could not wait for the truth to escape its covering; I was required to make decisions in the present.

Jesus spoke of being the truth, and indeed he may have been, for all others were carrying portfolios of self-interest. But the truth about what? Was he speaking of being innocent, being a god, or about my complicity in an unjust trial? Jesus identified himself as truth, and, in my current misery, I would welcome the revelation of such. Yet, even at a distance of thirty years, I see no blister or flake; the truth and its peace of certainty remain concealed.

I have no expectations; few things in life or death are without frayed ends. My decision at Gerizim,[cxiii] Simon's departure, trusting Flaccus,[cxiv] these and a hundred more are the unravelings that I carry to my grave. And, if you line up and use these tattered ends to define my life, you must include my Sphinx[cxv] too, for it has lived with me since that day in Jerusalem, tendering its question and waiting to place it upon my shroud. "What is truth?"

Note to Mac:

"What is truth?" This is one of the most debated Scriptures in the Holy Bible. Knowledgeable theologians have labeled Pilate's query as everything from sarcastic to inquisitive. This portion of the transcript is in close harmony with the Scriptures, and, having conducted a detailed comparison, I do not believe it definitively supports any aspect of conjecture. The definitive answer as to Pilate's state of mind when querying Jesus is not found here.

As to how the elder Pilate felt about the question of truth, I find his summation powerfully succinct and in no need of commentary. He draws a straight line between the lessons of truth as taught to him by Sejanus, and how those lessons were corrupted by the interplay of acumen and time. With the exception of his reference to the Sphinx, Pilate's clinical analysis invites little subjective interpretation.

Greek mythology is rife with powerful images, but none is more apropos to the topic of truth than the Sphinx of Thebes. Did Pilate carefully select this myth to punctuate his thoughts, or was it an image that he casually associated with the topic? In either case, it extends the meaning and questions surrounding his encounter with Jesus.

As the endnotes document, this Sphinx was a fierce winged creature that would swoop down and confront the unsuspecting with a riddle. Answer the riddle correctly and you live; answer it incorrectly and you die. Within the myth itself, the Sphinx is used only as a means of defining the qualities of Oedipus.[cxvi] The elder Pilate, on the other hand, claims the Sphinx as the central issue in stating, "And if you line up and use these tattered ends to define my life, you must include my Sphinx too."

Pilate avows the creature his own, i.e., "my Sphinx." But what does it represent: the elusiveness of truth, the deity of Jesus, or an errant decision? Pilate goes on to say that the Sphinx "has lived with me since that day in Jerusalem, tendering its question and waiting to place it upon my shroud." Here he separates the question from the creature, making it implausible that the Sphinx represents the elusiveness of truth. A similar case can be made against ascribing the Sphinx to an errant decision, for decisions are of our creation, not the delivery of another. So, in exhausting the other possibilities, am I claiming that Pilate was weighing the deity or authority of Jesus? No, all that can be said is that he saw the issue of truth brokered by something beyond himself.

I began this discussion seeking to bring clarity to Pilate's contemplation of truth. It was he, though, who reached forward to educate me. The questions confronting us both are the same. Is truth simply what we desire? Is it what we live? Is it a commonly agreed upon fact? Can it be fashioned, birthed, or destroyed? Does it hold a place? Can it be owned, sold, or changed? Is truth the same for everyone? Neither of us will ever know the answer to these questions, but Pilate saw more. He recognized that these riddles were external from him, that both the riddle and its answer are found not within us, but in our Sphinx.

This is his lesson to me, that the definition of truth is not as important as its source. From the fountainhead of what we believe springs both the questions and answers that define our life, our truth. So what was Pilate's fountainhead i.e., Sphinx? It may have been a budding faith in Jesus, or it may have been the despondency of regret. We are not privileged to know the hearts of others. God gives such matters their own economy, making them a mystery in life, a shroud in death, and a companion for eternity.

Chapter 12
Folio 11
Middle Vision

How merciful it would have been to address just this portion of Simon's transcript. I could have wrapped my full rationale and justification around the act of sentencing Jesus, and spared the reader the ocean of events that led to this island of my imprisonment. A harsh word "imprisonment," an odd word to use when speaking of an event. This event, though, has been nothing less, for all that I have lived since has been bound by its consequence.

My painful commitment to document the whole affair is the lesson from a centurion named Lucius. He was what every new commander receives, an experienced veteran assigned to help the new officer adjust to command. In the ranks, these men were known as milk nurses, not a title of derision but of respect. For both soldier and legion knew that their presence might be all that separated them from the rash inexperience of a new officer. This would prove to be the case for my first command, for all would have perished had it not been for Lucius.

My education and family station[cxvii] had marked me for command, just as the lack of such made Lucius twenty years a centurion.[cxviii] Lucius had served as milk nurse thrice before and would be assigned to my command for the requisite two years. It was just two weeks after beginning his service to me, however, that he would teach me the lesson that would have me create this document, and that would rescue six-hundred men from certain death.

As was tradition, my first command assignment was off mount. My first orders had me transport my men to Venetia[cxix] to assist a larger force in suppressing bandit activity in mountains near Forum Julia.[cxx] It was spring and favorable weather allowed us to sail without incident to Aquileia.[cxxi] Disembarking, we marched to Forum Julia, the base of operations against the bandits. At Forum Julia I received orders to relieve the garrison that was stationed a four-days march to the northwest.

We marched out of Forum Julia in perfect weather. The men were suitably equipped for the below-freezing temperatures and welcomed the sure footing that the frozen earth provided. It was near dusk on the second day when I ordered the men to make camp. I had selected a location to bivouac that offered some protection from a cold northeast wind that had plagued the last three hours of our march. The selected site was a large, clear oval of dry ground with the steep face of a mountain on one side and a thick stand of pines on the other. I thought it an ideal location since the thick pines dissipated whatever wind managed to swirl around the shelter of the mountain.

The men had already begun to cut boughs for shelter and gather firewood when Lucius arrived with the rear guard. "Pick up, we move on!" he commanded. I approached him and informed him that I had ordered the men to make camp. His reply was respectful but firm, "Not here." By now the other centurions had gathered and were awaiting orders. Lucius did not hesitate. "There is little light left; counter march the men double time back to that last pasture."

Still uneasy in my command, I said nothing as the men quickly packed and began to retrace their steps. Finally, I summoned the courage to confront Lucius. "I had the men protected from the wind, now they will spend the night cursing us in their misery."

Lucius looked away from me at the face of the mountain, "Up there, Commander, the ice and snow on that face will not hold long against this wind. It may break loose tonight or next week, but it will break loose. Better the men are cold than dead. We should join the men."

That night, as we attempted to sleep in the frigid pasture, we were awakened as the earth shook and a thunderous roar washed across us. Lucius was first up, barking orders to the other centurions, "Order your men at rest! It is the snow off of the mountain, nothing more." The men were quickly settled, and Lucius returned to our camp. I immediately began to express my gratitude, but he interrupted, "It will be a long march tomorrow, Commander. It is best for us to rest."

At dawn we received word from the scouts that an avalanche had completely filled the pass, burying and crushing the entire stand of pines. I elected to march the men half a day to the south rather than attempting to pick our way through the debris. By the time we made camp that night, we had circumvented the obstacle and were within one-day's march of our destination.

It was that night, as Lucius and I sat alone around a banked fire, that I offered the centurion my apology. Lucius made himself busy tending the fire and then stopped to face me. "Middle vision...you have the instincts of a field officer. No reason to apologize for that."

"Middle vision?"

That evening Lucius would explain the wisdom he had gained from scores of campaigns, while serving some of Rome's most revered officers. The most interesting of his observations pertained to the vision of command. He reasoned that all great commanders had what he termed middle vision. They focused on the objective, the adversary, and on caring for resources at their disposal. They devoted little time to what he called near vision: personal safety, glory, and such. And they were not prone to far vision, those elements large but not easily held. These larger things, rumors, motives, and weather, though heeded, are never allowed to preoccupy the decisions of command.

This then is Lucius' contribution to documenting this affair—that I give the middle vision, neither seeking self-deception nor lamenting the grander forces that robbed me of control. Yes, the crucifixion order is here, but so too is the middle that surrounded it, the mission, the adversaries, and the resources. It is these that you must be steeped in, along with all the treachery, noise, and cross-purposes. How easy it is to seek but a ladle full, but I immerse you in the entire stew. This is how it was served to me, and if you would understand, how you must be served.

***

The transcription of the Jesus affair:
Day 1,763 of Governor Pilate's administration
Prepared by Simon of Emmaus
Present:
Governor Pilate
Clephus, Officer of Internal Affairs
Dalaccus, Officer of Military Affairs
Curio, Captain of the Guards
Simon of Emmaus, Secretary to Governor Pilate
Jesus of Nazareth
Annas, Former High Priest
Caiaphas, High Priest and son-in-law of Annas
Claudia, Wife of Governor Pilate
Janus, Officer of Internal Surveillance

(After summoning Dalaccus, I accompanied the governor and Curio in a thorough inspection of the Praetorium[cxxii] defenses. The governor seemed pleased with Curio's preparations, adding only that additional water be provisioned in anticipation of a siege. When we returned to the governor's office, Dalaccus was waiting.)

Governor Pilate: (entering his office, not even waiting for Dalaccus to stand) What is the mood?

Dalaccus: It is better. The crowd seemed highly organized earlier. Sending the prisoner to Herod seems to have scattered their intent.

Governor Pilate: Herod was not part of Annas's plan; he will organize them and have them back here with the prisoner.

Dalaccus: The crowd has not dispersed; they have not yielded the courtyard. What I meant to say is that their empty bellies and full bladders have them uneasy.

Governor Pilate: Good. What of the equestrian corps, are they deployed?

Dalaccus: No, your orders were to keep the peace. The city has pockets of crowds that allow no room for free movement. I feared the consequence of a child or woman trampled.

Governor Pilate: Sound thinking. (the governor, eyes closed with both hands rubbing the back of his neck, said nothing for a five-count) If we leave the horses stalled, we run the risk of having them slaughtered.

Have the entire corps mounted and divided evenly outside the Ephraim, Sheep, and Horse Gates.[cxxiii] Have them lined up in show, but order them to avoid confrontation. We must not relinquish control of those gates. See to it immediately, Dalaccus; time draws short.

Dalaccus: (standing in salute) Will you have me stay with my men?

Governor Pilate: No, I will need you here. Also instruct your men to clean up Barabbas. (the governor leaning forward) I need him looking clean and well kept. I shall have any man that strikes him on the oars.[cxxiv] Do you understand?

Dalaccus: As you say, Governor.

Governor Pilate: (standing and looking down at the map) The prisoners, Barabbas and Jesus, are our best weapons this day. When you return I will need you to personally supervise their care.

Dalaccus: (again saluting, but stopping as he reached the door) May I suggest that your horse be quartered in one of the Praetorium grain stores until things have settled?

Governor Pilate: (smiling, looking at Dalaccus) My horse and yours to accompany him.

Dalaccus: Thank you, Governor.

(As Dalaccus left the room, the guard entered, informing the governor that his wife was waiting for an audience.)

Governor Pilate: Do not keep the lady waiting. I will see her now.

Claudia: Forgive me, but you know it is not my practice to disturb your work… (the governor's wife stopped as she made eye contact with me) How is your brother, Simon; is his leg healing?

(I looked to the governor who, looking at me with raised eyebrows, extending his hand toward his wife.)

Simon: The redness and heat have dissipated. He is beginning to walk again.

Claudia: (looking at me) Perhaps you should…

Governor Pilate: (in a tone of amusement) Did you come to see me?

Claudia: I came because I am concerned. I had a fitful night. I have been with the staff since you left early this morning. They are afraid; they fear that their service to us may put them in jeopardy.

Governor Pilate: (patiently) Whom do they fear?

Claudia: It is a mixture, the crowds, the prophet Jesus, the Zealots… it has them all frightened. Perhaps it is best to let them be with their families.

Governor Pilate: (firmly) No, they have service here; now is when they are most needed. Besides, would you think them safer here or on the streets? Settle them as best you can. Now forgive me, I have urgent matters.

Claudia: Will you reconsider if conditions deteriorate?

Governor Pilate: (quietly) My lily, I am a slave to conditions. Now go get some rest and let me return to my duties.

(The governor's wife walked to him and extended her right hand; he took it in his left.)

Claudia: I trust that you know what is right. I will tend to our staff.

(The governor's wife left the room.)

Governor Pilate: (looking at me) Her heart is too large to govern, Simon, yet it is most suitable for a good wife.

Has Clephus returned?

Simon: He is waiting.

Governor Pilate: Send him in and ask the guard to send food… anything but cakes.

(I informed the guard and summoned Clephus.)

Clephus: (entering the room) Governor, the prisoner is on his way back to the hall.

Governor Pilate: Did Herod receive you?

Clephus: Yes, most graciously. He examined Jesus and was quite curious,[cxxv] but Jesus would answer none of his questions. Annas and Caiaphas were relentless in their accusations.

Governor Pilate: And did Herod support the charges?

Clephus: Herod, frustrated by Jesus' refusal to defend himself, joined the others in mocking him, but in the end refused to rule. He sent him back to you. He was most flattering.

Governor Pilate: How so?

Clephus: He said your experience and judgement in such matters are without equal. That justice might best be found upon your lips.

Governor Pilate: It seems that the moron has acquired some tact and political acumen… an alliance with Herod is an attractive prospect.[cxxvi]

162

Clephus: I believe that is his intent. I will pursue the matter.

Governor Pilate: After Passover. We must not be…

(The guard entered and announced Curio.)

Curio: Forgive the interruption, but the prisoner has returned, and a larger crowd has gathered.

Governor Pilate: Where is the crowd?

Curio: As before, between the south porch and the temple.[cxxvii]

Governor Pilate: The Ephraim Gate? Is there a crowd there?

Curio: We control the gate, the crowd is isolated to the south porch.

Governor Pilate: Our good fortune, we will eat and then settle this Jesus affair.

Simon, where is the food? Curio, will you join us?

Curio: Thank you, Governor, but I will see to my men.

(Curio left and I sent a second message for food. In a short time the food arrived, as did Dalaccus. Dalaccus and the governor spent the meal in an unrelated but spirited discussion of equestrian strategy. Having completed the meal, the governor stood.)

Governor Pilate: Let us adjourn to the hall and be done with this matter. Dalaccus, I will need Barabbas at the ready, but keep him out of sight until I request him.

(The governor walked briskly to the Hall of Justice followed by Clephus and myself.)

Governor Pilate: (to the entrance guards at the door) Announce me.

(The large bronze doors were opened. The doors to the south porch opposite us were closed.)

Guard: Hail all, Pontius Pilate, prefect of Judea, prefect of Samaria, prefect of Idumea, hail Pontius Pilate!

(Again, as we entered the hall, only Curio and eight of his guards were present. The governor, instead of climbing the platform, walked straight to the porch doors.)

Governor Pilate: Open them.

(The guard looked to Curio, who, being assuaged by the outside guard, allowed the doors to be opened. The roar of the crowd was more deafening than before. This time, however, the priests were prepared and had the crowd silenced before the governor reached the bottom of the steps.)

Annas: (smiling) We have returned the prisoner to you, Governor.

Governor Pilate: (in the flat voice of command) You bring this man to me as one who misleads the people. I have examined him before you, and I find no fault in him regarding your accusations. I sent him to Herod, and he too found nothing in him deserving death.[cxxviii]

(The governor leaned over, saying something to Clephus that caused him to quickly ascend the steps.)

Annas: The crowd awaits your decision, Governor. Will you put him to death or not?

Governor Pilate: You have the crowd hungry to taste blood, Annas, and it would be foolish not to accommodate them. So I will give them a choice. I shall honor the Passover tradition of releasing one prisoner… let them choose. (the governor motioned to Clephus at the top of the stairs) Shall it be Jesus or Barabbas?[cxxix] (Barabbas and Jesus were both led to the porch at the top of the stairs.)

(Annas, visibly shaken, did not respond to the governor's question, but turned to consult the council. The crowd's roar was replaced with a murmured roar.)

Governor Pilate: Shall we ask the crowd? (climbing three steps and addressing the crowd in a loud voice) Would you have me release the King of the Jews or Barabbas?

(Governor Pilate looked down at Annas who was struggling to climb onto the cart, while the governor again addressed the crowd.)

Governor Pilate: Who is to be released?

Annas: (facing the crowd) Barabbas! Barabbas!

Crowd: (beginning to join in) Barabbas! (in full throat) Barabbas!

(The governor descended to the council. Annas, having quieted the crowd, was helped from the cart and faced the governor.)

Governor Pilate: Impressive, but the choice is mine.

Annas: You have your answer, Governor.

(Governor Pilate quickly climbed the stairs, entered the hall, and took the judgement seat.)

Governor Pilate: (pointing at Barabbas) Lock him up and bring Jesus forward. (pointing at the porch) And close the doors!

(Clephus assumed his position at the table to the right of the governor, and I had just settled at the scribe's table when Curio approached the governor.)

Curio: (reaching to hand the governor a small scroll) A message came for you, Governor.

Governor Pilate: From whom?

Curio: Your wife sent the message.

(The governor took the message and began to read it.)

Governor Pilate: (shaking his head, in a low but audible voice) If she dreamt me flying, should I have wings stitched to my back?[cxxx] (tossing the scroll to the floor, looking at Jesus) Have you nothing to say?

(Jesus looked up at the governor, but said nothing.)

Dalaccus, take this man and have him flogged, but see that he is not severely injured. Perhaps this will satisfy their thirst for his blood.

(Jesus was taken from the Hall of Justice, and the governor turned to Clephus.)

Am I to free the man who killed fourteen Romans so that Annas can see Jesus dead?

Clephus: It might be of little consequence, for if released, Barabbas will be killed by his former followers. Jesus? If he is let go, they will quickly bring a new charge against him. Both are dead men with a pulse.

Governor Pilate: (to Curio) Have your men find Dalaccus and have him bring Jesus to the porch. There might yet be room for Annas and me to agree on this matter.

I need some time to think.

(The governor rose and walked to the main door of the hall. Upon motioning to have it opened, Curio moved toward the governor.)

Curio: I will accompany...

Governor Pilate: (holding up his hand) Alone, I will walk alone. I need time to think.

Curio: I will not disturb the Governor. I only...

Governor Pilate: The Praetorium is secure; let me have peace. A short walk alone and I will return. (the governor exited alone)
(The governor's walk took longer than anticipated, and Curio had begun plans to search for him when the governor returned to the hall. Saying nothing, the governor motioned for Clephus and me to join him. Ordering the porch doors opened, he descended the steps to Annas.)

Annas: What is your judgement, Governor?

Governor Pilate: I deliver to you a double gift. I have had Jesus scourged, and will crucify the traitor.

(Suddenly a roar came from the crowd as Jesus was led to the porch. The governor seemed startled as he turned to look at the prisoner. Jesus had been severely beaten and was unable to stand without assistance. He wore a crown of briers and had a robe draped over him. Governor Pilate climbed three steps to face the crowd.)

Governor Pilate: (to the crowd) Behold the man![cxxxi]

Annas and the Council: Crucify him!

Crowd: (joining Annas and the council) Crucify him! Crucify him!

Governor Pilate: (returning to Annas) You take him and crucify him, I find no fault in him. What law has he transgressed?

Annas: We have a law, and according to the law he should die because he made claims to be the son of our God.

(The governor, still facing Annas, climbed two stairs.)

Governor Pilate: I will again hear the prisoner, and then I will judge.

(Reaching the top of the stairs, the governor ordered the prisoner inside and had the doors closed. Taking the Seat of Judgement, he turned to Dalaccus who had since returned to the room.)

Governor Pilate: (in a rage) This man is barely alive! I told you not to seriously injure him! The flesh hangs off of him… (standing and moving toward Dalaccus, still screaming) You make me want to put him out of his misery! (descending the platform and screaming into Dalaccus' face) I wanted sympathy! You made him an eyesore!

(The governor returned to the seat and motioned to the guards on either side of Jesus.)

Governor Pilate: Bring him here! (looking intently at Jesus and speaking in a measured tone) Where... are... you... from?

(Jesus, barely able to stand, looked up at the governor but said nothing. The governor leaned forward, his voice showing increased irritation.)

Are you not speaking to me? Do you expect to stare me down? I have the power to crucify you or to release you! Do you understand?

Jesus: (with no emotion) You would have no power against me had it not been given to you from above. Therefore, they that deliver me to you suffer the greater sin.[cxxxii]

Governor Pilate: (exasperated) I will not pass judgement on this man alone. Carry my seat to the pavement halfway down the steps. Set it up so that it faces the council.

(The governor stood and motioned to his seat.)

Take the prisoner down with the chair.

(The Seat of Judgement and Jesus were taken to a flat area known as the pavement, halfway down the south porch stairs.)

Curio: Governor, I do not think this wise. We do not have enough men...

Governor Pilate: Enough men to allow them to kill the prisoner? They do not want us Curio; they want him!

(The governor pointed toward Jesus as Jesus exited the hall.)

If it will make you feel better, bring your guard and join me.

(The governor waited for the seat and Jesus to be brought to the pavement. As soon as they were in place, he descended the stairs immediately followed by Curio, six guards, Dalaccus, Clephus, and me.)

Governor Pilate: (sitting and motioning toward Jesus in a mocking tone) Behold your king![cxxxiii]

(By now Jesus' face had become hideously disfigured from the swelling. His face and hair were a mat of torn flesh and drying blood. Those portions of his twitching arms and legs that were visible were equally caked with a mixture of dirt and blood.)

Council: Crucify him!

Crowd: (joining) Crucify him! Crucify him!

Governor Pilate: (to the crowd) Shall I crucify your king? And you have me do this for what reason?

(The crowd offered no response.)

Caiaphas and Council: We have no king but Caesar! If you let him go, you shun Caesar. Do you not know that whoever makes himself king rises against Caesar?[cxxxiv]

(The governor's face lost both expression and color. He turned to Curio.)

Governor Pilate: (in a slow quiet tone) Bring me a basin of water and a towel.

(Curio issued the order and a guard was dispatched. While waiting for the basin, the governor leaned back, but said nothing. He fixed his stare on Annas.)

Curio: The basin is here, Governor. Where would you have it placed?

Governor Pilate: Place it in front of the prisoner.

(The impatient crowd began to press toward the stationed guards. Seeing this, the governor stood and raised his arms, quieting the crowd.)

Governor Pilate: (washing his hands in the basin) I am innocent of this man's blood. It is as you have requested.[cxxxv]

(A group of younger men in the front of the crowd pushed forward.)

Young man: (screaming at full throat) Let his blood be on us…

Second man: (smirking, as he screams) And on our children!

(The governor looked at the men and then at the council.)

Governor Pilate: Release Barabbas. (motioning toward Jesus) Crucify him.[cxxxvi]

(The governor turned and began climbing the stairs while addressing Dalaccus) Get Jesus away from the Praetorium, out of the city. Disperse this crowd before it ignites.

Dalaccus: (leading) Release Barabbas?

Governor Pilate: I told you, release him. Clephus is right; he will be dead by tomorrow.

(Looking at Clephus.) It has been a long day.

(Turning to me) Simon, I will need you at my office, and then I will rest for a while. The rest of you I will summon when I am ready. Be available.

(Once inside the Hall of Justice, the governor walked to the scribe's table.)

Simon, write this out for Dalaccus.

(I took my place at the scribe's table.)

Write it out for Jew, Greek, and Roman. I want them all to be able to read it. Write this, "Jesus of Nazareth, the King of the Jews."[cxxxvii]

(All stood silent as I wrote out the message.)

Dalaccus: I do not understand, Governor.

Governor Pilate: (waving the scroll dry as he handed it to Dalaccus) Have it transferred to a plank and nailed to Jesus' cross.

(The governor stared at Dalaccus for a moment and then in a tone of controlled rage.) Now!

(Dalaccus saluted and left the hall. The governor turned to me and then to the others as he left the hall.)

You are with me, Simon, the rest of you be available.
(Saying nothing, the governor walked briskly to his office.)

Governor Pilate: (to the guard) Bring two plates of food. Sweet wine too.

(Looking at me) Prepare a report for Rome on the release of Barabbas. I will not have this twisted by senate politics. I will need writing implements. I will write of the matter to Sejanus in my own hand. Also, prepare an order for Dalaccus' return to Rome; he does me no good here. I want no laurel[cxxxviii] in that order, just his return.

Simon: If the governor would like to rest, I can prepare the letter to Sejanus to be appended later with your thoughts.

Governor Pilate: We will prepare them now. I am anxious to be done with this matter.

(I supplied the governor with the material he requested. The governor and I worked in silence until shortly after the first bell when the food arrived.)

Governor Pilate: (looking up from his correspondence to partake of his plate) It reads a tragedy when scribbled. They free the guilty, and have me condemn the innocent. It does not speak well of your people.

(I began to speak but returned to my work.)

Out with it, Simon. You have something to say?

Simon: Forgive me, Governor, but this matter speaks well of no one. I mourn only the innocent, and see only Jesus above this tragedy.

(I expected the governor's rebuke, but he responded in a surprisingly considerate tone.)

Governor Pilate: Your naiveté is refreshing, Simon. Jesus might have been the only innocent present. But he is not without culpability, for he offered no defense . . . in accepting his fate without protest he forfeits his claim as victim.

171

(The room grew increasing dark. The governor rose and walked to the window.)

A spring storm? Ask the guards to light the lamps.

(I so instructed the guards, who began tending the lights as I returned to my table.)

(Returning to his desk) It is a strange storm; I can barely see the courtyard wall, yet there is no wind. Most appropriate for the day... let us be done with this and then we can rest.

(The governor and I returned to our correspondence, but were interrupted by the guard delivering a message that brought a smile to the governor.)

It is from Dalaccus. Caiaphas and Annas are protesting the plank on Jesus' cross. They want it rewritten to say, "He claimed the title of King of the Jews."[cxxxix]

(To the guard) Is Dalaccus' man here?

Guard: Yes, Governor.

Governor Pilate: Send him in.

(Dalaccus' orderly entered and saluted the governor.)

Governor Pilate: (to the orderly) Tell Dalaccus to inform the priests that I have written what I have written. Can you remember that?

Orderly: Yes, Governor.

(The governor dismissed the orderly with a motion.)

Governor Pilate: (looking down at his work) Annas has grown to expect his own way; he must learn to accept disappointment.

(I worked until after the fourth bell,[cxl] recopying my text to Rome. It was not until the guard entered and announced Janus that I noticed the governor had fallen asleep at his desk.)

Janus: (noticing that the governor had been asleep) I can return later.

Governor Pilate: There is no need, I have had my rest. (with a small laugh, shaking his head) I fear that age no longer allows me full gallop with no sleep.

Your report?

Janus: Both Jesus and Barabbas[cxli] are dead.

Governor Pilate: (surprised) Are you sure? Already?[cxlii]

Janus: Barabbas' body was found near the Horse Gate with six Roman long daggers driven through it. He never made it outside the walls.

As for Jesus, he died quickly. The captain tells me he looked near death before he was hung. I had him opened up; the wound spilled water.[cxliii] What do you want us to do with the bodies?

Governor Pilate: Deliver Barabbas to Annas; it is his problem.

Janus: And Jesus?

Governor Pilate: Let him hang. Let them see their king for a day, and then give the body to his followers.

Janus: There is another matter. This darkness[cxliv] has the men anxious; they see it as an omen.

Governor Pilate: (weary, with a pronounced sigh) Tell them that it is a type of storm. That we have seen it before and it will pass by morning. Issue an extra ration of wine to those off guard.

Janus: And if it does not pass by morning?

Governor Pilate: You too, Janus? Look out the window, the sky lightens before your eyes. An anomaly... nothing more.

Janus: (smiling in embarrassment) I will pass on your orders. If I am not needed, I will return to my duties.

Governor Pilate: We will meet later. Be available.

(Standing, Janus saluted and left the room. Before the door could close behind him the guard entered and announced Joseph of Arimathea.[cxlv] [cxlvi])

Governor Pilate: (looking at me) Do I know this man?

Simon: He is a prominent member of the council.

Governor Pilate: I have had enough of the council. Send him away.

(The guard left the room, but returned almost immediately.)

Guard: Your pardon, Governor Pilate, he is accompanied by a man named Nicodemus[cxlvii] who says that you will receive him.

(The governor said nothing as he walked to the cold hearth, his hands clasped behind his back.)

Governor Pilate: (his back to the guard and me) Is there no end, no audience for Somnus?[cxlviii] This day brings two twilights... but no rest. (with a deep sigh) Let us spare tomorrow. I will see them now.

***

Though this portion of the transcript speaks of what was, it neglects any discussion of what might have been. Had I not effectively deployed my forces and controlled crowd movement, would Jerusalem have known riot? Had I not kept tight rein on Dalaccus, how long would it have taken to stack the bodies of both Jew and Roman? Had I not made Jesus the people's choice by offering a fashioned Barabbas, what martyr-inspired revolt might have followed?

I was in command, negotiating the balance of objectives, adversaries, and resources. You consider this matter on a grand scale, but all of it—deployments, crowds, trial, Herod, council, and sentence—was a blur smeared across a single morning. It was just one of over four-thousand mornings I served as governor.

I ordered the death of Jesus of Nazareth, and in doing so, some would say I created his following that now plagues the empire. Come forth with your argument; this old man has not the strength or influence to mount a defense. That morning I did not have the opportunity to look forward through the decades; I had but the middle vision of command. And where twenty-thousand could have died in revolt, I chose a path that led to the death of two, a murderer and Jesus.

There was no justice in Jesus' crucifixion, but peace was the treasure that day and justice the price. I offer no explanation beyond that offered in the beginning of this record. I considered death a reasonable lubricant on the axle of peace.

Note to Mac:

The aged Pilate's concluding remarks make a powerful argument for his exoneration. The act of sacrificing the innocent to attain peace is as old as recorded history. It is this logic that we have used to justify the millions of civilian causalities that have accompanied the numerous military actions of the twentieth century. But there must be more, for Pilate did more than kill an innocent. I believe that he killed the Son of God.

As I read these folios, I have gained an understanding of Pilate's values and his responsibilities. I have seen him address both trivial and profound duties within the context of his military experience. On the inside, this Pilate is a soldier. His values and thought processes were formed during that period of his life when he was a man of arms. And though I do not believe this pardons an unjust execution, it does bring a chilling sympathy and fear that accompanies the embrace of conditional morality.

I judge Pilate's morality within the context of my own. I believe in God and rightiousness as defined in the Scriptures, but from what vantage point? I spent my formative adult years as a computer salesman. Is that the ethical leaning of my morality? The fact that I judge all matters from a pro-business perspective would affirm such, but what infection does this bring to my moral code? Neither do I believe that I am alone in this conditional morality. Are not parents, clergy, doctors, babysitters, soldiers, and politicians conditionally held to a greater or lesser moral standard? Do we not empathize with a parent who avenges the slaying of their child? It is not as simple as we would have it; even "thou shall not murder"[cxlix] beckons conditional consideration.

I have no ready answer, just a shattered image of my moral superiority. This Pilate brings his evidence before me, pleading for conditional consideration. He was a soldier doing his job; and to him Jesus was just another man. The choice is binary. Am I to feel empathy or loathing? A question not easily answered, for this judgement falls not just on Pilate, but on the conditional morality of my own life.

Chapter 13
Folio 12
Choices

My father outlived his family and friends. His life spanned more than eighty years, with only one of his daughters and me alive to accompany his final decade. He damned his long life, believing that he had inherited the curse of the Greek's Prometheus.[cl] "I am chained to this old body," he would rage, "forced to endlessly relive my tragedies." I remember once trying to comfort him by reciting the accomplishments and joys of his life. He listened patiently, nodding agreement at the appropriate moments, and then crushed my effort with this admonishment, "Petition the gods that they will have you slain on the field of battle."

I too have inherited the Prometheus curse. Eighty years enfeebled within this bag of sagging skin, I now understand my father's exhortation. With this empathy I struggle to avoid his grinding remedy of self-recrimination. I discipline myself to make learning my medicament. I struggle to learn from the past, squeezing from it an elixir that I can give to my nephews and their children so they live a better fate. It is at every opportunity that I pass on my life's essence to these that still care. In return, I receive their gratitude, or is it that they humor an old man? It is of little consequence, for I have outlived my estate and it is the last of my currency.

If I were to squeeze any portion of Simon's transcript, the most precious elixir would come from this segment, for within its recitation is the deep and profound understanding of choices. I admonish those who read this not to confuse choice with decision, for though there are good and bad decisions and good and bad choices, they are not to be taken together, for decisions are things we act upon, but choices are not so constricted, they are the possibilities we allow to exist.

Hidden deep within the distinction between decision and choice is the lament of our old age. The fulcrum[cli] of my decision that day was the crucifixion or release of Jesus. That was the range of choices that I gave myself. Could I have sentenced him to the galleys? Could I have demanded that Herod pass judgement? Could I have allowed passions to cool by imprisoning him for a period of time before considering crucifixion? These and scores of other choices were within my grasp, but my selected choices presented a decision of extremes.

Should I have given the matter greater consideration? Was I somehow negligent in my choice? Only an idiot would condemn me of such, for Jesus was a man of no means and no support. He was a perfect sacrifice and deserved little consideration. Even if I had contemplated all the options available to me, the presence and mood of the crowd would have forestalled any consideration beyond his death. In this case, the choices were limited by a complexity of circumstance.

In saying this, I do not lessen the paramount impact of choices. Choice is the tender, spark, and fuel of our destiny. Even the most basic decision presents at least four alternatives. The first two are obvious, yea or nay. The third is to abstain from involvement, allowing events to dictate the result. The fourth choice is to abdicate the decision to others who have a more passionate interest.

The transcript speaks for itself; I managed my decision around the limited choice of circumstance. Here Simon documents Nicodemus' disappointment in my actions, but with neither a vision of the future, nor the luxury of idealism, I occupied the point of decision. The old man speaks of valor, but it was I who stood on the steps of the south porch between Jesus and the council, while he was hidden among the crowd.

This portion of the text presents the most vivid of my memories regarding the Jesus affair. I see it as clearly today as I did then, the ancient Nicodemus, the treachery of Annas, and the body.[clii] Here too are the sounds and smells of Jerusalem, but now accompanied by a strange longing in the present—a wish to share my noon meal with Nicodemus. We are just two old men who understood that moment, and who now want nothing more than an afternoon in the warm sun.

***

The transcription of the Jesus affair:
Day 1,763 of Governor Pilate's administration
Prepared by Simon of Emmaus
Present:
Governor Pilate
Clephus, Officer of Internal Affairs
Dalaccus, Officer of Military Affairs
Curio, Captain of the Guards
Simon of Emmaus, Secretary to Governor Pilate
Annas, Former High Priest
Caiaphas, High Priest and son-in-law of Annas
Janus, Officer of Internal Surveillance

Joseph of Arimathea, Member of the Council
Nicodemus, Representative of the Council and a Pharisee

(The governor poured himself a cup of sweet wine as the guard left the room to summon the awaiting petitioners. Returning to his seat, the governor sat silently rubbing his hands together.)

Governor Pilate: (clasping his hands and looking at me in a manner that suggested that he already knew the answer) What do suppose your people want, Simon?

Simon: I would have no way of knowing, Governor; I have been with you all day.

Governor Pilate: They want the body, Simon; they do not wish to see the birds peck at their king.

Janus: These men openly challenge Annas. Are we not foolish to receive them and risk provoking a satiated foe?

Governor Pilate: (coldly) You would have me live in fear of Annas? That I should govern around his likes and dislikes? (sarcastically) Would it not be more efficient to have him take my seat? I will meet with whom I choose.

Janus: I was in no way suggesting any subservience to Annas…

Governor Pilate: (curtly) I know what you were suggesting. To satiate Annas, protecting his favor. I will curry to Annas only when there is increased favor for Rome. (leaning toward Janus) I will not bend this government to maintain quiet waters; such conditions advantage only the crocodile.

(The guard had entered the room and, after waiting for the governor to complete his thought, announced Joseph of Arimathea and Nicodemus.)

Nicodemus: (solemn) I am grateful for the audience, Governor. May I present Joseph of Arimathea, a member of the council and a disciple of Jesus.

(The governor left the men standing.)

Governor Pilate: (addressing Joseph of Arimathea in a tone of authority) I have granted you this audience. What is it that you want?

Joseph of Arimathea: I ask that you allow me to claim the body of Jesus and place it in my tomb.[cliii]

Governor Pilate: (appearing disinterested) I have ordered that the body be taken down tomorrow, after noon.

Joseph of Arimathea: I beg the Governor's consideration, for our Sabbath begins in but a few hours,[cliv] and if the body is not taken now, it will remain through sunset tomorrow. With your consideration...

Governor Pilate: It seems that your concern for the body is greater than your concern for the man. Did I hear from either of you on the steps this morning? You should have made your claim then.

The body will hang until tomorrow. It will then be yours to claim. You have had your audience; now I have work.

(As the governor looked down at the papers before him, Joseph of Arimathea looked at Nicodemus and then turned toward the door.)

Nicodemus: (not moving) Governor, we seek no favor beyond sparing Jesus a final indignity at the hands of Annas. Our request brings no harm to Rome, but does bring honor to the innocent. I am asking...

Governor Pilate: (leaning toward Nicodemus) Are you asking that I remove Annas' injustice from the sight of the people? Let the body hang and scream the name of those responsible!

Nicodemus: (responding immediately) Jesus hangs upon a Roman cross. Do you suppose Annas will claim the act, or return the cross to you?

Governor Pilate: (saying nothing, searching Nicodemus for a five-count, then turning to me) Have the guard find Curio.

(I made the guard aware of the governor's request.)

Nicodemus: Will the Governor...

Governor Pilate: (with expressed curiosity) Save your breath, old man. I will give you the body, but only with an explanation. Where were you this morning; where was your voice during the trial? Was it not you who lauded Jesus, who encouraged me to engage him?

Nicodemus: (fumbling to compose his words) Do you... Do you suppose the whole council was present at the pavement? There were those on the council who spoke for Jesus, or at least of his innocence, but their numbers were small. Annas saw that we were pushed to the back of the crowd.

Governor Pilate: Most convenient for both you and Annas. But you Jews blend convenience and connivance into a skill. What do you make of a people who welcome their prophet into Jerusalem, throwing their robes before his ass... and in the same week scream to have him crucified?

The fluidity of your passions sickens me. Your people hold us to be savages, but even the most inconstant Roman has the integrity to hold a loyalty for a week.

(The governor sat silently waiting for Nicodemus' response, but no response was offered.)

Have you no thrust and parry Nicodemus? Where is your considered objection, your high morality? Does your wisdom abandon you when forced to fashion your people a bloodthirsty mob? Was it not you that spoke of Rome crushing innocents?

(The old man looked down at the floor; he somehow looked smaller than when he first entered the room. After a long pause he raised his eyes to meet the governor's.)

Nicodemus: Would you have me attempt to defend an act of gross injustice? I could say that Jesus' body hangs on a Roman cross. I could defend my people by pointing out that Annas had the south-porch courtyard packed with Pharisees and temple merchants... those who hated Jesus. I could recount the prophecy that has our God inevitably claiming Jesus as a sacrifice for my people.[clv]

(The governor's posture noticeably stiffened as he looked to Janus. Nicodemus reached for the back of a chair for balance.)

Thrust and parry? I am too ashamed and grieved to entertain such, for Jew and Roman, you and I had our part. I heard your words this morning; you had no stomach for innocent blood. And the people, those who sang hosannas to Jesus earlier this week, they were not there. But did they surround the wall outside the courtyard and demand his release? And we? We may try to heap this upon others, but we wear the fine linen[clvi] of power and the blood of this day most sorely stains our garments.

You seek to beat me into contrition, Governor. There is no need, I am already broken. I stood without struggle and watched God's anointed[clvii] crucified.

Governor Pilate: (pounding his questions on Nicodemus) The crowd, Annas had culled the crowd? Is that why they never left… Annas feared them losing their place to those sympathetic to Jesus?

(Joseph of Arimathea, who had paused halfway between the governor and the door, took a step forward.)

Joseph of Arimathea: Forgive me, Governor, but the hour grows late. There is little time before sunset and if we are to prepare the body…

Governor Pilate: Simon, have the guard summon Curio. (looking at Joseph of Arimathea) I have given you the body; do with it what you will. (Curio enters and salutes the governor.)

(Looking at Curio) Send your best centurion and fifty soldiers with this man to claim the body. Allow the Jews to handle the corpse; the troops are there only to afford access. Understood?

Curio: Yes, Governor. Should I report back?

Governor Pilate: Only if there is a problem. Your men are not to take any aggressive action unless ordered by me. (looking at Joseph of Arimathea) Go with the captain and claim your body. Nicodemus will join you when we are finished.

Nicodemus: (looking at Joseph of Arimathea) I will be along in a moment. I will join you at the tomb.[clviii]

(Curio saluted, motioned to Joseph of Arimathea, and the two left the room.)

Governor Pilate: (motioning to the chair that Nicodemus leaned against) Sit, old man, I will not have you fall and be accused of your injury.

(Nicodemus managed a weak smile and seemed grateful for the governor's courtesy.)

Nicodemus: Sunset is near; I must not abide.

Governor Pilate: I will not keep you long. The crowd... they were but tassels on Annas' robe?

Nicodemus: Annas had not the numbers to fill the courtyard with his Pharisees and Saducees, so he enlisted the temple merchants and their servants. Jesus had offended...

Governor Pilate: I know of Jesus' actions in the temple. Did Annas so fear his own people that he had to pack the courtyard with his supporters?

Nicodemus: The crowd was for you, Governor. He reasoned that as a military man you would be most influenced by the argument of a superior force.

Governor Pilate: (obviously angry, looking at Janus) Is this your idea of effective surveillance? I will not be outmaneuvered by a...

Nicodemus: (struggling to his feet) It was not my intent to upset you, Governor. There was no way for your people to know...

Janus: (angry, addressing Nicodemus) I do not need you to defend me, old...

(The governor held up his hand, interrupting Janus.)

Governor Pilate: (aggressive, looking at Janus) Listen!
(He then looked at Nicodemus.)

Nicodemus: As I was saying, Annas pulled the crowd together at the last moment. He rightly feared that one of us might discover his ruse. He thought our thoughts, and had us both at his mercy. It was such a struggle to make it in through the Horse Gate that I never noticed the composition of the crowd. I didn't learn what Annas had done until it was all over. Now I beg your leave, for as in all struggles, it falls upon the coward to bury the innocent.

Governor Pilate: (surprised by Nicodemus last comment) You quit too early, old man. Annas does not control our fate, and we shall have other opportunities.

Nicodemus: The prophets called out my opportunity for thousands of years. Moses, Isaiah, Micah, Zechariah, King David[clix]... all of them announcing the coming of God's anointed. I... I touched him, and allowed his blood to be spilled before my own. That is my fate.

Governor Pilate: I see no opportunity lost that cannot be recovered. You bury your fate too early; I see mine before me.

Nicodemus: I do not suppose to know the mind of God; what future you have is in his hands. But how I mourn your loss of valor, for what price is it that a man steps away from immortal heroism?

Governor Pilate: (agitated) That I save your anointed so that tomorrow he might be killed? That brings me valorous immortality? Did you not speak of the inevitability of Jesus' death? You confuse me, old man. You have me subverting the will of your God and becoming a hero? And if you are wrong, and he is not your anointed, then what has been lost?

Nicodemus: You ask too much of me, Governor. I am a simple man. I only know the prophecy to be true, that the anointed be sacrificed. But your fate was not so spoken. For you could have released the anointed Jesus and become the man the ages forever recognized as the guardian of righteousness. And if Jesus be only a man, then you would be a hero to yourself. For in denying the crowd the blood of an innocent, you would have climbed above the squalidness of humanity.

Governor Pilate: (smiling while slowly shaking his head) It may make sense to you, old man, but do not trouble yourself over me. Have you forgotten? I am the most hated man in Judaea. One more cross will hardly determine my fate.

Simon, have Curio accompany Nicodemus to the tomb.

Nicodemus: I do not need a guard, Governor. I am a man of peace.

Governor Pilate: (standing, looking first at Nicodemus then to me) So was Jesus. See that he is accompanied.

(I escorted Nicodemus to the door and so instructed the guard as the governor walked to the window.)

(Looking out the window) Quiet for now, I will be glad to get back to Caesarea. Janus, tell the others what we have learned and that they will not be needed until tomorrow. We will start at first light.

Janus: Governor, I think it important that you understand…

Governor Pilate: (turning to face Janus) Save your excuses Janus; just pile your mistake upon the rest. Dalaccus' severe beating of the prisoner, not demanding a decision from Herod, playing to Annas' picked crowd, which one is most sore? Which one made us an instrument of the Jews? You seem to have a hunger for this day. I am gorged with it. I want no more. Go brief the others. I will see you all here at first light.

(Janus stood, saluted the governor, and left the room.)

Simon: Do you wish me to bring work to your quarters?

Governor Pilate: No. I am going to soak this day off of me in a hot bath, have my meal, and sleep.

Simon: With the Governor's permission, I will transcribe today's business tomorrow evening in order that I might take the Sabbath meal with my family.[clx]

Governor Pilate: (walking toward the door) I will not need you until first light.

Simon: Thank you, Governor.

The transcription of the Jesus affair:
Day 1,764 of Governor Pilate's administration
Prepared by Simon of Emmaus
Present:
Governor Pilate
Janus, Officer of Internal Surveillance
Clephus, Officer of Internal Affairs
Dalaccus, Officer of Military Affairs
Curio, Captain of the Guards
Simon of Emmaus, Secretary to Governor Pilate
Annas, Former High Priest
Caiaphas, High Priest and son-in-law of Annas

(Shortly after sunup the governor entered his office through the rear door. Dalaccus, Clephus, and Janus stood as the governor took his place at the table.)

Governor Pilate: Sit. You have been briefed?

Janus: I told them of our meeting yesterday.

Governor Pilate: It appears that our policy of dealing with the Jews in a consultative fashion has been a failure. From this point forward we will act independently, confining our contact with their leadership to addressing grievances.

We will no longer be seduced into their web or assist in the stability of their government. The Herodians aside, we will separate the head from the body creating enmity between the leadership and the masses.

(The guard entered, informing me that a large delegation from the Sanhedrin had come to see the governor in regard to Jesus.)

Governor Pilate: What is it, Simon?

Simon: There is a large delegation from the Sanhedrin here to see you about Jesus.

Clephus: I will have them dismissed.

Governor Pilate: Not yet. Simon, I will see Annas and Caiaphas, no one else.[clxi]

Clephus: Are we not discontinuing such contact?

Governor Pilate: A little at a time. For the moment, let them think they have the upper hand.

(Annas and Caiaphas enter the room.)

Annas: Thank you for seeing us, Governor Pilate.

Governor Pilate: I see that you have grown accustomed to traveling with your own crowd.

Annas: I am not certain that I understand.

Governor Pilate: (coldly) What have you come for, Annas?

Annas: The people are vulnerable to…

Governor Pilate: (louder) What have you come for, Annas?

Annas: Sir, we seek only that you make the tomb secure lest Jesus' disciples come during the night and steal him away.[clxii]

Governor Pilate: And their reason for desiring a rotting corpse?

Annas: The disciples would then proclaim that he has risen from the dead, making the last deception worse than the first.[clxiii]

Governor Pilate: (to Dalaccus) Give them a guard. (to Annas) Make it as secure as you know how.[clxiv] I am finished with it.[clxv]

Annas: You should…

Governor Pilate: (loud) I am finished with it! Is there something else?

Annas: No. (with a slight bow) Thank you, governor.

(As Annas and Caiaphas left the room, the Governor stood.)

Governor Pilate: We are done with this Jesus affair. It is now a Jewish matter to be handled by the Jews. But you see… we again spend our time around Annas' actions when we should be tending to Rome's interests.

(Looking at Dalaccus) I have prepared orders for your return to Rome. Take the week to organize an interim command structure and bring it to me for approval.

Dalaccus: (smiling) Thank you, Governor, I will…

Governor Pilate: You are not needed here. Get started.

(Dalaccus, sensing the governor's displeasure, stood and began to speak, but instead saluted and left the room.)

Clephus: If you like, I can prepare a list of command candidates for your consideration.

Governor Pilate: Dalaccus knows his men; I will hear his counsel. It is only an interim… With Sejanus falling[clxvi] out of favor we can expect Tiberius' court to appoint his successor.

No, Clephus, I need you to spend your time encouraging discussions with Flaccus. Even without the influence of Sejanus we may be able to crush the Jewish interests.

Janus: If our friend in Egypt[clxvii] were to apply pressure from the south, we would have a great advantage in Samaria.

Governor Pilate: (speaking to me) Do you continue to transcribe?

Simon: Yes, Governor.

Governor Pilate: Stop. We are finished with Jesus.

***

My last words of the transcript are hardly fitting. For thirty years I have struggled to separate myself from a man who died young and never penned a single thought. But there is a residual power in a corpse: it can speak more loudly than the life it once embodied. Moldering remains bring forth extremes in men, either the prostration of total defeat, or hope beyond reason. It is Jesus' ghost, not the man, which has spawned the unreasoned hope that washes across the empire. An apparition that will not endure the might of Rome, but is destined to accompany me to my grave.

Old age has brought me little peace as both sides harass me seeking evidence of Jesus. Did he, could he, would he? It was simpler than that. The transcript speaks of what I know of the man. The rest, including his healing of my wife, the spontaneous fire,[clxviii] and like hearsay are the creation of those seeking to fabricate a deity. Equally ludicrous are those who dismiss the entire affair as a fabrication. I met and spoke with Jesus, a man with a powerful presence whose death was accompanied by an unnatural darkness.[clxix] Both the transcript of the moment and my memory place these matters beyond dispute.

And what can be said of those things that I did not personally experience? It is difficult to dismiss Jesus' ability to heal the sick. The preponderance of fully witnessed encounters had even his enemies considering such matters as fact. As for the raising of the dead, though confirmed by Janus' men, I believe it a hoax. Finally, did the earth shake at the moment of Jesus' death? I had no such personal experience, however, reported damage to the temple and trusted witnesses at the crucifixion site speak contrary.

This considered, it must be known that I do not lament my decision that day. Decisions must be made, and those who occupy the breach must make them. Nicodemus spoke of valor as if it were a bloom easily plucked. I never saw the flower, for my choices had me traveling a different route. Choices, decisions, duties, circumstance—a cacophony of conflict that converges on a moment. And to those who now judge my actions as too lenient or severe, I offer the following paradox. I ordered the crucifixion of Jesus of Nazareth. I offered his only defense.

Note to Mac:

This folio presents the corpse and asks the question, "Who is responsible?" I imagine myself in a darkened room staring at a lit stage as the various suspects are paraded before me in some form of surreal modern-day police line up. "Bring in number one," a voice bellows from behind, and an aged Annas shuffles across the stage. He stands before the markings that identify him as a little over five and one-half feet tall, holding a "1" placard, squinting into the lights. "Number two," the voice calls, and in comes Pilate to take his place on the stage. "Three," and Nicodemus appears. "Four," and somehow the crowd that welcomed Jesus on Palm Sunday fits in place. "Can you identify the one responsible," the voice asks? I struggle to answer, but cannot decide. "You must pick one," the voice booms, "pick one!"

I have studied these folios, the Scriptures, and my soul, but have no answer for "the voice." Each of the accused has culpability apart from the others, yet each has a claim of innocence. It all appears as some grand conspiracy with all suspects having a unique part in the death, while draping themselves in plausible denial. I struggle to rationalize them all, both guilty and victims, but the voice will not accept this haven. "You must pick one, which one will you hang?"

When considering the accused one at a time it is easy to assign guilt. Pilate issued the order, Nicodemus fully understood the stakes and stood mute, and Annas had the willful intent. As for the crowd, they alone had the power to override the others and prevent the execution. But if only one is to be identified, then let it be their testimony that singles them out.

"This considered, it must be known that I do not lament my decision that day. Decisions must be made, and those who occupy the breach must make them." These are the words of the elder Pilate that assume the responsibility for Jesus' death. The words are cold, purposeful, and without remorse. I have no recourse but to select Pilate from the lineup, and in so doing, imagine him following my voice, attempting to make eye contact with the darkness. With a tight smile of composure he steps forward, and with neither fear nor anger looks in my direction. "You hang me for doing my job," he chortles. "You hang the only one who tried to save him."

Chapter 14
Folio 13
Clear Waters

The night calls me, speaking of my fall; it is a welcomed darkness. It is hard to live the end, as visitors bring and offer only pity. I do not fault them, for they see only the last of me, the part that soils the bed and must eat crushed food. Should I, like others, end the struggle and burden by taking the poison of rest?[clxx] Perhaps, but I would leave just as it becomes clear. I do not know if it is the enfeeblement of old age or a last gasp of clarity, but it is before me. The stirred sediment of life settles, and through the clear waters the totality of matters becomes visible.

Like most, I viewed life as beginning with a thrust from the womb and ending at the fate of life's decisions; a straight line traveling an undetermined length. But having stopped to look straight down into the waters, I know it all to be an illusion, for we are born to an event. Our place, our life, is but a pinnacle moment with our past inevitably leading us there and our future cascading from its peak. Are we but actors reading our lines? No. The moment is ours and we live it as we choose, but once lived we are destined to ride its flow of consequence unto death.

My moment was the day of Jesus' trial. From it flowed the suffering of my wife, the disgrace of my service, and the loss of Simon. It is all clear now, but too late to be of purpose. We are never afforded an understanding of our pinnacle moment until the end. We live day to day, year to year, never knowing which of our encounters will be that moment, nor that our life is so defined. A twisted irony, we see the prize only after it is beyond our grasp.

As I read of Annas' deceit in the last of Simon's transcripts, the flush of rage returned to my loins. But I blame myself in no small measure, for I knew the Jews to be a race of mongrels, and Annas' insidious duplicity was an expected consequence of such ill breeding. I was equally enraged as I pondered these matters the night of Jesus' death.

Until that day I had pursued a policy of stabilization in Judaea.[clxxi] For five years I had used my meager military contingent to maintain a reasoned tranquility, resisting pressure from Sejanus and Falaccus who encouraged the destruction of the Jews. But Annas' treachery that day had made me the fool and further appeasement untenable. That night, I drafted a plan that would occupy my next five years as governor of Judaea.

The plan was straightforward and sound. I would create tension between the Jews and their leadership, fracturing their solidarity and making Rome a source of relief. I would no longer negotiate, but rather make demands that were more onerous to the leaders than the people, making certain to punish the latter for non-compliance. Still, lacking ample military support to execute my plan in Jerusalem, I chose to begin the new initiative in Samaria.[clxxii]

By beginning operations in Samaria I gained several advantages. First, the leadership in Jerusalem viewed Samaria as a bastard child.[clxxiii] I reasoned correctly that the Jews of Jerusalem would not intervene to support their illegitimate brethren. Further, I secured an alliance in the south to have similar policies pursued against the Jews in Egypt. This placed an insensible Jerusalem between tumultuous Jewish populations to her north and south.

The strategy in Samaria was one of probe and feint, never provoking enough activity to ignite an organized response, but ever creating enough action to maintain tensions between the Jews and their leaders. For two years after the treachery of Jesus' trial I held all the mongrels in the tight grip of cross-purposes. I had gained control of the territory with minimal military resources, and in spite of Sejanus' fall had gained favor within Tiberius' court. This was the last of my success, for shortly after Simon's death my life would begin its slide into an abyss of impoverished disgrace.

Simon and I, along with an appropriate military contingent, had traveled from Caesarea Maritima to the city of Samaria[clxxiv] to adjudicate a dispute. During the journey I had noticed an attractive parcel of land that was well watered with deep wells. I reasoned that once Palestine was under heel, commerce would flourish between Caesarea Maritima and Samaria, making the land's water invaluable to the livestock trade. Upon arriving at the city of Samaria, I sent Simon back to negotiate a price for the parcel.

I had spent my first two days in the city inspecting military and engineering projects and meeting with the Herodians. As court was scheduled to be held the next day, I became concerned when Simon had yet to return from his errand. Accordingly, I instructed a centurion to have his men retrace Simon's route and escort him back to Samaria.

When they delivered Simon's body it was white and bloated. His murderers had plucked out his eyes and had stuffed the sockets with coins, the emperor's image facing out. As he lay before me, I could not help notice the whip still tied to his wrist. It was a gift that I had given him when he first learned to ride, now but a cord that attempted to sever his swollen arm.

Later at my trial,[clxxv] Clephus would testify that my increasingly aggressive actions toward the Jews came from my anger over Simon's death. He would say that I had behaved irrationally from that point forward, seeking to punish all Jews. As in all believable lies, there was a thread of truth in

Clephus' accusations. I did in fact vigorously pursue those who murdered Simon. The murderers and their families were brought to the Seat of Judgement, found guilty of murder and conspiracy, and were ordered crucified at the place of their heinous act. I attended that crucifixion, and forbade their legs broken.[clxxvi] My motive was not vengeance but justice. And if the records of that day are searched, you will also find mercy in my actions, for twenty-three were found guilty, but only seventeen crucified. Six, being under the age of eight, received a full pardon.

The remaining three years of my service in Judaea were contentious. I often missed Simon's insight, but I think it of little consequence. The Jews by this time had committed themselves to sacrificial aggression. Every sword drawn, every banner hung, and every written decree, somehow found Jewish blood on it. The final year and a half was nothing but an escalation of wills. I was seeking control and they were seeking to make Rome a butcher.

I will not deny that their tactics were sound. Even I was affected by the courage of their stand in Caesarea.[clxxvii] But there was no cause or courage at Mt. Gerizim;[clxxviii] the Jews sought only provocation and I had no option but to respond. Did I order battlefield executions on Mt. Gerizim? Yes. Was there a full confrontation of forces? No. I had correctly calculated that a bloody battle might be avoided by a targeted attack on their leaders. This strategy saved hundreds of lives and conspired with other events to see me disgraced.

Sejanus' fall from favor four years earlier, Flaccus and Clephus' betrayal at the trial, the treasury report, all these came together to crush any hope of vindication. This was the end of my service; a trial where I was ordered executed. It was only Dalaccus' influence with Caligula[clxxix] that saw my life spared, and my wife's property reinstated.

For years afterward, I was never certain who had endured the greatest, me for being spared an execution, or my wife for silently enduring my disgrace. Now, ten years past her death, I am even more certain that no man has held a more loyal or loving woman than she. Each day that I knew her she became more beautiful to me; even the last day there was a beautiful light of life about her.

The end was kind to her. I remember sitting in the shade of a near tree watching her tend her flowers. The morning passed without incident when she came to me speaking of fatigue. I put her to bed and brought her a cup of warm wine. It was as if she knew that the end was near, for she bade me to sit on the bed next to her and took my hand. "You are so special to me, I count myself favored to have been your wife." She brought my hand to her lips and kissed it. I told her that I had brought us both disgrace, but she interrupted me. " No, you lived and did what you thought best. You learned to love me and thought me beautiful. I so love you. Please understand that I know that Jesus…" She struggled to wipe her tears, taking a deep breath. "Please understand, and know that I love you." Those were her last words.

I have often wondered how she might have completed the thought. "Please understand that I know Jesus…" Know that Jesus deserved to die? Know that Jesus was innocent? Know that Jesus was a god? The topic of Jesus was the only distance between us. Her dreams persisted after his crucifixion, creating a divisive friction. It wasn't until Simon was murdered that she agreed to no longer discuss the topic. And so it lay dormant for almost thirty years, surfacing only to punctuate the end of her life. It is of little matter though, for whatever her thoughts, I claim them as my own. I so long to share more with her and to once again feel her near.

But these are the longings of an old man, and I took this task in order to document, not piffle. I was a soldier; I was trained to govern; and I was at the center of Judaea when Jesus was crucified. Jesus had a power that threatened the Sanhedrin. The deceit of the Jews had me crucify him. This treachery led to a more aggressive policy. The tension of that policy resulted in Simon's murder. Simon's murder became the excuse of my enemies—the distortion of my enemies a convenient means of shielding the empire from its failed policy of thirty years. Now they prepare to decimate Judaea and polish tarnish off this Roman vassal.

As for the tarnish of my life, I can summon no conclusion more eloquent than my wife tendered at her last. "You lived and did what you thought best." That is the sum of it all; I lived within the same corruption of circumstance that all men must endure. For what man does not adopt the morality of his calling? What man's decisions are not twisted by circumstance? Who has not lashed out in fear or retribution? And where is he who does not feel the seductive lust of power?

I have spent my final months documenting an event that cumulatively occupied less than a day of my life.[clxxx] All this, that you might know that I was not a fool, butcher, or bungler, but simply a man looking to make his way. I face death knowing that a corpse receives no justice. So I leave you this complete turn of the wheel, all aspects of the Jesus affair. It is offered with no excuse or edit, the truth alone must carry my cause. Is it as Nicodemus, Annas, or Metellus would recount it? No, but it is true to what I experienced; that is all the wisdom of old age will allow me to say. For all truth hangs from the experience of those crafting a reality. Jesus confidently claimed to bring truth;[clxxxi] I hold no such certainty.

I awoke this morning to discover my bowels spewing blood. I will die soon; there is nothing left for me. Some grand thought or pronouncement is in order, but there is only a void. Looking back I see it all as a sack of tragic uncertainty. My legacy . . . to be a forgotten excuse of derision. Make of it what you will, for I am the dead seeking only to be rid of that baneful question that stalked my every turn. I leave it with you. What is truth?

Chapter 15
Final Thoughts

This effort began when Mac thrust this document at me imploring, "Let me know what you think." I had surmised from his request that he wanted my opinion as to the authenticity of the manuscript, but after months of study, I understand that he wanted something more. Mac's question was not about the hand that wrote it, but about himself, and about me. The question that caused Mac to abandon the document, and me to attempt exorcism through the publishing of this book is fundamental. Would I, operating within the same time period and under the same pressures, have ordered the crucifixion of Jesus?

It is easy to snap off a self-serving "there is no way," until you are confronted with the layers and logic of this chronology. The transcript frames Pilate's actions with Jesus as but a moment in the governor's tenure. All of this occupied less than twenty-four hours out of four thousand days he served as prefect. No doubt Pilate made tens of thousands of decisions while serving in Judaea. And even if we imagine every decision self-serving, we must grudgingly recognize that he served with some distinction, for he administered eleven years of stable government.

I find myself sounding like a Pilate apologist; I have no such agenda. The man's brutality is evidenced throughout the transcript. He knew Jesus to be innocent, yet ordered him killed. My Christianity allows no sympathy for the man who killed the Son of God! But here too the manuscript allays, for Pilate was a pagan and saw no divinity in Jesus.

I dance around and attempt to satiate my inner struggle, but the question persists. In Pilate's position, would I have given in to the pressures of my job, the threat of the crowd, and the allure of sacrificing one to save thousands? Would I have ordered the crucifixion? Honestly, I don't know.

This manuscript has taken me on a journey deep within myself. It has broken through my crust of professed morality and shown me the worldly pressures and rationalizations that I hold at the center of my life. It has immersed me in my own corruption, and having done so, has transformed God's saving grace from concept to necessity.

I cling to the promise and hope of John 3:16-17. "For God so loved the world that he gave His only begotten Son, that whoever believes in Him should not perish but have everlasting life. For God did not send His Son into the world to condemn the world, but that the world through Him might be saved." This is both the hope and the paradox that Mac and I embrace—that

Jesus has saved us from the very corruption that, given the opportunity, may have seen us execute Him.

It is a realization that cannot be given away, nor one that can be exorcised by having it published. Mac and I have read the transcript and know that we share a value system with the man who ordered the death of Jesus Christ.

I am sorry Mac; the matter is indelible. May God have mercy on our souls.

Endnotes

[i] In later conversations the professor denied receiving payment.

[ii] According to the tradition of the Eastern Church, both Pontius Pilate and his wife converted to Christianity. Specifically, both the Coptic and Ethiopic Church canonized Pilate and his wife as saints. The Greek branch of the Eastern Church bestowed sainthood upon Claudia Procula (Pilate's wife), with her feast celebrated October 27.

[iii] A reference to David Irving's forged "Hitler diaries" that were "found" in 1983. When discovered to be a fraud, the diary proved to be a career-impacting embarrassment for those who had authenticated it.

[iv] Judaea was part of the imperial province of Syria. Imperial provinces (unlike senatorial provinces) were considered hostile to Rome and were directly ruled by an ambassador who was appointed by the Roman emperor. Pilate, as governor of Judaea, reported to the ambassador of Syria. Oddly, during the first years of Pilate's term as governor, there was no Syrian legate (prime minister) stationed in Syria. L. Aelius Lamia held the position of Syrian legate, but he was kept in Rome by the Emperor Tiberius. As governor of Judaea, Pilate would have kept both the ambassador and his patron in Rome (Sejanus, chief administrator of the empire) advised of his actions.

[v] The author of this document correctly (though sarcastically) uses "Christ" as a title (i.e., King).

[vi] It is likely that Simon would have used a papyrus roll to document conversations. These rolls (mounted to become scrolls) had a maximum length of approximately thirty feet.

Ironically, the rapid growth of Christianity and the need for greater accessibility to the Holy Bible led to the codex (early form of books). The earliest known codex is a Greek Bible manuscript from the fourth century A.D.

[vii] A religious group drawn from members of Israel's upper class. As both wealthy landowners and members of the priesthood, they derived their status from wealth and power. Their religious beliefs were exclusively based on the Pentateuch (the first five books of the Bible). Their rejection of other traditions and prophets put them in conflict with other religious groups of the day.

[viii] A religious group that derived its status from their knowledge of the Scripture and from keeping a complex set of religious laws. Pharisees based their beliefs on both the Pentateuch (the first five books of the Bible) and the oral tradition and teachings of the prophets. Pharisees were the most populous of the religious parties and served as religious authority for most Jews.

[ix] Devoted to copying and studying religious law, the Essenes were recognized as living highly virtuous lives that were centered on self-discipline and the rejection of worldly pleasures.

[x] In A.D. 70, the Roman general Titus would destroy Jerusalem. The author refers to this event as being imminent, thus establishing the alleged date of authorship at approximately A.D. 69. See timeline preceding Chapter 1.

[xi] The Zealots were the most militant group in Israel. During Pilate's tenure this group was focused on the overthrow of Roman rule, often using violent means to attain their objectives.

[xii] Jesus called a Zealot (Simon) to be one of His twelve disciples (Luke 6:15).

[xiii] This date properly places these events 4.7 years into Pilate's eleven-year term as governor.

[xiv] Isaiah 11:6-9.

[xv] This is not an exact quote from Isaiah 65:25, but is the essence of the passage referenced. The difference in content could be attributed to versions, translations, or a misquote from the speaker.

[xvi] Juxtaposing a hill for a mountain and attributing it to Rome would have come easily to a true Roman. The city of Rome was founded on a hill (the Palatine), one of seven hills known as the seven hills of Rome.

[xvii] In both the Old and New Testaments, time is divided into "watches," as in the period of time a soldier stood watch. The Jews of the Old Testament had three watches, the Romans four. By this date Jerusalem (as documented in the New Testament) had adopted the Roman four-watch system. Prior to Roman influence, the Jews had no inclination to track time to the hourly level.

[xviii] Janus' being there since the cock-crowing watch would indicate a significant level of interest in seeing the governor. The cock-crowing watch was the third watch, lasting from midnight to 3 A.M.

[xix] A character from Greek mythology that was half man, half bull. Knowledge of the Greek system of gods was common among the Romans as most Roman gods were based on Greek mythology.

[xx] During this period, Rome still relied on the water clock as a means of dividing both day and night into twelve equal parts. This system resulted in a "variable hour" as days became shorter or longer with the seasons. The "bells" mentioned here are probably some form of local announcement of the hour.

[xxi] Traditional accounts document Pilate as a Roman equestrian (middle rank of nobility) of the Pontii clan (thus the first name Pontius). There is no specific record of his military service, but serving under mount (on horseback) would be in keeping with his station.

[xxii] Lacus Asphaltites i.e., Dead or Salt Sea.

[xxiii] Although the servant's name (Caius) is never mentioned in the Scriptures, an encounter between Jesus and a centurion is documented in Matthew 8:5-13 and Luke 7:1-10. These Scripture references are supportive of the encounter as described in the folio.

[xxiv] This event, as recorded in the New Testament, occurred halfway through Jesus' Galilean ministry, in approximately A.D. 28. This timing is in sync with the events as documented in the transcript.

[xxv] The New Testament documents Jesus raising a little girl from the dead (Mark 5:21-43, Luke 8:40-56). The father of the little girl (Jairus) is identified as a ruler of a local synagogue, but is never identified as knowing or being associated with a centurion.

[xxvi] Dalaccus, his wife, and Marcus lack any historical reference. Sejanus, however, is known to have been the chief administrator to Emperor Tiberius. It is also known that Sejanus was Pilate's patron and probably responsible for his appointment as governor of Judaea.

[xxvii] Pilate had sent the senators to his official residence. The palace of Herod, in Caesarea Maritima, was the official residence for the governor of Judaea. Pilate is reported to have spent the majority of his time in the "less Jewish" Caesarea Maritima, journeying to Jerusalem only on high holidays. His presence during those holidays was not a show of respect but a desire to be near the dangerous tensions that developed in Jerusalem during the feasts. The reference to Herod's "court" is a likely reference to Herod Agrippa 1, who had a residence there (Acts 12:19-23).

[xxviii] As the weather this time of year would have prevented sea passage from Rome, it is likely that the senators had wintered in Alexandria (considered one of Rome's jewels) and made a side trip to Jerusalem.

[xxix] Jerusalem's population of 55,000 swelled to more than 180,000 during the Passover festival, while the military contingent at Pilate's disposal remained static at between 3,000 to 4,000 troops.

[xxx]The Jewish historian Josephus mentions a Roman theater in the city of Jerusalem. The specific location of the theater has never been established by archaeologists.

[xxxi] The Sanhedrin was the supreme Jewish council. It was presided over by a high priest (appointed by the Romans) and included both Pharisees and Sadducees. The Romans allowed the Sanhedrin significant power and authority over Jewish matters. The Romans kept a watchful eye on the Sanhedrin's activities. Significant to this document is the fact that the Sanhedrin did not have the authority to issue a death sentence. Some scholars in reading the Scriptures see this constraint incongruous with the death of Stephen (Acts 6:12-15; 7:54-60), but Stephen's death can also be explained as an act of mob violence.

xxxii In response to a Jewish revolt in A.D. 70 (approximately forty years after this conversation), the Roman legions would exercise such retribution.

xxxiii Here Pilate exhibits an astonishing understanding of Israel's history. In 586 B.C. the Babylonians, under the rule of Nebuchadnezzar, crushed Israel. Israel's southern neighbor (Edom) rejoiced at her suffering. The prophets Obadiah, Jeremiah, Isaiah, and Amos spoke of God's future retribution against Edom. This retribution would take place in the second century B.C. when a powerful Israel, under the Maccabees, would defeat Edom. The Edomites would be forced to convert to Judaism and would be pushed into southern Israel. The defeated Edomites were called Idumeans, the place of their exile, Idumea.

xxxiv Two competing brothers, Jacob and Esau, founded Israel and Edom. Jacob, who would have his name changed by God to Israel, would father the twelve tribes of Israel. Esau and his descendants would establish the nation of Edom. One of Esau's sons, Teman, would have his name become synonymous with the nation of Edom.

xxxv Qumran (located eight miles south of Jericho) was inhabited between 130 B.C. and A.D. 70 by a sect known as the Essenes. It is believed that the Essenes were the authors of the Dead Sea Scrolls, which they hid in nearby caves during the Roman invasion of A.D. 70. Why they may have needed an escort to the Passover feast is unclear.

xxxvi Bethabara (east southeast of Jericho) is on the Jordan River approximately one mile north of the Salt Sea. As Romans were industrious builders of water systems, both in Rome and in outlying provinces, it is plausible that the soldiers were assigned to such a task. When nearby Qumran was excavated in 1956, an extensive water system was discovered. Likely it was planned or engineered by the Romans.

xxxvii Approximate wording of Isaiah 55:8-9.

xxxviii Nicodemus does not identify which of the Bible's covenants (promises) is the basis of his faith. Likely the covenant about which he is speaking is found in Genesis 17:1-27. In this passage God makes an everlasting covenant with Abraham's descendants and promises to give the land (Judaea/Israel) as an everlasting possession.

xxxix The Sadducees were the upper class of the Jewish hierarchy and held most of the leadership positions on the Sanhedrin. They had a strong interest in holding power and, therefore, were more willing to negotiate with Roman authority. Here Nicodemus, as a Pharisee, is probably speaking in a tone of derision.

xl The death and resurrection of Lazarus is documented in John 11:1-44. It is interesting to note that the conversation between Nicodemus and Pilate took place in the spring of A.D. 30. Lazarus died and was resurrected in the winter of A.D. 29. Considering the pace of events, his death must have created quite a stir to remain a topic of conversation for such an extended period of time.

xli Evidence that the Lazarus affair had threatened the power base of the Jewish leaders includes the chief priest's plot to kill Lazarus (John 12:9-11).

xlii Nicodemus' encounter with Jesus is documented in John 3:1-21. It was to Nicodemus that Jesus succinctly summarized the purpose for his life and death: "For God so loved the world that He gave His only begotten Son, that whoever believes in Him should not perish but have everlasting life." (John 3:16.)

xliii This is the approximate answer that Jesus gave to the disciples of John the Baptist (Luke 7:22-23) when John sent them to question Jesus' credentials. It may have been a stock answer that Jesus offered to any questioner who was knowledgeable of the Scriptures, as the answer reflects the prophesy of the Old Testament (Isaiah 35:5, Isaiah 61:1-3, Psalm 2:12).

xliv Public works projects were part of Rome's plan in building loyalty to the empire. Such projects were financed via tributes paid to Rome. These tributes (taxes) also covered administration and military expenses.

xlv A Roman coin equal to a day's wage for a laborer. About $20.

xlvi Under the Roman system this would be between midnight and 3 A.M.

xlvii In John 10:11, Jesus speaks of Himself as the "good shepherd."

xlviii "Other sheep" in this case refers to the gentiles. In Jesus' time gentiles were not part of God's chosen family at birth. The more radical Jews of Jesus' day would view all gentiles as pagans.

xlix John 10:16 has Jesus delivering a message inclusive of both Jews and gentiles.

l Adoption was a substantial part of Roman culture during the time of Christ. An adopted child had the same rights (including full citizenship) and duties as a blood heir. Augustus (considered the greatest Roman emperor) was the adopted son and selected heir of Julius Caesar.

[li] Almost all public projects in Imperial territories were built with local labor. Pilate's threat was to have the project managed by locals, possibly preventing the Roman engineer from personally profitting from the venture.

[lii] Annas was likely to take the threat seriously, as Pilate had previously spilled Jewish blood at the temple (Luke 13:1).

[liii] During his eleven years as governor of Judaea, Pilate likely attended numerous meetings in Alexandria (Egypt) where he would have had exposure to the wildlife of the Nile River. In addition, the most common sea route to and from Rome was via Alexandria.

[liv] The story of Lazarus is only told in the Gospel of John. John 11:5 states that "Jesus loved Martha and her sister (Mary) and Lazarus."

[lv] John 11:6 documents Jesus waiting two days before going to Lazarus.

[lvi] John 11:17-19 describes Lazarus as being dead for four days when Jesus arrived. Upon arriving Jesus was greeted by Mary, Martha, and a large crowd that was there to comfort them.

[lvii] John 11:43-53 speaks of a conspiracy to kill Jesus that resulted from His raising Lazarus from the dead. The conspiracy was between the chief priests, who were mostly Sadducees, and the Pharisees. The plot to kill Jesus is also documented in Matthew 26:1-5, Mark 14:1-2, and in Luke 22:1-2.

[lviii] Jesus had many confrontations with the Pharisees. Likely the one that drove them into an alliance with the Sadducees was an incident that occurred just before the death of Lazarus. The Pharisees excommunicated a blind

man because Jesus had healed him (worked) on the Sabbath. Jesus rebuked the Pharisees, which led to their attempted stoning of Him (John 9:1-10:39).

[lix] Matthew 22:15-22, Mark 12:13-17, and Luke 20:20-26—this meeting would occur on Tuesday in the week of Jesus' death.

[lx] Numbers 15:39—four tassels were worn on the outer garment of observant Jews. These tassels were a reminder of covenant obligations (i.e., a shared promise with God). Simon's observation of the tassels as "long" is interesting as Jesus would later (Matthew 23:5) denounce those who wore excessively long tassels as a means of calling attention to their piety.

[lxi] The fact that Pilate was negotiating with Annas rather than the High Priest Caiaphas (Annas' son-in-law) lends credibility to the transcript. Annas was high priest between A.D. 7-14 when he was deposed by Gratus (governor) and replaced with Caiaphas. There is no doubt, however, that Annas continued to wield the real power during Jesus' final days (A.D. 29-30). This is evidenced by his numerous mentions in the Scriptures and by the fact that all of Annas' five sons eventually served as high priest.

[lxii] There is no mention in the Scriptures or other historical documents of Barabbas being involved in the murder of Roman troops, though he is identified as a murderer and insurrectionist that was in custody at the time of Jesus' trial (Mark 15:7).

[lxiii] It was Roman policy to give provinces the authority to govern their own day-to-day matters. This was more than an act of generosity as it allowed Rome to rule while committing minimal resources.

[lxiv] A group who followed the politics of Herod Antipas (an ally of Rome). It was generally recognized that the Herodians actively supported the policies of Rome. It is highly plausible that Pilate, being short-handed and nearing Passover, would have been especially careful to preserve this alliance.

[lxv] As early as A.D. 28, the Scriptures identify the Herodians and Pharisees as having a common hatred of Jesus (Mark 3:6).

[lxvi] Today Lake Asphaltites is known as the Dead Sea or Salt Sea.

[lxvii] Pilate's headquarters were in Caesarea Maritima, but he spent his winters and most of the major Jewish holidays in Jerusalem. The peacetime route between Caesarea Maritima and Jerusalem covered approximately sixty miles. The likely route (from Jerusalem) proceeded northwest almost to Lydda (twenty miles) and then north through Antipatris to Caesarea Maritima (forty miles). Considering the terrain, the journey likely would have taken two and one-half days.

[lxviii] Augustus was the grandnephew and adopted heir of Julius Caesar. He ruled Rome from 31 B.C. to A.D. 14 and is considered to be the founder of the Roman Empire. At his death, the Roman Senate declared him a god.

[lxix] Paper, as we know, was invented in China around the time of Christ but would not find its way to the West for several hundred years. References to paper here may be a translation from papyrus (paper-like material made from the papyrus plant) or a translation of the word "parchment" (skins of sheep and goats made into a writing material). In this case, absent the original Greek manuscript, there is no way to distinguish between a factual and a translation error.

[lxx] Travel to Rome (via the Mediterranean Sea) during the winter months was weather restricted. The preparation of a tax summary in early spring would coincide with a practical means of delivering it via sea passage.

[lxxi] Under Jewish law, annual festivals required that all Jewish males visit the temple in Jerusalem (Exodus 34:23, Deuteronomy 16:16-17). There were three annual festivals: Passover, Feast of Weeks, and The Day of Atonement. In Jesus' time, many Jewish males had lessened this obligation to a requirement of each male attending the temple once each year.

[lxxii] This would be a substantial indication of Pilate's concern for the unrest that existed in Jerusalem, as the seat of government and most of the wealth entrusted to him was in Caesarea Maritima. It should be noted that Caesarea Maritima had a more pagan and stable population.

[lxxiii] Pilate's military contingent of between 2,700 and 3,700 troops would (in a full-fledged revolt) be confronting a male fighting force in excess of 100,000.

[lxxiv] Rome collected import taxes (customs) at seaports and city gates. The collection of taxes was most often contracted to Roman citizens, but sometimes to locals. Collectors would pay Rome a sum in advance for the right to collect taxes in a location. Rome paid little attention to how much profit the collector made, and thus tax collectors were considered harlots or extortionists by much of Jewish society.

[lxxv] The governor possessed supreme judicial authority. Much of his authority he delegated to native courts. There is a body of evidence that suggests that the governor maintained control of political offences. It is reasonable to

assume that the Jews tried to make Jesus a political threat in order to place Jesus under Roman jurisdiction.

[lxxvi] "Death took my friend and mentor Sejanus," is an odd phrasing since Sejanus was executed by the Emperor Tiberius in A.D. 31. His alleged crimes included the murder of Tiberius' only son (Drusus Caesar), and plotting to overthrow Tiberius. Upon Sejanus' death, the populace and the senate reportedly rejoiced and had his body dragged through the streets of Rome.

[lxxvii] Being an acknowledged friend of Sejanus was dangerous. A long reign of terror ensued against Sejanus' followers after his execution. Pilate's wife, Claudia Procula, (daughter of Emperor Tiberius and granddaughter of the revered Augustus) may have been responsible for shielding Pilate from retribution.

[lxxviii] Certain ranks were required to serve ten years in the military before they could hold positions of responsibility within the empire. It is unclear if this requirement was in place during Pilate's youth, however, the transcript infers such a requirement.

[lxxix] The Romans defined a foot as being made up of twelve unciae (inches). The Roman inch (during the time of Christ) was likely 25 percent smaller than today's inch. A pace being five Roman feet, would be approximately forty-five of our inches. A wall two paces high would be ninety modern inches or 7.5 feet.

[lxxx] Under Roman authority, flogging (whipping) could take many forms. This threatened, severe flogging, as well as the later flogging of Jesus (Luke 23:16), probably involved a whip that had sharp pieces of bone embedded in the leather. Being beaten with such a device often left the recipient dead or near death.

[lxxxi] Modern archaeologists have identified the ruins of four fortress sites in the Jericho Region.

[lxxxii] Olive presses were a common instrument of the day. Turning the press brought the pressure of a great stone weight upon the olives, squeezing the oil from them.

[lxxxiii] Annas's son-in-law, Caiaphas is known to have been the high priest during Jesus' crucifixion (Matthew 26:3).

[lxxxiv] There were dozens that rose to prominence during Jesus' time by claiming to be the messiah. Jesus, unlike the others, fulfilled the prophesy of the Jewish cannon (Old Testament). Barabbas (like the Pharisees and Sadducees) might have been too consumed with his own mission to give Jesus serious consideration.

[lxxxv] This comment places this meeting one week before Jesus' death (the Friday before Good Friday). Jesus would enter Jerusalem just two days (Palm Sunday) after this meeting.

[lxxxvi] Trade reports would be of special interest to the governor as the Romans financed their control of provinces though two means, a general tax on the population and customs (trade) duties.

[lxxxvii] This exchange would have taken place on the Tuesday before Jesus' death. Numerous references in the Scriptures document Jesus entering Jerusalem on Sunday (John 12:1 in conjunction with John 12:12-13) and being crucified on Friday (Mark 15:42). The reference here to Jesus entering Jerusalem four days earlier would place it in harmony with the Scripture's chronology.

[lxxxviii] Although Simon's transcript shows no special emphasis, Pilate's specific question about the donkey may have significance. Within the region, the donkey was the mount of kings and princes (Judges 5:10, 10:4, 12:14 and 2 Samuel 16:1-2). Pilate's next comment supports the possibility that he had knowledge of the donkey's significance.

[lxxxix] Bethany is two miles southeast of Jerusalem. It was a logical place for Jesus to retreat (Mark 11:11) as it was the home of Jesus' good friends Mary, Martha, and Lazarus (whom Jesus raised from the dead). Bethany is on the eastern slope of the Mount of Olives making it about a fifty-five-minute walk from Jerusalem.

[xc] Although Jesus' confrontation with the moneychangers is documented in the Gospels of Matthew, Mark, and Luke, the transcript most closely follows the chronology recounted in Mark 11:5-15.

[xci] As coins with pagan symbols were not acceptable currency in the temple, moneychangers set up shop and charged an unfair premium for swapping such coins for an acceptable currency.

[xcii] This incident is documented in Matthew 22:15-22, Mark 12:13-17, and Luke 20:20-26.

[xciii] Pilate, in addressing Jesus as a Nazarene, touched on prophecy. His affirmation concerns prophesy found in Judges 13:5-7, "...the child shall be a Nazirite to God from the womb; and he shall begin to deliver Israel out of the hand of the Philistines." This was an extraordinary prophecy considering that Nazareth in 1100 B.C. was little more than an obscure watering station. New Testament references to this prophecy can be found in Matthew 2:23 and John 1:45-46.

[xciv] Pilate's reference also held a meaning to the Roman military. A Roman military garrison was located near Nazareth. The entire region around Nazareth was suspected of being sympathetic with the enemy (Zealots).

[xcv] It is known that Pilate was recalled to Rome in A.D. 36 and that in A.D. 70, Rome reaffirmed its control over Judaea by invading and destroying Jerusalem. The manuscript indicates that Rome is massing its resources for this attack, thus dating Pilate's reflections to around A.D. 69. If correct, Pilate would likely be seventy-eight years old when writing this portion of the folio.

[xcvi] In A.D. 70, Rome would extract a severe payment for the years of Jewish rebellion. The Roman campaign would see the temple in Jerusalem dismantled stone by stone, 100,000 Jewish fugitives sold as slaves, and between 600,000 and 1,197,000 Jews killed. (Tacitus, a Roman, reports the lower number, the Jewish historian, Josephus, the higher.)

[xcvii] There is some evidence that the Apostle Peter was in Rome spreading the Gospel of Jesus (The Way) as early as A.D. 42. Both Peter and the Apostle Paul labored to convert the Romans to Christianity until their deaths. Historical accounts have them both suffering a martyr's death at the hands of the Romans in A.D. 64.

[xcviii] Although there was still a strong economy based on the Roman gods, a large portion of Rome had become disenchanted with the belief system. By the second half of the first century, both Greek and Roman poets were openly mocking the Roman pantheon.

[xcix] The Praetorium was the official Jerusalem residence of the Roman governor. Although its exact location has never been established, experts place it beside or near the temple

complex.

[c] Judas brought a detachment (possibly 200 men) of troops to arrest Jesus (John 18:3). Pilate seems surprised at Jesus' arrest and does not mention the use of Roman troops. The most likely explanation is that they were not Roman soldiers, but Temple troops acting under the authority of the high priest.

[ci] John 18:28—Although the main Passover meal had taken place the night before, there were many more ceremonial meals and events that would take place during Passover week.

[cii] Here Simon appears to give Governor Pilate a "shorthand" version of the Jewish law. It was not entering the house of a gentile that made a Jew unclean, but entering a house (during Passover) where there was leaven (yeast). As most gentile homes had yeast as part of their stores, gentile homes became off limits during Passover.

[ciii] As governor of Judaea, Pilate was responsible for three territories: Judaea, Samaria, and Idumea. Judaea (or Judea) was in the center with Samaria to the north and Idumea to the south.

[civ] The title of prefect (praefectus) had a military connotation that showed the determination of the empire to subdue a province.

[cv] To this point, the encounter follows the Scripture as recorded in the Book of Mark 15:1-5.

[cvi] This closely follows the spirit of the dialog of John 18:29, but adds Pilate's concern about "facts."

[cvii] Comments regarding Galilee are found only in Luke 23:5. The term sedition is not included in the Luke text.

[cviii] This encounter follows events as recorded in John 18:34.

[cix] Although specific wording differs, the intent closely follows John 18:35-36

[cx] John 18:38

[cxi] There is a confusion of "Herods" in both the Holy Bible and historical documents. This was no doubt Herod Antipas, a Jew assigned by the Romans to rule over Galilee. (Galilee, located north of Samaria, was not under Pilate's authority.) It was Herod Antipas who ordered the beheading of John the Baptist and killed the Apostle James.

[cxii] Jesus being taken before Herod appears only in the Gospel of Luke (Luke 23:6-12). Although transcript encounters between Jesus and Pilate bounce between events covered in the four Gospels (Matthew, Mark, Luke, John), there are no substantial conflicts with the Gospel's record. In some ways, the transcript provides a structure that brings together the various renditions of Jesus' trial.

[cxiii] This probably refers to Mount Gerizim, which is located in Samaria (thirty miles north of Jerusalem). In his last year as governor, Pilate had a bloody confrontation with the Samaritans on Mount Gerizim. It is widely held that this event led to Pilate's recall to Rome.

[cxiv] Avillius Flaccus was the Roman governor of Egypt. He, Sejanus, and Pilate were known to be hostile toward the Jewish people. Flaccus' harsh acts against the Jews would result in him being recalled to Rome in A.D. 40. Pilate's remorse in trusting Flaccus is without historical reference.

[cxv] Pilate is likely referring to the Sphinx of Boeotian Thebes (Greek mythology). This winged, ferocious creature would unexpectedly swoop down and demand an answer to a question. If the question (riddle) were answered incorrectly, the creature would devour its victim.

[cxvi] In Greek mythology, Oedipus was the king of Thebes who unwittingly killed his father and married his mother. One of the trials that Oedipus faced was solving the riddle of the Sphinx.

[cxvii] Traditional accounts have Pilate as a Roman equestrian (middle rank of nobility). Under the Emperor Augustus, both the governors of lesser imperial provinces and military commands were filled from this rank. With the exception of Felix, all the governors of Judaea appear to have been drawn from the equestrian rank.

[cxviii] A centurion was in command of 100 men (later 200 men). As first-line officer of command, Pilate was likely to have had five to seven centurions and 500 to 600 troops under his command.

[cxix] Venetia is identified on ancient maps as being a province (county) that surrounded the northern point of the Adriatic Sea and extended fifty miles north into the Alps.

[cxx] Forum Julia is approximately eighty miles northeast of modern-day Venice and forty miles north of Aquileia.

[cxxi] Aquileia was a city located on the coast of the Adriatic Sea approximately forty miles east of modern-day Venice.

[cxxii] In addition to being the governor's official residence in Jerusalem, the Praetorium also housed the barracks

complex where Jesus would be beaten prior to His crucifixion (Mark 15:16).

cxxiii During Christ's time, Jerusalem was a walled city. Holding certain gates would have been strategic in controlling the crowd and in securing the Praetorium.

cxxiv Forced labor was a common punishment within the Roman military. Being assigned to serve as an oarsman in the belly of a galley (war ship) was no doubt severe punishment.

cxxv Herod's curiosity concerning Jesus is documented in Luke 23:8-9.

cxxvi Luke 23:12 documents this event as creating a friendship between Pilate and Herod.

cxxvii Layouts of the city at that time vary, but respected archaeological maps estimate the distance between the south porch of the Praetorium and the temple to be an area of 200 by 400 yards.

cxxviii This closely follows the account given in Luke 23:13-16.

cxxix Pilate giving the crowd a choice between Jesus and Barabbas is chronicled in all four Gospels (Matthew, Mark. Luke, John). The account covered in the manuscript includes unique aspects from each of the Gospels (e.g., Herod is only mentioned in Luke, Pilate's wife only in Matthew, etc.). Though the transcript presents dialogue and action that are not covered in the Scriptures, that which is held in common is without substantial conflict.

cxxx The note from Pilate's wife warned him to "Have nothing to do with that just Man for I have suffered many things today in a dream because of Him." (Matthew 27:19).

cxxxi Here, Pilate introduces Jesus to the crowd as a man (John 19:5) in hopes of garnering the crowd's sympathy. Later in the trial he introduces Jesus to the crowd as their "king" (John 19:14), hoping to shame the crowd.

cxxxii With the exception of the word suffer (vs. has), this closely approximates Jesus' response as recorded in John 19:11.

cxxxiii John 19:14.

cxxxiv The essence of this dialog is found in John 19:12-16, although the order of delivery is juxtaposed. This dialogue defines the level of hate the Jewish leaders had for Jesus in that they willingly proclaimed their loyalty to a pagan emperor as a means of having Jesus killed.

cxxxv A combination of Matthew 27:24 and Luke 23:24.

cxxxvi Within this directive, the meaning of Barabbas' name gains special significance for Christians. The name Barabbas means "son of the father," i.e., anybody. Jesus, dying in Barabbas' place, was taking the place of "everyone."

cxxxvii John 19:19-20—The words were written in Hebrew, Greek, and Latin.

cxxxviii Laurel is a small evergreen shrub native to the Mediterranean region. Roman generals returning from a victorious campaign were adorned with a branch of laurel as a symbol of victory.

cxxxix John 19:21-22—Although not the exact wording, this exchange closely tracks the Scriptures.

[cxl] I can find no reference to Roman timekeeping in Judaea. Using the Scriptures and the chronology of events, the Jewish sixth-hour (after sunrise) can be calibrated to the mentioned first bell (noon), thus making the fourth bell 4 P.M. Using this assumption, the events of the Bible are in harmony with the manuscript.

[cxli] The fate of Barabbas after his release is not included in the Scriptures.

[cxlii] Crucifixions were designed to be a long, painful ordeal. Those being crucified would often suffer days of agony before dying.

[cxliii] John 19:34—Before the days of modern medicine it was difficult to tell if someone was dead. One method that proved reliable was to pierce the body. If blood came from the wound, the person was alive. If water and blood flowed (the blood had settled and separated), the person was dead.

[cxliv] Matthew 27:45, Mark 15:33-34, and Luke 23:44 document an unnatural darkness that preceded Jesus' death by three hours.

[cxlv] Arimathea is a small town twenty miles northwest of Jerusalem.

[cxlvi] Matthew 27:57 identifies Joseph of Arimathea as a rich man who was a follower of Jesus. Mark 15:43 describes him as a prominent council member who was waiting for the kingdom of God. Luke 23:50 calls him a council member and a good and just man. John 19:38 simply addresses him as a disciple of Jesus.

[cxlvii] The Scriptures do not include Nicodemus in the meeting between Pilate and Joseph of Arimathea, though John 19:39 has Nicodemus assisting Joseph (at the tomb)

with the preparation of the body. Although the Scriptures do not specifically include Nicodemus at this meeting, his presence would explain why Pilate would grant an audience to a stranger and then release Jesus' body to him.

[cxlviii] Somnus (Greek, Hypnos): The Greco-Roman god of sleep.

[cxlix] Exodus 20:13—The second commandment of the Ten Commandments issued by God.

[cl] In Greek mythology, Prometheus was the God of fire. Zeus (the chief Greek God), upon discovering that Prometheus had given fire to mankind, punished him by chaining him and sending an eagle to rip the liver from his body. Each morning the immortal Prometheus would awake to find his liver regenerated and the eagle returning.

[cli] The fulcrum is the point against which leverage is applied. The mechanics of the fulcrum were formally defined by Archimedes in 280 B.C. By the time of Christ, Archimedes' principles were part of a formal Roman education.

[clii] There is no evidence, in either the Scriptures or the transcript, of Pilate seeing Jesus' body after his death. This statement may refer to seeing the beaten Jesus, or may allude to an event that is not detailed elsewhere.

[cliii] Matthew 27:59-60 states that the tomb belonged to Joseph of Arimathea. Seven hundred years earlier, Isaiah prophesied that the Messiah would be buried in a rich man's tomb (Isaiah 53:9).

[cliv] Mark 15:42, Luke 23:54, and John 19:42 each identify the day as being "preparation day," i.e., the day before the Sabbath. Because the Jewish law prohibited preparing or

interring the dead on the Sabbath, if Jesus' body were not claimed before sundown it would remain unclaimed until sundown the next day (Saturday).

[clv] There are numerous prophecies of Jesus' death being a sacrifice to atone for the sins of the people. It is impossible to tell which of these Nicodemus may have been referencing, however Isaiah 53:6 and 53:8 have a striking applicability to the situation.

[clvi] In Jesus' time the rich and powerful wore an expensive grade of linen that was woven so finely that it had the look and feel of silk.

[clvii] In calling Jesus God's anointed, Nicodemus may be referring to the prophesy of Daniel (Daniel 9:24).

[clviii] John 19:39 documents Nicodemus' presence at the tomb.

[clix] Old Testament prophesy concerning Jesus includes Exodus 24:6, Psalms 8:5-8, 18:43, 22:11-15, 89:19, Isaiah 42:1, 53:3, 53:4, 53:10, Micah 5:3, and Zechariah 9:9-10.

[clx] Simon's request shows a split in his life. He requests time to take the Sabbath meal with his family, yet returns the next morning (breaking the Jewish law) to work on the Sabbath.

[clxi] Matthew 27:62 documents this encounter with a slight variation. The Scriptures have the "chief priests and Pharisees" before Pilate. The transcript has this same group coming to Pilate, but the governor only receiving the chief priests.

[clxii] Closely follows the encounter described in Matthew

27:64.

[clxiii] Matthew 27:64.

[clxiv] Matthew 27:65.

[clxv] According to the Scriptures, when Jesus was discovered to have risen, the chief priests did not return to Pilate, but instead bribed the soldiers guarding the tomb (Matthew 28:11-15). Thus, the Scriptures are supportive of the transcript's dialogue regarding Pilate being finished with the matter.

[clxvi] Dates are interesting here as Sejanus (suspected of trying to overthrow Emperor Tiberius) was arrested and executed in A.D. 31. Dates of Jesus' death vary with most sources listing the year of his death as A.D. 30. If a later date (i.e., post A.D. 31) of Jesus' death is presumed, the manuscript's timeline becomes suspect.

[clxvii] "Friend" may refer to Flaccus, who, as governor of Egypt in A.D. 38, supported mob violence against the Jews of Alexandria. In addition to allowing the destruction of Jewish homes and public scourging of Jewish leaders, he had the Jews of Alexandria stripped of their citizenship. It is known that Flaccus and Pilate had an alliance later in Pilate's tenure as governor (A.D. 36-38?), but an association with Flaccus at this early date is undocumented.

[clxviii] The Scriptures do not reference any direct contact between Jesus and Pilate's wife, nor any event involving Jesus and spontaneous fire.

[clxix] Roman (non-Christian) documentation exists from the middle of the first century that references the unnatural darkness that accompanied Jesus' death. The writer Thallus accounts for the darkness as a natural phenomenon. His

seemingly logical argument that the event may have been a solar eclipse must be discounted as Jesus was crucified over Passover, a holiday that is defined by a full moon.

[clxx] In first-century Rome, suicide was neither a crime nor a dishonorable act, in fact, the state usually gave criminals condemned to death the option of suicide. Over the next fifty years, the acceptance of suicide would decline as large numbers of slaves took their lives, depriving their owners of valuable property.

[clxxi] Most historical accounts portray Pilate to be a shrewd and ruthless ruler. Pilate's claim of conducting a passive policy in the first half of his administration may not ring true with some historical accounts, but it was by all accounts far more passive than the second half of his service.

[clxxii] Some accounts have Pilate first hanging banners in the temple in Jerusalem. This can be reconciled by labeling it an inaccuracy, the self-serving memory of an old man, or as a less important detail that was omitted. In any case, all accounts ultimately attribute Pilate's fate to his oppressive action in Samaria.

[clxxiii] Though Samaritans were Jews, they held a belief system that ostracized them from the Jews of Judaea. Part of the animosity toward Jesus was due to His tolerance of the Samaritans.

[clxxiv] Samaria was a district of Palestine during this period; its primary city was also named Samaria.

[clxxv] Respected historical accounts trace Pilate's disgrace and his recall to Rome to the reign of Tiberius. Tiberius would die before Pilate reached Rome, however, and a reliable record of Pilate's future ends with Tiberius' life.

Unsubstantiated materials offer numerous outcomes including: suicide, trial, exile, reassignment, and conversion to Christianity.

[clxxvi] Breaking of the legs during a crucifixion was considered a merciful act as it hastened death via suffocation. Absent such an "act of mercy," a normal individual might live and suffer for days on the cross.

[clxxvii] Pilate had ordered his troops to encamp within the walls of Jerusalem, sending his troops in with images of the emperor attached to their banners. This caused a massive demonstration in Caesarea. The historian Josephus reports that Pilate was deeply moved by the Jews' willingness to die for their beliefs and consequently ordered the images removed.

[clxxviii] After the Samaritans accused Pilate of attacking them on Mount Gerizim they protested to Vitellius (legate of Syria) that Pilate had executed men without a trial. Pilate was recalled to Rome.

[clxxix] Roman emperor of A.D. 37-41.

[clxxx] An approximate survey of the folios has me count twenty hours of Pilate's involvement in matters relating to Jesus. The majority of this time was spent during the day of Jesus' crucifixion. No doubt Pilate's point is that it was a trivial matter when measured against his eleven-year tenure as governor.

[clxxxi] "... I have come into the world that I should bear witness to the truth." (John 18:37).